Touch of the Whimsy

JULES OLIVER WILKINSON

First Published in Great Britain in 2024.

Published by Julubukes.

A CIP catalogue record for this book is available from the British Library

Paperback : ISBN 978-1-0683219-0-0

Ebook: ISBN 978-1-0683219-1-7

Cover Design and Typesetting by Creative Covers

'Cece! Oh, my Cece!
There are none so blind,
As those who won't see!
See?'

Anon

Touch of the whimsy is dedicated to my mother… who never undertook any outing without a pack-away rain-hood in her handbag.

And to Pete, always my hero, who has undertaken to join me on my literary journey… and who has done his best to resolve all the issues I have encountered along the way.

And many thanks to my alpha reader Wendy, for her patience, perseverance and encouragement!

And many thanks to Creative Covers, for Mr.K Dawson's invaluable support in helping me to turn a story into a book!

Prologue

Man shaped, but star filled, the figure emerged unseen from the ink-sea, making its way unfalteringly across sand, shingle, and kelp-covered rocks, then onwards into an entanglement of trees.

It did not pause, nor was its progress slowed by the dense undergrowth, as it penetrated the black of the night jungle.

Nor did it leave any trace of its presence on the fresh wet sand.

A stranded starfish, patiently awaiting the turn of the tide, briefly experienced a sense of rapport with the passing figure, before being snatched up as a late fish supper by a hungry gull.

It's feelings of affinity with the other starry being slipped down in order of priority in its tiny mind, as it wondered at the aerial view; it had never before witnessed the sea from above!

It was turning out to be quite the night for firsts!

Part One
Castaway!
Chapter One

Coughing and choking up salt-bile, and water-battle weary, the figure that collapsed onto fine white sand was distinctly female shaped. Barely far enough out of the water to be safe, and uncaring of the vagaries of the storm-fuelled waves still lapping at her sea-battered body, she sank into oblivion.

By the end of that long, sunburnt day, as the cloud-whipped tropical sky drew a last deep breath, and blew away storm remnants, neither cotton-floss traces, nor scutterings of cirrus wisps, remained to interfere with the stars' view of the fragile form left abandoned on the beach.

...And some miles out to sea... but from a gazillion miles away... a luminescent shimmer briefly manifested on the bottom of the ocean floor, noted, really, only by a vaguely curious octopus.

Solid barely long enough to make an impression on the silt-world of the bottom dwellers, the domed, and saucer-shaped object, interrupted the relative peace of the casually savage dominion of 'large, eats small... eats smaller'.

The nature of the interruption stemmed from the universally recognised intonations of individuals having 'an exchange of words,' drifting out from the portholes, rather than from the almost-audible drone of its hydro-powered motors.

Anything within earshot, and with ears, may have picked up on tones of annoyance, frustration, and eventual petulance, before the shape shimmied back out of existence.

The vaguely curious octopus had been furtively making its way over to investigate the basin, stopping every few seconds to morph, first into a threatening looking rock, then into a beautifully variegated sea-anemone.

It had just struck a pose as the latest disguise in its repertoire, and the one of which it was most proud, that being, the ubiquitous 'discarded drinks can', when it suffered a momentary loss of dignity, as it suddenly found itself being dragged, suckering and bubble-blowing, into the vacuum created by the abrupt non-existence of the shimmering saucer.

Using a still trembling tentacle to lasso the one actual rock which was sturdy enough to have withstood the very local phenomenon, it levered itself unsteadily out of the indentation left behind.

It chose not to feel embarrassed by the huge cloud of blue ink it found itself leaving in its wake, and spurted off, a far less inquisitive, but somewhat more wary, cephalopod than it had been before its experience.

Chapter Two

The ferocity of the scorching sunlight burning through her grit-encrusted lids forced Cece Fontaine to her senses, and feeling neither refreshed nor restored, she slowly surfaced from the exhausted state, more akin to a prelude to death than sleep, which had consumed her last few hours.

Rubbing the back of gravel caked hands across her face did little to dislodge silt and sand from her mouth and her nostrils. However, she did find, as she fully emerged from her salt-drenched stupor, that spluttering out a goodly collection of harsh expletives and profanities went some way to clearing her airways!

And then the briny flood of tears, which coursed down her face, helped to wash away some of the blinding sand from scratched and stinging eyes, as hazy fragments of memory sloshed around her waterlogged brain, and Cece tried to make sense of her situation.

"Narcece! Get away ... the rail! You're ... soaked... skin!"

"Cece! CEECEE! You'll ... up...overboard!"

The voices had come to her as if from a distance, fractured by roaring sea-sound.

Laughing!

And that last word was still ringing in her ears!

'Overboard!'

Salt-licked and breathless, she had gloried in standing so close to the rail, watching the gigantic waves rolling in towards the massive cruise ship, and its vast bulk had seemed to be easily absorbing the swells which were coming in from a distant storm, causing little more than minimal turbulence on deck.

Nothing about the manner of the well-drilled crew had suggested anything untoward was about to happen!

There had been no call for lifejackets!

The band had not started to play the last waltz!

So the freak wave had materialised without warning really, and Cece's emotions had had no time to evolve from thrill to terror, before a freezing shock crashed over her head, and ice-water hands were grabbing and pulling her under the azure waves for what, in that instant, felt like her final moment.

Her mind's eye replayed her water-journey, carried atop of the crest of the giant wave, before being unceremoniously dumped, on what was possibly, and remarkably, the only barely habitable piece of land around for thousands of square miles. Cece vaguely remembered an awareness of crashing down onto dry land, and dragging herself a few feet out of the water.

She had no memory of progressing further up the beach towards the treeline, and figured her self-preservation instincts must have kicked in, leading her to drag herself, in a semi-conscious state, up above the tide line, and out of danger of drowning.

But still very much in danger, it seemed, of being eaten alive!

Or at the very least, being *bitten* alive, by a whole microcosm of creeping, crawling, and flying things, which were now fighting to sample the new delicatessen which had been delivered to their doorstep.

The shape of a man, that wasn't a man, watched, as he had watched all night, as the woman pushed herself to a semi-sitting position, to be better able to look about herself.

He observed her shade sea-green eyes with grimy hands as she peered round, taking in the length of the beach, and the proximity to the jungle's edge, as she assessed her situation.

He observed her struggle unsteadily to her feet and start to edge away from the trees, slapping at her upper and lower limbs as she did so, then closely exploring the skin where she had slapped, and then scratching at herself.

He observed, and registered, but drew no conclusions from her behaviour.

Without moving from his position in the treeline, the figure was able to monitor Cece as she made her way back down to the water's edge, and watched as she again raised her hand above her eyes, facing the sea, staying in that position for several heart beats, before turning her gaze this way and that, and then settled once again, to face out towards the direction of the storm-dirtied ocean.

Then, as she turned her head to start scanning the beach again, he observed her begin to move slowly along the shingle and sand, and noted her steps quicken each time she neared another sea-wrack covered rock, intermittently emitting cries of "Hello! HELLO!" as she ran.

Eventually the frenetic dashing from one kelp mound to the next slowed and faltered, and the increasingly hoarse bleating faded. She was still within his view when she eventually sank to her knees and, barring for her ragged breathing, fell quiet.

He noted that the sounds that she made then changed to low harsh sobs which caused her breast to rise and fall convulsively as each gasping sound forced its way out of her body.

He recorded the changes in her activities, and neither knowing nor caring what her erratic behaviour meant, he stored and transmitted the information, and awaited further instructions.

Chapter Three

Not too far from Cece's position, an immortal entity, from a species older than the universe, and almost as old as time itself, and who will more latterly be known as 'Dave', flitting somewhere between existence, and thought, briefly materialised, and tutted.

Soon-to-be-Dave's still developing manifestation took place in a vague, non-descript, protoplasmic-form, inside a submerged vehicle that his companion had assured him was a 'contemporary transportation device', and which, he had informed him, was 'infinitely appropriate' for the corporeal manifestations that they would be taking on their current assignment.

He checked out the decor, then de-materialised again.

A few micro-seconds after the protoplasmic-form had disappeared, an early pro-simian figure fleetingly replaced his presence, then that too was gone.

The small primate then *re*-materialized, as though having just remembered why it had been there in the first place, tutted again, insofar as an unevolved monkey can tut, replied to a few incoming transmissions, then flickered back out of existence one more time.

Chapter Four

Cece wandered disconsolately along the water's edge.

Scouring the beach hoping that she was going to find a shipmate washed up along the shoreline, did not feel selfish to Cece, even if it did mean wishing her own fate on someone else!

She did not know whether the ship had gone down, with that last enormous wave, or whether she had just been unfortunate enough, or careless enough, to have gone over the side, but the thought of being alone, anywhere, for any length of time, was terrifying to Cece.

Let alone being on a deserted island in the middle of the Pacific Ocean!

Cece had been almost as shocked as everyone else in her circle when she had suddenly announced, during one prosecco fuelled girls' night at The Little Chickadee's, that she intended to take advantage of being 'between jobs' … unplanned, and in the run up to Christmas to boot…and feeling flush with redundancy money, had decided, as she was 'currently single', to book herself on to a month-long Tropical Myster Cruise!

If anyone wanted to accompany her, she would work her cruise round their convenience, she had announced magnanimously, but if not, she would go alone!

After the initial surprise at her proclamation, the enthusiastic responses from the gaggle of alcohol-merry females had varied from declarations of mass resignations, in order to accompany her and to 'get themselves a fresh start' too, to promises of trying to arrange 'a bit of time off' to 'go with', to those who more realistically settled for wishing her the most fantastic time, because 'she deserved it!'

When the dust had settled on her invitation however, and the alcohol had evaporated, offers to 'come with' seemed to have been no more substantial than the alcohol fumes that had prompted them, but with the fear of losing face with her friends trumping her fear of making such a mammoth trip alone, she had set about arranging a protracted once in a life-time Christmas Cruise for herself.

And, against all her own expectations, she had actually been starting to enjoy the experience!

Torn between feeling the need to spend time alone contemplating what was happening with her life, and trying to work out what she *should* be doing with it, and the fear of spending too much time alone inside her own head, especially during the festive period, had resulted in Cece managing to inveigle herself into several groups of cruise-tropico aficionados who didn't mind her tagging along; when it suited her.

This meant that she did not have to commit herself to any *one* individual or group, she had concluded happily, so no-one would miss her when she wanted to opt out of any of their activities, and spend time contemplating life and the universe!

But now, Cece had to wonder, how long would it take any of her cruise-mates to notice her absence if, for example, she happened to get herself washed overboard?

And Cece didn't even know if that was what her fate had been!

If she had been washed overboard, at least the cruiser was still out there!

Hopefully no longer *cruising*, but going full steam ahead, or full *engines* ahead at any rate, scouring the seas for her!

Or at least exploring any likely land masses that she might have been washed up on!

But what if she was indeed the sole survivor of a now sunken cruise-ship?

The whole situation seemed unfathomable to Cece, and did not bear too much more thinking about!

Pivoting on her heel, Cece made the sudden decision to head back up the beach towards the tree line.

It was unlikely, Cece decided, that she was going to find a knight in shining armour materialising on the beach, so she supposed she had better start to think about what she needed to do to survive!

Realizing that although there was a lot she did not know about her situation, what she did know for sure was that she was very, *very* thirsty, and that she could not survive for long without fresh water.

And that soon she was also going to need food! And shelter!

She wished too that she could get rid of the damned biting insects which despite not being the most pressing of her current problems and, admittedly, not nearly as bad since she had come away from the water's edge were, nonetheless, greatly adding to her misery!

As Cece made her way determinedly towards the jungle, a chill breeze crawled along her skin, coming unexpectedly out of what had turned into a sweltering and stifling day, after the previous day's storm, causing goosebumps to run along her forearms, and she felt a slight tremor course through her body.

The man-shape watched from the trees as Cece made her way off the beach and into the jungle, detecting every nuance of her behaviour, despite his distance.

He blended back into the trees as she drew near, then moved beyond him, even observing the hair raise on her skin, and the slight tremor as she passed.

He did not move, but shifted his gaze slightly to watch her progress, as Cece, feeling like she was in a wildlife documentary, and trying hard to remember any random pieces of survival trivia she may have heard over the years, started making her way along a well-used animal spoor, which allowed her access into the dense brush.

Cece's overriding thought was water, the need for which was becoming more desperate.

Her throat was sore from retching up salt-water, her lips dry and cracked already from sun and lack of sun cream.

She would have given a lot for the stick of lip balm which had been in her lovely canvas messenger bag, which she had had on deck with her, and which was now probably gagging a fish somewhere!

Yes, Cece thought dejectedly, she would have exchanged everything she had for a glass of water, and her lip-balm.

If she had had anything to exchange.

Which she didn't.

Chapter Five

Water!

Cece could hear trickling water! At least she *thought* she could hear trickling water, *almost* definitely thought she could, anyway, amongst the continuous cacophony of jungle-sounds.

She stood poised, head cocked, trying to determine the direction of the source.

So much noise! Not least of which was the pounding sound inside her own dehydrated and stressed-out head!

It was impossible to tell what she was listening to.

Impulsively Cece clapped her hands in a quick staccato of applause, achieving the desired result of a lull in the noise around her.

The jungle had paused to assess!

In the moment of sudden calm Cece was able to hone in on the steady trickling sound and hastened her step, tripping and stumbling over protruding roots and breaking into a run, as the sound became more distinct, and definitely recognisable as trickling water!

The ground had become wet and marshy underfoot, as she neared the source, and one plimsolled foot suddenly disappeared up to the ankle, bringing her to her knees, as she fell face first into the manna from heaven she had been racing towards.

Ignoring the pain in the ankle that she had twisted as she had fallen awkwardly to the ground, Cece buried her face into the water where she landed, and started dog-lapping it up.

And then promptly threw it back up into thc strcam.

Cece twisted herself into a sitting position, and wiped saltwater and vomit from her face. Sobbing dry sobs, too de-hydrated to produce tears, she felt almost as desperate as when she had first awoken on the shore.

Her head banging, she was now fully aware of the screaming pain in her ankle, and the taste of acrid stomach acid and salt-ditch water in her mouth.

Could things get any worse?

Silent eyes, watching this new player in its arena, from the shadow of undergrowth, would suggest that it could.

Cece's clapping, and the mad dash she had made to what she had mistakenly taken for a watering hole, had served to direct more than one interested party to her current location.

One *particularly* interested party now stood just feet away from this strange animal, new to its territory, stretched out prone on the ground, heaving into a salt-pool. Retching and sobbing were unfamiliar behaviours to it, so for a moment it just narrowed the yellow-green eyes which peered out from a tawny face, and watched.

...And a face without eyes, but which nonetheless saw everything, gathered information; it saw the stalking feline, it saw Cece, it transmitted the information, and awaited instructions...

Cats tend to be curious creatures by nature, and this one was no exception; it had felt surprised by the arrival of the new animal on its turf.

But that surprise was nothing, compared to the surprise it felt about two minutes after that.

Chapter Six

Gathering her wits, and her senses, Cece sank her swollen ankle again into the cool water.

It may be no good for drinking, Cece acknowledged wryly, seemingly being too near to the sea's edge, and a mixture of fresh water, trickling down from between the trees, and coastal water, pooled in the shallows from the last spring tide, but it *was* very soothing to her poor ankle!

She contemplated her fast-swelling lower limb, and decided that she was going to have to sacrifice what had been her favourite wraparound dress, which had so far survived her current ordeal intact, by ripping strips off the bottom to make some sort of strapping to support it.

Cece soon found this task not nearly as easy as popular fiction might have you believe, however. After several attempts at trying to make an indent to the hemline with her teeth, gagging as the material stuck to her parched mouth, and then almost cutting off the circulation in her fingers by trying to pull the material apart with her bare hands, she gave up.

"Better made than I thought", she had to concede begrudgingly. "I'll have to give them five-stars when I get home. *If* I get home."

Hobbling on her painful ankle, still unstrapped and unsupported, following the stream further inland to its source, Cece tracked the trickle of water far enough away from the marshy ground to risk tasting it again, more tentatively this time, and managing to avoid the face-plant approach.

She realised, thankfully, that the water seemed fresh, was cold, and any potential critters it may have contained, were too small for her to see or worry about.

It was only after having drunk as much water as her stomach could take, that Cece suddenly noticed how dark it was.

She had assumed the day was still young when she had made her way into the trees, although she now realised that she had no sure way of knowing that, as she actually had no idea what time it was when she had regained consciousness on the beach.

Nor did she have any way of tracking how long she had wandered up and down the beach, hoping to find signs of other castaways, before giving up and deciding to venture into the jungle!

Although Cece realised that it was quite possible that the darkness was likely to be due to the density of the trees around her, rather than approaching nightfall, she began to worry all the same, about just how far into the jungle she had gone, in her quest for water!

Her exhaustion made it even more difficult for her to assess, as it felt to Cece as though she had walked for miles!

She realised that, up until her undignified and calamitous sprint towards the sound of water, she had been making her way very warily through the trees and undergrowth, and so was aware that she may not have walked quite as far as she felt she had.

However, although Cece did not relish the idea of spending the night alone on the beach, she found the prospect infinitely preferable to spending the night alone in a jungle!

Or, rather more to the point, spending the night *not* alone, in a jungle!

With her thirst assuaged, Cece started to become more acutely aware of other concerns.

Hungry as she was, thinking about potential dangers that any jungle animals may present, her need for shelter of some description suddenly took precedence, in her mind, over her need for food.

Craning her neck back as far as she could, without toppling over, Cece could make out glimpses of dazzling sunlight between the tall treetops.

So, it was still daylight out there somewhere, she thought, grateful at least for this small mercy!

The animal spoor on which she had previously been relying, had been lost during her ungainly dash for water, so instead Cece started to track the trickling stream, in what she hoped was the direction of the beach.

Her mind could not help but dwell on what sort of animals might be author to the clamour of sounds which echoed through the trees around her.

And she had seen enough wild life documentaries to know that it was the ones that she could not hear which were more likely to be of danger to her, than the ones that she was listening to!

She was totally oblivious to the narrow escape that she had already had!

And she could have no knowledge, or comprehension, that the most dangerous being currently residing in the jungle hovered mere feet away from her present location, observing her every move!

Trying to scour the bushes and trees for anything remotely edible, while simultaneously trying to keep her eyes on the ground to avoid tripping herself up over numerous protruding roots, did not make Cece's progress easy.

It also made her feel a bit sick, and was giving her a pain behind her eyes!

As the trees thinned out enough to allow her to see the ground under her feet, Cece narrowly avoided mashing underfoot something which was barely recognisable as a piece of fruit.

Although the dim light did not allow her to get a good look at it, Cece wiped the fruit's surface with one filthy hand, then wiped it down her even more filthy dress, then hesitating for only a second more, sank her teeth into it.

The shocking sourness momentarily made Cece gag, and her recently re- hydrated eyeballs made a point of proving that they were still able to produce tears! She managed to swallow anyway, and even more impressively, keep it down.

Grimacing, she took another bite, then another, almost breaking a tooth as she crunched into the large stone at the fruit's centre.

She looked about the floor for more of the fruit, and finding another two pieces, stuffed them in her pockets for later. She hoped against hope that she would find a more palatable source of sustenance before she was desperate enough to actually have to eat them!

Feeling only slightly less hollow, Cece limped on, until she suddenly stumbled out onto the sunlit beach.

Chapter Seven

More man than monkey now, the nicely-percolating-into-a-Dave form perched himself on what, with a bit of tinkering, could become a very serviceable swivel chair.

From here he could monitor the functionality and progress of the 'avatar' that he had just finished tweaking, after having created it on a whim, then fine-tuned it on a capricious impulse, on realizing that it could, if he had got his calculations correct...and he was fairly sure he had...independently calculate and predict outcomes which would, to say the very least, give him more time to work on his various other pieces of allocated assignments.

Not to mention the many arduous and time-consuming tasks that he tirelessly took on of his own accord, he thought, virtuously.

Not least of which was trying to get the right height and tilt on this swivel chair!

Time was not as important to an almost immortal entity as to, well, let's say, a non-immortal entity.

But to mortal and immortal beings alike, a wrongly positioned tilt on a swivel chair can make a duty shift feel like an eternity!

Chapter Eight

"Urgh! This day is fast turning into the twelve Labours of Heracles, or Hercules, or whatever name he might go under these days!" Cece said out loud to herself, as she dragged the largest pieces of undergrowth that she could manage to haul from the jungles edge, down onto the beach.

"Now that I've found water I don't have anything to carry it in!" she chuntered on. "So, guess who is going to have to drag their Aris through a mile of jungle every time I want to drink!"

"And I've found food, if you can count sour unidentifiable fruit as food, and you don't count the fact that I'm trying *really* hard to ignore the fact that my guts have been gurgling something chronic ever since I ate it!

"But then again that could just be the microbes in the ditch water that I drank, that are trying to get out!"

She paused, putting her hand to her stomach for a moment, then went back to her complaining.

"If I don't find water any nearer, and if I get desperate enough to eat them, at least the fruit is full of water! Well, it made my mouth water anyway... not necessarily in a good way, though!"

She grimaced again at the memory.

Then, again to herself, but still out loud, "So, Heracles, for your next labour, you've just got your shelter to build, and you'll be all set for the night!"

Studying the pile of leafy branches that she had accumulated, Cece was suddenly overcome by exhaustion, and flopped down next to her spoils.

She dragged in a deep breath, and sighed.

"And I have absolutely no idea what I am going to do with any of this stuff! How am I supposed to weave myself a shelter out of all this lot?"

She drew her knee up to her chest so that she could study the injured ankle that had become progressively more swollen over the course of the afternoon, as she had continued to hobble around on it.

It did not look any better up close, and again she wished she had something with which to bind it. Or a paracetamol or two!

She thought longingly of her shoulder-bag, which contained everything barring the kitchen sink, lying at the bottom of the ocean floor, and contemplated another of her pieces of fruit.

She decided her guts were not yet desperate enough for that particular challenge, and instead lay them out ceremoniously next to the pile of shrubbery.

"Bugger!" she said, contemplating the pile of leaves and branches again. "I'll just have to use it as a mattress for tonight, and knit myself a shed tomorrow!"

Despite a niggling memory from a long-ago first aid course, trying to tell her she might regret the action later, Cece released her swollen ankle from her plimsoll, then threw herself on top of the shrubs.

Too tired to even notice a hundred twigs sticking into her entire body, within a very short time she had fallen in to a deep, exhausted, sleep.

A hungry blue crab, sidling along the beach, on its usual route, came across a most unusual object.

It paused in front of the pile of branches and shrubs, climbed up and over the greenery, and stopped at the wrapped-up fleshy creature reclining on the shrubs.

It tentatively nipped at the juiciest looking of five pink protuberances attached to the end of one of the long limbs, and was surprised to find itself in sudden contact with the pointy end of the other long limb.

It was much sharper than its tentative pincer squeeze to the other limb had led it to believe.

The crab was also surprised to realise that it had got to the advanced age that it had, and it *was* quite advanced, for a crab, without having before realised that it could fly!

If only for short distances.

And with no power of self-navigation!

But it found itself doing so now, before crash-landing, with a thwack of its hard carapace, against a nearby rock.

Shaking itself off, and deciding to give the fleshy package-with-a-kick a wide berth, it pierced one of the pieces of fruit on its large pincer instead, and rolled the other piece along ahead of itself, or more accurately, beside itself, as it sidled off down the beach with its fruit supper, still wondering what had just happened.

Cece's activities had all been monitored, and reported upon, as had the crab's activities; information had been responded to by the recipient, and further instructions ... deliberated upon.

Chapter Nine

In response to the ongoing transmissions, and after the afore-mentioned deliberations, and a lot more tweaking of the tilt of an almost perfectly tilted swivel-chair, the working-on-becoming-a-Dave entity fed several vaguely defined directives into the program, along the lines of, 'Continue to ensure the ongoing functionality of the primary study subject!' and, 'Well done, that avatar!"

He also instructed the avatar to use whatever means it had at its disposal, preferably favouring local resources. And using minimal energy output.

The Dave-in-progress being was more than a little aware that he had already exceeded the resources budget that was allowed on a personal project, in creating the avatar.

But he had been frugality itself, he reassured himself, utilising bits of barely developed spare cosmic matter that had been lying around unused, and certainly not likely to be needed, at least until after he had finished his project, at any rate.

And more importantly, he knew he could return the raw material of his avatar back to where he had got it from when he had finished with it, before it was even missed!

By *his* calculation, anyway!

And it wasn't like he hadn't done this before!

He was good at calculations, and projecting outcomes!

It was what he *did*!

His role within his society of self-elected space overlords was, after all, to observe developing species, gather data about them, and make forecasts, predictions, and projections, about how these other species might one day impact upon his own kind, to enable them, when needed, to be able to steer their own almost immortal species out of the line of fire, so to speak!

But to do so within budget!

He was currently using only one small part of his consciousness to continue the exchange of information with his avatar, about the activities of one strangely intriguing castaway, whilst simultaneously observing and analysing the remainder of the planet… and also keeping a vague eye on the rest of the universe!

Whilst also adjusting the tilt of his chair!

So, creating an avatar to do his information gathering for him on this one small project, allowing him more time to devote to the main assignment, as well as his other various private projects, was… economical… to say the least.

And to say the *most*, he thought smugly, nothing short of *genius*!

Carrying out private projects alongside the bigger assignments, enhanced the effectiveness of the larger scaled projects, and so helped them stay more relevant, so Dave-to-be reflected.

They also tended to be more fun!

He would have liked to give himself a pat on the back, while he had a back to pat, but his temporarily almost-human shaped arm could not quite reach.

After a moment's thought, nearly-Dave briefly sprouted a three-foot long Hadaspian appendage from his left ear, just long enough to achieve the required back-patting.

"Where there's a will, there's a way!"

Chapter Ten

When Cece awoke in an unknown place several hours later, her first thought was to panic, and when she had come to a little more, and remembered where she was, and why, her second thought was to *really* panic!

Having talked herself out of panicking, even though she could think of no sane grounds on which to do this, she divided her conscious thoughts into two main categories.

Firstly, she had to decide which pain to prioritise!

Just about every joint and bone in her body had decided to simultaneously register the facts that over the last, who knew how many hours, she had battled the sea, (and won!) as well as having pruned, and gardened, half a desert island; to say nothing of then having slept on a bed of thorns!

In addition to all this, not only had her ankle, which having been released the previous night from the confines of her snugly fitting footwear, swollen to twice the size it had been, but to add to the mix, and for no reason Cece could think of, her big toe was even more swollen and painful than her ankle!

Not to mention being red and shiny!

"Either it's spreading or I'm starting with gout!" she thought glumly, as she frowned down at it.

Secondly, when she had gone to reach for one of the disgusting fruits she had collected from the jungle, with which to freshen her dry mouth, and to provide herself with a paltry breakfast, she had discovered that where she had left two pieces of fruit the previous night, there was now a huge pile of the things!

What the heck!

Had they bred in the night?

Had she been out collecting them in her sleep?

Or had they rolled down from the trees and into, what she laughingly thought of as her 'camp', by themselves?

Her head feeling too woozy to make sense of anything, and too ravenous to care much, Cece decided to do a Scarlett O'Hara, and think about it tomorrow.

She grabbed one of the pieces of fruit, much bigger than the ones she had managed to squeeze into her pockets the day before, and recognising them in the daylight as mangoes, sank her teeth into it, grimacing in anticipation of the sour taste that her experience of the previous day had led her to expect.

She was very pleasantly surprised to find the fruit softer and sweeter than the one she had eaten before, and realised she must have previously eaten an unripe one!

Rather than having dropped from the tree of its own accord, when it had ripened, it had probably been discarded by some wildlife or other, she realised.

Probably because it was unripe, and not fit even for a monkey to eat!

"I've eaten a monkey's leavings!" she mused out loud, starting to giggle, as she munched on what she now concluded was the most delicious food she had ever eaten.

It must be exhaustion, Cece thought, as her giggles threatened to get out of control. She finished the mango and stood up to stretch her muscles, trying to ease some of her aches and pains.

Letting out a sharp cry as she unthinkingly put her full weight on her ankle, she collapsed back to the floor.

"Bugger", she said, when the pain had subsided enough to allow her to speak again. "That's not good!"

Cece knew she was not going to be able to squeeze her swollen foot back into what had already been quite a snug-fitting pair of slip-on pumps, and having already failed at ripping her dress to bits to make bandages, she decided there was nothing else for it, but to try to make a strap out of the entire dress; it was after all, a wraparound dress!

She would just have to wrap it around her foot!

It did not occur to Cece to feel self-conscious about taking off her dress on a deserted island, with no-one there to see her stripped down to her underwear.

However, she did worry about de-vesting herself of the last shred of protection which lay between her and the biting, stinging, and in addition, more recently, although unbeknownst to Cece, *nipping*, army, that were back on full attack mode, since she had been awake enough to worry about them.

She had already accumulated enough bites, she decided, to constitute what she hoped was a full set, and so was in no hurry to collect any more!

She found that the dress, when creatively applied, actually made quite a serviceable bandage, and she managed to manipulate the stitched-in belt of the wraparound, around the rest of the material of the dress, creating quite a firm support for her poor beleaguered foot.

When she tentatively stood up, experimentally putting her weight on it, she found she could do so relatively easily, and the pain was relatively bearable.

Well, everything is relative!

Looking then at the pile of branches and shrubs which had given her a very painful night's sleep, and no protection, with no idea how to turn it into something that would give her some semblance of shelter, Cece felt in equal parts, hopeless and helpless!

She then had the sudden thought that she might be able to glean something slightly more useful from the beach than she had managed to scavenge from the woodland.

The beach was a treasure trove of all things useful if you knew how to look; she knew this for a fact, as she had seen it on tv.

She thought she must have missed the episode on *how* to look though, as nothing came to mind.

Casting another look at the various branches that she had dragged down to the beach, and what she was now beginning to think of as her bonfire pile, without having put too much thought into how she was going to create fire, she thought beachcombing must be at least worth a try!

Cece could not believe her luck however, when almost as soon as she started to scour the beach, in the immediate vicinity of what she had decided to keep as her 'base camp', she stumbled across her very own messenger bag!

Algae-green, and waterlogged, but still fastened! And by the look of it, with the contents still intact!

She lunged for the bag, wrenched open the clasp, and delved inside, dragging out first her lip balm, and caking her lips with it, then routing in a zipped-up side compartment, she looked for, and found, her emergency chocolate stash!

She ripped open the wrapper, her dry mouth suddenly moistening with anticipation, and sank her teeth into a soggy, salt drenched mouthful, of the most disgusting chocolate bar she had ever had the misfortune to put in her mouth.

Spitting out the sea-soaked mess of confectionary, and scraping her tongue on the back of her arm, Cece felt torn between tears and hysterical laughter.

"Well, what did you expect, you idiot? It's probably been eaten by something nasty, and thrown back, since you last laid hands on it!

"Or worse!"

Her mouth scrunched into a grimace, Cece tossed the rest of the spoiled chocolate into the sea, before screwing up the wrapper and throwing it down with all the disdain it deserved.

She then guiltily chased after the only piece of litter on the otherwise pristine island, as a light breeze sent it scurrying across the beach.

She straightened the foil out and tucked it back into the side pocket of her bag, before returning to search through the rest of the compartments.

Various other potentially lifesaving items had survived relatively unscathed, to a greater or lesser degree, as well as a number of useless items, such as her purse, with plastic cards and polymer bank notes, as new!

Her waterlogged mobile phone did not look as though it would be reminding her that she could be having a better service if she just coughed up a little more cash, anytime soon! But a packet of safety pins was remarkably rust free.

The pins would probably be of more use to her than the phone anyway, even if it had survived, she thought.

It was not like she had even had a signal when she was aboard the ship!

Unlike the phone, her pack-away rain-hood seemed to have survived in perfect condition!

Of course it had!

Cece wasn't entirely sure what you were supposed to do with a pack-away rain-hood, except her Nanna had never gone anywhere without one.

Cece had spent years of her early youth rolling her eyes at her Nanna, every time she asked if Cece had her rain-hood, whenever she went anywhere, rain or shine. Because, apparently, you never knew.

This was usually just after she asked if she had been for a wee, and just before she asked if she had decent underwear on, in case she got run over.

And if she had a hanky, just...well... just in case.

She had been in the habit of teasing her Nanna over the queries, saying that they had been out-dated even when her great-gran had been the one chasing her Nanna to the door with them!

But since none of the generations of matriarchs who had invested in Cece's future were around to mind Cece, she had found herself going through almost identical mantras with herself, whenever she walked through the door.

"Had a wee, got tissues, no holes in my kecks."

And in addition to this soothing self-talk, Cece had also started popping the much-maligned rain-hood in her bag, whenever she went away.

Well, you never knew, she'd thought defensively, as she had included it in her cruise luggage. They must get showers in the tropics! She'd tried to remember what read about rain-forests and tropical storms. Yes, the rain-hood might finally have its day!

Her manicure set, a souvenir from Whitby, containing tiny tweezers, a tiny nail file, tiny tinny scissors, two tiny needles and a thoughtfully provided tiny needle threader, due to the even tinier needle eyes that practically no-one could possibly see, along with tiny amounts of black and white thread, and two tiny buttons, all also seemed to have survived relatively intact.

If she needed to repair a doll's out-fit while on the island she was set-up!

And if they hadn't had so thoughtfully provided the needle threader, she thought peevishly, for anyone who does not have 20-20 vision, and super-nimble fingers, they might even have been able to fit in some real sized needles and thread!

'But what are the odds of it not only being washed up, but being washed up on my bit of beach?' her thoughts ran on. 'I mean, *really*! What *are* the odds...?'

Cece suddenly looked about her, having experienced the strangest sensation, almost as though she was being watched, and for the first time she became self-conscious about the fact that she was standing on a beach in the middle of no-where, in nothing but her underwear.

She hugged her arms around her almost naked body.

But even if there *was* anyone else around, she rationalized, she wasn't doing anything other than wearing the equivalent of a bikini on a beach! What could be more natural than that?

But what *were* the odds that her bag should turn up here, by itself?

Almost infinitesimal against it, probably, she thought!

But then again, she reckoned, she was due *something* going in her favour! She had had the infinitesimally bad luck of been washed overboard! Maybe this was the universe's way of settling up!

She must have had the bag over her shoulder when she fell in the water, she decided, and it must have hung on in there with her during her nautical saga, and been thrown out of the water with her!

She had obviously not seen it when she first came round, as she had immediately started walking up the beach.

Yes, that would account for it!

That *must* be it!

Since waking up, she had not yet made the trek up through the jungle for water, on her injured ankle, as she had decided the juicy fruit stash - and her mind again slid away from wondering where that generous pile had appeared from - would suffice for the moment, to keep her hydrated, as well as fed.

Two Herculean Labours, covered in one!

Or should that be Heraclesian Labours, she thought? Hercules? Heracles?

"Well, they are all Greek to me!" she concluded out loud. "Or should that be Roman?"

Either way, she still had some mammoth tasks ahead of her, she knew, and now that she had the fruit, however it had got there, trying to make herself some sort of shelter from the green-stuff she had gathered the previous day, had to take priority.

Cece started to strip the smaller twigs from the larger branches, scratching and blistering her hands as she did so, and all without the help of her 'tools'! She had decided that the tiny nail scissors and nail file, might have survived an epic voyage, but were unlikely to survive introductory shack-building!

Cece continued to grumble her woes to herself.

"Some Labour of Heracles!" she complained. "Making a house from nothing! In game shows at least they give them stuff! Or leave stuff for them to find!"

Like a handbag full of… even if for the most part useless… emergency gear?

Cece decided to continue with her Scarlett approach, and dismiss that thought, as she could not quite get her head around finding her bag, including contents, not only washed up, intact, but right on 'her' bit of beach!

And there were bits and pieces in there she had not even remembered packing in it!

Although she had always packed her handbag with enough 'just in case' items to cater for all emergencies, never in her wildest dreams had she ever anticipated this one!

And she had some pretty wild dreams!

Cece thought ruefully about the small zipped plastic bag in her handbag, full of safety pins and such, which she had thought she might have been able to bring even a mouthful or so of water back with her when she did her next water-run, but to her frustration had realised, on closer inspection, that the bag had been punctured by its contents, and so was no longer watertight.

She had even unfolded the fold-away rain-hood, for the first time ever, since she had had it, only to find that 10 years of being folded in the same creases does nothing for the integrity of polythene! And so despite what she thought she knew about the longevity of plastic, and polyurethanes, and the environmental implications, this particular lifetime product apparently only lasted a lifetime if you did not use it!

But to be fair, she mused to herself, if she had not pitched up on a desert island it probably would have lasted a lifetime, as it would have remained unopened in one handbag or another for pretty much the rest of her life!

But as it was, the polythene had started to break-down along the fold lines of the hood, so, much like Cece's explanation to herself, as to how her handbag had turned up, it would not hold water!

She struggled to yank a massive piece of branch out of her pile, grunting loudly as she did so, thinking it might help her to release some of her frustrations onto the job.

"I AM HERACLES!" She bellowed to the world, as she finally managed to extricate the bough and throw it down onto the sand.

"No, ***I*** am Heracles!" she then shouted, pushing her head back and dipping her chin onto her chest to force out deeper, rumbling tones.

"No, *I* am Heracles", she continued in yet another tone, then… "Oh no! That's Spartacus, isn't it? Wrong film! You're mixing up your Greek myths with your Roaming leg-ends again Cece!

"And also, I have absolutely no idea what I am supposed to do with all these branches once I've stripped them!" she continued muttering out loud to herself. "Sleep on a pile of stripped branches rather than a pile of branches with twigs sticking out of them? Well at least that might be a bit more comfortable!

"And I'm going to need a *lot* more than this to make anything other than a door mat!" she chuntered, looking ruefully at the large pile of foliage which had become a much smaller pile of stripped sticks.

She piled up the leaves separately.

"My mattress," she muttered, then, on further inspection, after scrunching them up together, "Well, my pillow, at any rate".

Realizing she was going to have to trek back up into the jungle, and drag down many more branches and such, before she could start to construct anything of any use, she decided to first eat some more fruit for sustenance, and maybe re-strap her throbbing foot and ankle, before she tackled the task

She stretched out her aching back, then thumping her chest, Tarzan- style, and mixing her metaphors, as well as her myths, yelled to the beach,

"I am Heracles!" and then in yet another tone, "No, *I* am Heracles!"

"No," said a quiet voice in the trees. "*I* am Heracles."

Chapter Eleven

The first crewman of the submersible-saucer, who had yet to land upon the moniker of 'John', raised what would have been an eyebrow, if he had had eyebrows, as he looked at the second crewmate, who had already chosen, but not yet quite adapted to, the name 'Dave'.

And if the second crewman, nearly-Dave, had had lips to bite, and teeth with which to bite them, he would have been chewing on them, in what, for all the worlds, would have appeared to be consternation.

However, he had not yet quite perfected those fine facial features, so he did not.

And if anyone who had had a common language with the individuals who were yet to become John and Dave had been in earshot, they may have overheard a conversation that went something like...

"You seem to be spending an awful lot of time and resources on one tiny part of the project, crewman. You're not getting... *over involved*... again... are you?"

"No! Of course I'm not! I'm just interacting with an… avatar... that I created to oversee a particularly interesting subject, and which I have put in place for the exact purpose of ensuring that I *don't* get 'over involved', as you so delicately put it!

"Anyway, I wouldn't dare! Not after getting demoted to Beyond the Lowliest of the Low, the last time I got *involved*, and was deemed to have *interfered* in the natural progress of a developing lifeform."

"Are you implying that you *didn't* interfere with the progress of a developing lifeform?" The first crewman's incredulity would have been apparent in any language.

"You wiped out an entire species!"

Soon-to-be-Dave managed, with or without a face, to aim a disgruntled scowl in almost-John's direction, before that character continued his remonstrations, "And anyway, you did *not* get demoted to *beyond* the Lowliest of the Low, you got demoted to the *exact* same rank as Lowliest of the Low!

"I ought to know! I have been a Lowliest of the Low for my entire career! But, if you *don't* mind, I would *rather* that you refer to me by my full title which is *Junior Assistant Researcher* -Lowliest of the Low, or preferably, just JAR- LOL, if you will! It's more dignified!"

This time it was the entity-who-would-be-Dave's turn for non-existent eyebrows to disappear into a non-existent hairline. "If you say so, crewman!"

"And if I can also point out," not-yet-John continued indignantly, "even being a JAR -LOL in an organisation as prestigious as ours is still an honour! Although it does rankle a bit, I admit, still being graded as a *junior* research assistant, after all these millennia of flawless service!"

"And that, my friend, is exactly what holds you back from promotion, if you ask me!" the second crewman could not help but re-join, "Because your *flawless* service is a result of you never having taken a risk!

"You don't think outside the box, or get close enough to the subjects to work out what makes them *tick*! You are way too good at following instructions!"

-And I *did* get demoted to *beyond* the Lowliest of the Low, the second crewman, yet-to-become-Dave, thought glumly. But that had been on an entirely different occasion of him having been taken to task for 'using his initiative' to resolve a problem.

But the soon-to-be-John entity did not know about that little escapade, so he was not aware that his erstwhile senior had not just been demoted to being his equal in rank, but was now his junior.

Nor was he aware that an entire new grading had had to be created to allow an additional demotion for his colleague, who was now quite literally entitled *Beyond* the Lowliest of the Low!

But pre-Dave felt sure he would soon climb back up through the ranks without there ever being a need for his colleague to find out about this latest humiliation, because, he reflected smugly, unlike his rule-following colleague, he *did* actually understand how the system worked!

They were allowed enough freedom to make the mistakes without which no real advancements were ever likely to be made.

But the powers-that-be were never going to take responsibility when things went wrong!

They would plead shocked ignorance to his rule bendings when problems came to light!

And would penalise him accordingly, to 'save face'... if they had *had* faces...

But whilst acknowledging the risks to the multitude of species, on innumerable planets, that thirst for knowledge, which all from his almost immortal species possessed, could not quite be sated by observation, and making projections alone.

The dark and desperate need for illicit interactions, even vicarious ones, with some of the fascinating species they chose to study, sometimes became too overwhelming for some members of their old and jaded race.

Research teams' tendencies to stray from the rule books in order to test out hypotheses, had been observed from afar (very afar!) by senior supervisors, on countless occasions, and been allowed to proceed, unchecked.

The crewman soon-to-be-known-as-Dave, for example, had enough of a reputation for creating such a multitude of myths and legends, on so many planets, by his spontaneous appearances among mortals, to make him a bit of a legend in his own right!

And he had received innumerable plaudits for his discoveries and theories!

But as soon as a minor indiscretion resulted in a fairly harmless, and easily rectified situation, he was usually hauled over the proverbial coals, and left to carry all the blame!

He would not put up with it, except...he did so love the opportunities his position afforded him!

There was nothing quite like it really, when you have all eternity to fill!

But demoting him to Beyond the Lowliest of Low was totally uncalled for! *Just* for wiping out a minor civilisation!

Or two...

***... And** a 45,000-year-old memory of a fascinating and beautiful creature crept unbidden into Dave's mind...*

...Blinding light lit up the night sky, and Mica pressed herself up against Roc's sinewy back, her fingers entwining themselves into the thick tanned hide hanging over his shoul-

der. He placed a large calloused hand over her smaller, but equally rough one, and was troubled to realise that it was trembling beneath his own.

Roc had rarely known his beautiful and fearless Neanderthal mate to be afraid of anything before. Often choosing to hunt alongside him and the other men rather than gather roots and tanning animal hides with the women, she had saved his life as many times as he had hers.

The only other time he could remember Mica being afraid, was after yet another battle between the ferocious sky warriors, whose deafening drums and brilliant white spears often appeared during the rains, chasing off their prey, and ruining their hunts!

Mica had disappeared from his side, as the spears of light had torn through the sky, startling the herd of mammoth they had been hunting into a full-blown stampede!

She had not reappeared until several days later, telling him she did not know where she had been, and keeping her head down, and her eyes averted.

He suspected that, in the confusion of the stampede, she had been taken by a warrior from another tribe, and had fought her way free and back to him, but was unwilling to tell him in case he rejected her.

He would not do that. Roc was as happy and relieved to have Mica back, as she was to be back, but he did not ask her about it again, and did not complain that she now chose to stay by his side, hunting, every day.

And it was as though it had not happened… until the lightning returned, and he now found her trembling and clinging to him like a child.

Mica could not tell Roc where she had been, or what had happened to her.

The experience had been so far out of her understanding that she could not even process it herself, but she knew that Roc would *throw her off if he knew what had happened!*

She was glad he did not ask questions, and had put it out of her mind, until she eventually decided that the memory had been nothing other than one of the visions which often came to lighten up the darkness of the night, as she lay sleeping in Roc's arms.

Until the weird lightning returned, and Mica somehow knew it was here for her!

She trembled more than she had at her first hunt as a child, when an injured and half crazed smilodon had started picking off the tribe's youngsters from the caves during the nights, and Mica's father had decided that it was safer to bring his plucky young daughter along on the hunt, than to leave her under the safeguard of the elders.

He had almost lost his own life in that ferocious battle with the desperate and mortally wounded cat, encouraging his young warrior child to finish the animal off, when it was all but dead anyway.

She had relished being part of the hunt, and with her father having earned the right to smear the great beast's blood on his daughter's face, Mica had tasted the lifeblood from her first kill as proudly as though she had slain the gigantic cat all by herself!

But as the lightning tore across the sky, Mica waited for she knew not what, cowering behind Roc, feeling like a helpless elder, knowing that she would not be able to fight it when it came for her again.

***This** time, however, the bright streaks that ripped apart the skies were just lightning; the start of a wild electrical storm which had been brewing for days, and would likely continue* *to ravage the valley that Mica and Roc called home for some days to come.*

The storm would result in poor hunting, but it would also deter many of the larger beasts from tracking them to their own lair among the deep caves which lent them some protection against the elements and, to some lesser degree, from the wild beasts with whom they shared the valley.

Roc eyed his mate from time to time over the stormy days, but said nothing, and Mica, in her turn, stayed close to Roc throughout several days of lightning-strike; nor did he deter her from doing so.

And as the fierce storms started to diminish, she nodded gratefully to the lightning god, thanking him for sparing her, this time.

Roc saw the gesture, and his heavy brow furrowed into a frown.

Chapter Twelve

Cece managed to detach a huge bough from a tree quite near the forest edge, by half climbing up, and swinging from it, emitting a shrill tarzanesque yodel, followed by an even shriller, "*Ouch*!" as she landed unceremoniously on the tree's prominent roots.

As she was making her way backwards, down to her 'campsite', dragging the heavy piece of foliage behind her, and glancing only occasionally over her shoulder to orientate herself, Cece did not immediately see the massive pile of stripped branches awaiting her return.

As she neared the pile of wood she had left, she did a sudden double-take, thinking for a moment she was dragging her spoils towards a mound of sea-drift instead of her camp.

She turned, and started walking forwards, still pulling the dead weight of wood behind her, her steps slowing, until she came to a full stop some meters away from the pile, now higher than her own height, of stripped and neatly stacked branches.

Her stomach clenched as she dropped her own branch and swung round to scan the beach, her eyes settling on the treeline from which she herself had just emerged.

Her heart pounding almost out of her chest, she shouted out,

"Hello! *Hello*! HELLO! Who's there? *Who's there*?" Her voice cracked at her last yell, and after taking a deep breath to try again, she suddenly stopped herself.

Who *exactly* was on the island with her?

And should she be attracting their attention?

Well, clearly, they already knew she was there!

And had been watching her!

Waiting till she left her site, to deliver the branches!

And must also have left her the fruit!

So, they could not mean her any harm! Could they?

But why had they not come to speak to her? Surely it could not be anyone from the ship?

She suddenly realised how stupid she had been in assuming that she was on a *deserted*, desert island!

She could be anywhere!

Absolutely anywhere!

Not only did she have *no clue* as to how long she had been in the water, or how far she may have conceivably been carried by the sea, she had very little idea as to how far the ship had been from any known, or unknown, land masses when the wave hit!

She had been keeping her eye on the schedule, of course, as to when they were due to next dock and explore the various destinations on the agenda, but that didn't mean they were not near other smaller islands!

Maybe ones not set up for the tourist trade? Or maybe not very friendly to tourists? She decided not to worry about that one.

They were clearly not *un*friendly towards tourists. Her mouth twisted in wry humour. Was she seriously considering herself to be a *tourist* on this island now?

Anyway, someone had seen fit to gather fruit for her, and strip half a forest worth of branches to help her in her endeavours!

An invite to their village would have been *nicer*, she thought, but gratitude and small mercies, and all that; and *maybe* it was just a small, shy boy?

"Please come out! There's just little old me!" she called encouragingly.

Then, glancing again at the size of the wood-pile, another thought pushed aside her momentary elation; maybe *several* small, shy boys?

Or several large, timid men?

"Yes, there's just... me..." more hesitantly, and then, feigning confidence "*...and my army!*"

She got to the edge of the jungle, and stopped; her courage didn't quite reach into the trees.

She could see no movement in the treeline, and the bird and insect sounds, and what was possibly the occasional primate call, all of which she was becoming accustomed to, were the only sounds she could make out.

The sense she had had earlier of someone watching her had returned, making the hair stand up on her arms again, but this time she knew she was not imagining it.

"I'm heading back to my camp. To make my shelter. You know, with the wood you got me? If you want to come say hello, I would really love for you to come and talk to me!"

She doubted that whoever was out there spoke English, and they clearly did not want to speak to her, but she felt she should try to communicate anyway.

If there were potential friends here, she was obviously going to need to win over their trust!

She needed all the help she could get!

And she missed not having anyone to talk to. A ridiculous amount!

And if there were potential *enemies* out there, well, they obviously already knew she was there!

She made her way back to her wood pile, and set about trying to work out how to fashion herself some sort of shelter.

She sat with her back to the sea, facing the trees so that she would see anyone emerge from there.

The sun was beating down quite relentlessly, when, after two hours of trying to twist and weave the green sinewy branches into a panel of some description, and her glances up towards the trees had become less frequent, Cece eventually straightened up from her toils, and declared to herself,

"Well! I have a door! I don't have anything to hang it on, or hang it with, for that matter, but I have a door!"

Hunger and thirst were again becoming an issue, and although her ankle was not throbbing as violently as it had previously, she knew she had to try not to put her weight on it any more than she had to, to give it time to recover.

She weighed up her options.

The massive pile of fruit would provide her with both food and fluid, unless the flies and insects that had already tried to make several meals out of them finished them off first.

She had even discovered a small packet of pain-relief tablets in her miraculously recovered shoulder-bag, but thought she ought to keep these for emergencies.

Cece realised that she seemed to have raised the bar quite significantly as to what constituted an emergency since landing on the island.

Her ankle was nowhere near as painful as it had been the previous day when she had first injured it, so she didn't feel she could justify taking one, but she spent a moment cherishing them, and touching the packet to her lips!

Never did she think she would feel so sentimental about a packet of analgesia.

She should unwrap her ankle, and see how the swelling was doing, Cece decided. It was only as she started to unwrap the wrap-around dress from her ankle that it occurred to her that she had been trying to have her dialogue with strange island dwellers in her underwear!

She was as covered up as she would have been if she was in a bikini, she knew, and she *was* on a beach after all! But she felt suddenly self-conscious, and even found herself crossing her arms across her chest again, as she glanced once more up towards the trees.

"Stupid!" she told herself. "Anyone out there has seen all there is to see now anyway! But my dress might protect me from the sun a bit, if my ankle can manage without it now, so I might as well alternate between wearing it and using it for a bandage for a bit."

And with that justification Cece finished unwrapping the sand-filthy black dress from her swollen foot, shook it out, and wrapped it back round her body.

Her ankle did not look too bad, but it suddenly occurred to her that soaking it in cold sea-water, which was not too far away now, as the tide was quite high, might help reduce the swelling further.

Searching among the pile of stripped branches, Cece selected one of the sturdiest ones to help her hobble down to the water's edge without having to put her full weight on the unstrapped limb.

Tucking her dress up into her underwear, Cece waded into the water.

Not as cold as the cool North Sea that she was used to paddling in, but the tide washing in from the vast Pacific Ocean was still cool enough to offer instant relief to the poor offended ankle.

Cece bent down so that she could also dip her sore hands into the gently lapping surf, taking a moment to enjoy the soothing water.

She examined the variety of bites and scratches she was collecting, mainly on her arms, and was relieved to see, that irritating as they were, nothing seemed to be infected.

She was undecided, however, as to whether the sea-salt would help, or hinder, the wounds, and concluded that as her ankle had had enough of a soak, she ought to make her way back to her unbuilt shack anyway.

Turning away from the mesmerising view of azure sky and aquamarine water lapping up onto the golden sands, she came to a stock-still stance, as she immediately realised something about her campsite had changed.

As Cece headed back towards where she had left the stack of branches, and one rough finished panel, she was starting to make out that the pile of stripped branches had been replaced, by a whole stack of panels!

Dozens of rough finished panels, *identical* to the one she had just taken hours to weave, were now stacked up against each other!

Chapter Thirteen

"**This** is nice John," said Dave, pouring himself a cup of tea from a tartan thermos flask, and standing it on the panel in front of his swivel seat.

He paused for a moment, peering out of the large viewscreen, which was currently functioning as a porthole, and watched a large mottled grouper fish, which, without any real interest, was watching him back.

"If you say so...Dave." 'John' was less enamoured with the 'immersive research' approach they had agreed to intermittently trial.

"And I'm calling you Dave, seeing as how you are in 'Dave mode', but really, as you know, I'm not too sure about this one."

It was one thing, he acknowledged, imitating their research subjects to minimise interference in the natural progression of a species.

He understood the logic of that!

There were innumerable examples of how researchers had inadvertently interfered with the development of a species, just by having been seen, or, as in the case of the lethargic, but surprisingly sensitive, Dallydorfs in the Thadiae galaxy, for example, where one of his own kind had not so much been *seen*, but having been somehow *sensed* or otherwise 'detected', in their natural, non-corporeal state.

These encounters had invariably led to a whole range of difficulties.

After one such brief experience the Dallydorfs had been inspired to go away and invent a *polymorph* detector, which had effectively advanced their civilisation by some millennia beyond which any projections had predicted!

Fortunately, in that particular instance, the species had inexplicably died out, at a rate greatly in advance of the projection anyway, so the skewed data had not been as much of an issue as it could have been!

If not for that fortunate happenstance, the researcher's reputation could have been ruined, due to one random encounter with the wrong individual!

That had also been one of 'Dave's' assignments, John remembered, glancing sideways at his colleague, and feeling an inexplicable urge to purse his lips.

Dave always seemed to land on his feet, or whatever he was using as stabilising appendages at any given moment!

But it was quite another thing, John felt, being asked to actually *assume the identity* of an individual that the species they were observing could relate to, *just in case* contact occurred!

And John was not convinced that they had totally understood this assignment anyway, nor indeed that they had got the environment *one hundred* percent accurate!

Also, John could not help but think that one of their characters ought to have a more senior position to the other, just to add *depth*, or another dimension, to their interactions.

He could also not help but think that as he had taken on the bulk of researching, designing, and creating the ship, that he should be the one to take on the role of senior crewmen!

And much as he was trying to immerse himself in the whole 'John' personae, he could not quite work out what his *motivation* was supposed to be!

He would just have to give the whole situation more thought.

Or possibly do more research.

Or maybe just take another look at the instructions on the assignment!

Chapter Fourteen

Cece stood frozen to the spot, staring at the woven panels.

How could that even be? She had only been away from the place for half an hour, if that!

What on earth was happening?

Just exactly how many people were out there watching her?

And who *were* they?

A team of panel weaving DIY experts?

The sturdy branch that Cece had used to help her hobble to the water was nowhere near strong enough to support her injured ankle, as well as her suddenly jellied legs, and Cece flopped to her knees, her mouth gaping, goldfish-like, the better to drag in enough oxygen to try to steady herself.

Trying to be pragmatic, Cece eventually decided, that for the moment at least, she had to make the most of this dreamlike existence that she seemed to be living in, and rather than look this strange gift-horse in the mouth, whatever its nature, she had better take advantage of it.

"O*kaayy* ..." the word left her mouth on a deep exhalation. "Well…I need food, water, shelter… food, water, shelter..." she found reverting to mantra helped her to calm herself, "but not necessarily in that order! And I think I need to add … *getting a grip of my marbles…* to the list!"

Another steadying inhalation, then, "Right, I have a massive pile of … festering … fruit, which will provide me with enough food and drink, I suppose, to be going on with.

"And I also have a whole shed load of panels, apparently, now, as well!"

Cece suddenly realised that she could not bring herself to look in the direction of the treeline, where she felt her Secret Santa must be lurking, probably waiting for some sign of gratitude, or at least a sign of her acceptance of the gift.

But as though trapped in a nightmare, unable to turn to see what was in the dark, her neck felt rigid, her eyes unable to swivel in the direction where who-knew-what was hiding.

Keeping her eyes firmly down, she decided to distract herself by juggling the pile of panels into a shelter. Picking up a piece of the less insect nibbled fruit to munch on, as she dragged the panels out across the beach, she assessed what she had.

Without anything to attach the panels to each other, after an hour of hobbling round mainly on her knees to give her ankle a rest, she realised that the most she was going to achieve was a very large house of cards, which would, as a best-case scenario, provide her with the most minimal amount of shelter!

And as a worst-case scenario would come tumbling in on her and do her a serious injury!

Closing her eyes and puffing out another breath, and then turning her head with her eyes still closed in the direction of the treeline, she determined to head back to the jungle to try to find vines, or whatever was this season's wilderness 'string' offering.

Forcing her eyes open, and seeing nothing untoward, she ventured a searching scan up and down along the beach, where sand ran into scrub, and scrub ran into shrub, and seeing nothing to further add to her consternation, she put practicality to the forefront of her mind, and modesty to the back, and slipped off her much-abused dress, to again securely bind up her throbbing ankle.

Then bending to pick up her sturdy bough, she started to hobble purposefully back up to the trees.

The shape in the woods continued its observation as she approached, remaining totally immobile, even as she passed within feet of its position, only turning to continue its observation after she had passed by.

Following the animal track she had followed the previous day; this time it didn't seem to take Cece nearly as long to reach the fresh water source.

Thirstily gulping down as much water as she could when she found it, and cursing again that she had nothing to enable her to carry any water back to her camp, she sat down to rest her ankle and consider her situation.

The ripe juicy mangoes, of which she already had copious amounts back at the camp, she now knew were abundantly available to her, since she had realised that she only needed to lift her eyes and to look up above her head occasionally; so she knew she would not starve!

But despite several Tarzan films clearly indicating that various versatile vines hung conveniently and conspicuously from every tree top, in every wooded area, this was not proving to be the case!

She may have realized that if she had actually looked a little higher, that indeed it *was* the case, but Cece's often tunnel vision approach to life had never lent itself to her developing the skill of looking further than the end of her nose!

And so she remained oblivious to the swathes of vines dangling above her head!

Cece realised she needed a plan if she was not to spend another night in the open air on the beach, snuggled up on her bush mattress, doing a good impersonation of a person-in-a-basket meal.

Scanning the trees around her, her eyes suddenly alighted on the long wide leaves, seeming, to Cece, to be growing straight out of the trunk of the tree straight opposite her.

The leaves seemed to lap over each other, like one of those trees you could make from paper, by rolling a sheet up very tightly, snipping downwards into the top, then telescoping the whole thing out, until you had a tall white frilly paper tree!

Pushing herself to her feet, Cece got a good hold of one of the leaves, and with much effort, managed to peel it off the tree, causing a host of ants, among other tiny lifeforms, to respond to the sudden emergency in their microscopic world, by spilling out, in drill formation, and pouring down the tree.

Cece jumped back with a yell, and slapped defensively at her arms, despite none of the creatures being anywhere near her skin.

Making a small grimace with her mouth, she girded her loins and finished ripping the leaf off the tree trunk, and studied it.

She tried stripping it lengthways, using her fingernail to make a nick at the top of the leaf to help her endeavours, and was relieved when her first attempt resulted in the leaf splitting neatly from end to end, with very little effort.

She went on to shredding the leaf into several long thin pieces, and then; moment of truth time!

She wrapped either end of one of the pieces around the fingers of either hand and gave it a sharp yank!

It snapped in her hand.

"Arghh!" She growled, then, "Bugger!"

Realizing she was in no position to give up, she looked around again, and noticed large leaves were the going trend, and settled on a rather large shrub whose leaves were not quite as big as the paper telescope tree, and did not grow directly out of the trunk.

She pulled off one of these leaves, with much more ease than the last one, and again shredded, then wrapped a strand around her fingers. She gave it a good hard tug, and the yell she let out this time was one of pure joy!

Well maybe not *pure* joy, as it had also cut into her fingers!

Gleefully Cece shredded the one leaf into several two-foot strips, and tried the experiment several times to make sure the first one had not been a fluke.

Success had rarely tasted so sweet to Cece, as she started to gather arms full of the stuff, and still trying to hang on to her stick, even though it was now mostly lost among the arms-full of foliage, she started to limp back to camp.

Several minutes later, and having lost half of her bounty already, and her throbbing ankle telling her she needed the support of her stick, she tried to shuffle what was left of her load under one arm, to better enable her to use her makeshift crutch, when a sudden thought occurred to her.

"BUGGER!", she said loudly, to no-one in particular, while attempting to surreptitiously peer into the trees.

"I'll probably need a lot more of these strippable leaves, but this is all I can carry!" and she let some of the ones that she was struggling with drop to the floor.

And with another glance around, and a more manageable load under one arm, and her sturdy stick solidly supporting her from the other hand, she set off back to camp.

"Bugger!" no-one in particular said quietly to himself, before turning to head back deeper into the jungle, pushing several low dangling vines out of his way as he made his way back to where the strippable leaves grew.

Chapter Fifteen

Cece did not feel overly surprised to see a small mountain of large leaves awaiting her when she got back to her camp.

She did, however, feel a little surprised that the larger of the leaves she had slept on the previous night had also been diligently separated from the pile of other foliage which had constituted her mattress, and put rather conspicuously to one side.

She felt catered for, but at the same time rebuked, for having shown a lack of initiative!

Starting to take these strange phenomena for granted, she quietly shredded several of the larger leaves into thin sinewy threads.

After contemplating the pile of roughly woven palettes for a few moments, Cece worked out a way, by using the threads and a small twig that she had fashioned into an implement with which to poke the threads between the woven branches, and with some huffing and puffing to herself, to secure two, then three, panels together.

Then, deliberately leaving the task half done, she limped off towards the water's edge, and away from her camp.

She walked down as far as the shoreline and stood soaking her ankle in the cool water, her back to her camp, staring out to sea.

She allowed the allure of the water to captivate her for a moment, before turning her gaze to scanning the shallows again, checking for any sign of debris.

There was no sign of anything having washed ashore, other than herself and her bag, so she had to conclude that she alone had been knocked overboard, which obviously, looking at the bigger picture, was preferable than signs of the ship having gone down in a freak wave.

But she could not help but think that, looking at the *smaller* picture, she would have been much better off if more than just herself had been tipped from a ship!

It was unlikely now, she thought to herself, that anyone else was going to wash up. Not alive anyway

But a regular supply of flotsam washing ashore would not have gone amiss

At this stage, she would have even settled for a bit of jetsam!

Pausing a moment before turning back to the camp, she suddenly decided to think out loud, "It would be really helpful if the odd box of supplies, or a first aid box, or matches, or something I could carry water in, got washed up!

She realised that she thought out loud a lot more than she used to. And more loudly, too.

What was she hoping for anyway?

A miracle?

Sighing heavily, she decided that she had given her unseen friend, or friends, long enough to prove, or disprove her theories, and she turned slowly back to face her camp, to be met by the sight of a row of three-sided roofless shacks, like so many toilet cubicles, lined up where she had left the one three-sided cubicle.

"Okaayy...." Cece drew the word out, as though that would give the situation more gravitas. "Well, that's something…not as useful as supplies from the ship would have been, but definitely...something!"

…And the wind carried away the sound of another heavy sigh, followed by an almost imperceptible splashing, as of footsteps plodding resignedly into the depths of the ocean.

Chapter Sixteen

Cece limped back up the beach, to further assess the situation. Most of the panels had been strung together in groups of three, but two remaining panels, being short of a third to make another three-sided shelter, had been abandoned alongside a pile of spare, as yet unshredded, leaves.

Cece managed to manhandle two of the three sided constructions together, making a six-sided shack, one of the sides being manoeuvrable enough on its leafy hinge to serve as a door, and after forcing the whole structure down into the packed sand as far as she was able, she wedged the two spare panels into the packed sand either side of the construction, lending it some small degree of stability.

She then managed to flatten out another one of the three-sided cubicles, and hoist it aloft on top of the shack, making a fair representation, visually at least, of a windowless, hexagonal, wicker cabin!

"I don't know if it would stand up to a storm," Cece thought, "but tonight at least I have some semblance of a shelter to rest my bone-weary bod".

Wrapped up in dealing with the very harsh reality of surviving the moment, and a natural devotee of never put off until tomorrow what you can reasonably put off till next week, Cece had almost managed to avoid thinking, in too much detail at any rate, about the direness of her situation.

But there was one thought that even Cece had been having trouble avoiding altogether, as she had been trailing through the jungle looking for seemingly non-existent vines, and which came back to her yet again, briefly, before she dragged her mashings of bedding into her new shack and threw down her exhausted, wiry frame onto the insect riddled bedding.

She may have been washed overboard, alone, or she may be one of hundreds who were victims of a freak sinking, but how long would it be before anyone seriously noticed that she was missing?

The various parties on board with whom Cece had affiliated herself, would probably assume she had decided to spend time with one of the other groups; if they thought of her at all!

Even the girls she was with when it happened, unless they had actually seen her being washed overboard, would probably assume she had nipped off to get dry clothes on, and then swapped groups!

She had made such a point of not being tied to anyone!

And who, from her life back home, would miss her, really?

Cece had no family, since Nanna, the grandmother who had raised her, and who Cece had considered to be eternally youthful, it transpired, had been neither that, nor, sadly, immortal, leaving Cece, barely out of her teens, to fend for herself; a young woman, suddenly older than her years.

She had made a point of sending out her Christmas cards early, and to everyone she knew, bragging about the upcoming trip!

Pride had led her to imply that the extended nature of her luxurious break was more of an indication of an unexpected windfall, rather than an unexpected state of joblessness, so distant family and friends alike may assume she was making the best of her good fortune, and certainly not in need of rescuing!

The prosecco crowd knew she was on ventures bold, but would probably just come to the conclusion that she had decided to extend the adventure, if they noticed she was over-due back, or absent from their next payday gathering.

Or they might assume that she had eventually met someone!

Or could no longer afford the nights out, with no pay packet coming in!

Or that she had found another job, and was in with a new crowd!

Or just decided life offered more interesting opportunities than alcohol and late nights!

And she was not that close to any of them that they were likely to be ringing to check which of those boxes she was ticking!

With a shock, she realised that there wasn't really anyone she could think of who would either know, or particularly care, if she disappeared off the face of the earth!

For someone who had once considered herself to be a people person, how had she managed to create a life for herself, where no-one would really miss her if she wasn't there?

She assumed that at some stage there might be an investigation into why her rent and bills were not being paid, once her bank account ran dry, but as she had left enough of her redundancy money in there to see her over for a couple of months while she job hunted after her holiday, that might not be any time soon!

There were probably takeaway food delivery people who would notice her absence first!

She had left all her house plants with watering sticks stuck in their pots, and felt a pang of guilt for her poor plants when she realised that they were only set up to be fed and watered for a month!

Misery vied with exhaustion as she tried to plump up a pile of leaves into something resembling a pillow, and unwrapping her ankle, hugged the multi-purpose dress around her, as she tried to avoid the realization that not only was it unlikely that anyone was going to be sending out a search party any time soon, but that the individuals who were likely to most miss her presence in their lives, if she did not return, were her landlady and a potted geranium!

"If I survive this, I really need to make more of an effort to make a proper friend or two!" she snuffled to herself, self-pity draining her of her last bit of energy, as she fell into deep dreamless oblivion.

Chapter Seventeen

Cece awoke from her exhausted sleep hungry, thirsty, and stiff, and itching in innumerable places, where she had scratched at her various bites in her sleep.

But considering the darkness which had surrounded her thoughts the night before, as well as the darkness which she wrongly assumed had surrounded her tired body as she slept, she was surprised to realise she was feeling strangely buoyant, and eager to see what the day would bring.

Still not knowing what to make of the strange goings on, on her island, she decided to do another Scarlett, and 'think about it tomorrow'.

She ate as many of the juicy mangos as were still edible, and then said out loud to the fresh air, "I could really do with some more of these!"

Then, just to be clear, held a sample piece out at arm's length.

"Fruit," she clarified, "I'll need more fresh fruit. The insects have eaten most of mine."

Then, more quietly to herself, "Well that's dinner sorted!"

She stood then, hands on hips, surveying her handywork of the day before; it had at least survived the night!

Testing her weight on her injured ankle, she was relieved to note it was nowhere near as tender as it had been. She also noted that it was not as swollen, and so decided she could manage without her stick on her ventures today, and without re-wrapping her ankle.

Feeling quietly hopeful, Cece headed down to the beach to see what the tide might have brought in.

Drifting along the water's edge, the first thing that she happened across came as more of a surprise than her own suitcase packed full of all her worldly belongings would have done.

Although the suitcase would have been more useful.

What she actually came across, glistening in the water's edge, brought to her attention by the sun catching on its spiralised pattern, was an almost perfect ammonoid fossil, eddying back and forth on the edge of the gentle outgoing waves.

"Oh!" she said pouncing on it, the worries of her situation momentarily forgotten in the wonder of the find!

"An ammonite! Oh! *What a beauty*!"

She snatched it up, first examining the crisp lines of the intricate spiralling form, then automatically turning round as if to share the excitement of the find with a companion, before realizing with a jolt, that she had no-one with whom to share the find; or indeed, anything else!

The joy leached somewhat out of the moment, but not quite able to deprive herself of the small treasure, despite the impracticality of hanging on to it, she tucked it down the front of her dress, giving herself a lopsided-boob effect, and carried on her beachcombing.

Trying to redress the balance of the sheer frivolity of collecting the fossil, whilst also redressing the balance of the lop-sided boob effect, Cece went on to scoop up a large clam shell, and tucked that down the other side of the top of her dress.

'That would make a good cup' she thought, 'if I had anything to drink.'

She then bent down again and picked up a tiny, but beautiful, colourful stone, that had caught her eye as she bent to collect the clam, and tucked that into her cleavage also.

She wasn't quite sure what that might come in useful for, but after a lifelong love of beachcombing for fossils and unusual coloured stones and shells in her 'other' life, old habits die hard; and it certainly was pretty!

Cece would have been more than a little surprised, and perhaps somewhat gratified, to have known that her finds, and her reaction to them, had indeed been shared, noted, reported upon, and filed away.

Chapter Eighteen

Dave swivelled on his swivel chair, and idly scanned the screen in front of him, twisting the view-screen channel dial. The dial did not actually function, but helped to give him the impression of flicking between visual summaries of his various projects, whilst also watching the colourful tropical fish pass by, which he found oddly relaxing; he knew not why!

But he did also find the rows of figures, viewed in this two-dimensional visual format, oddly mesmeric, and was feeling complacently 'immersed' in his new personae.

He had skimmed through a sample selection of the reports, sent in by the avatar.

Nothing of any great significance to analyse there yet, he thought, languorously giving his chair a full 360-degree spin, as the combination of information and queries danced across the screen.

Reading words, and using *eyes*, might not be as efficient as absorbing infinite masses of spontaneously available information, Dave reflected, but there was something eminently satisfying about the experience. He felt he was doing some real, *quality* research.

He might even get some sort of extra credit for the authenticity of his research methodology, he mused.

Obviously, there wasn't much for the avatar to report yet, he acknowledged, as the research subject needed to settle in to the situation that he had instructed the avatar to place her in; a remote, deserted island, without any *physical* contact from Dave, or anyone else, for that matter.

She should be well out of harm's way there, he concluded happily to himself.

And more to the point, highly unlikely to get him into any more bother!

But he and John and the ship were able to hang around in the vicinity; near enough to pop over and introduce himself in his new Dave form if he wanted to... although, no… maybe not.

Dave continued to swivel for a moment longer trying not to dwell on his past mistakes, in particular the infamous 'Missing Link' fiasco... not his finest hour!

Dave had to remind himself why he was still having to lie low, 45,000 years after that whole Neanderthal debacle!

The screen in front of his swivel chair seemed to lose transmission, for a moment, and wavy lines interfered with the images on the screen, as a momentary lapse of concentration on Dave's part led to a presentation of what was on the back of his mind, rather than what was supposed to be in the fore-front of his thoughts, and he suddenly found himself unhappily re-visiting a series of grainy black and white images, depicting more slices of the history that had led to his humiliating demotion.

...Mica *shivered uncontrollably, despite being buried under the thick mammoth pelt, and a slick sheen of sweat covered the pale face, which was the only part of the emaciated body* *visible to her mother, who squatted by her side on the pile of skins.*

The old woman extracted from her own mouth a piece of meat that she had diligently chewed for her daughter, and tried to push it between the girl's lips, but Mica found the energy to turn her head away, refusing the nourishment her desperate mother tried to give her.

She lifted her head to try to drink the water that her mother brought her in a large conch shell, but gave up after a couple of sips, the effort too much.

Mica clutched the old gnarled hand, and looked thankfully into her eyes for a moment, before even that effort was too much, and she allowed her heavy lids to close, as she drifted off into a fitful sleep.

Roc looked on; the deep frown etched in to his heavy overhanging brow, causing his deep-set eyes to appear deeper still. His mate was not the only one to be suffering from this strange affliction.

Although she was the first to show signs of whatever ailed her, the disease had spread quickly throughout the tribe, some of the elders having already succumbed.

He did not know what to do for his beautiful mate, once so strong, now so very frail, but he did know if she and the others did not eat, they would die.

So, he did what he knew best, and went back out to join the others in another hunt.

Only a few wavy lines on the screen separated the scenes in the unfortunate sequence of events that had played out, so many years ago, and to avoid watching the next images, Dave mastered dropping his gaze, as well as hanging his head, but despite this, and the fact that he had also more or less got the hang of lowering lids over the human

-looking eyes, he was not able to avoid being aware of the images which continued to play on in front of him.

Roc *still mourned his mate, but he was very aware that more than half the tribe had now gone to be with the sky gods, including the old chief, and many of the elders.*

After brief skirmishes among the survivors, many of whom were weakened themselves by the illness that had gone through the tribe like nothing they had ever known before, Roc had fought his way to chieftain.

Feeling weak and exhausted he set off, with those of the tribe able to travel, to find other tribes to join with, and to find new mates, to increase their numbers…

…A small amount of static heralded the slight shift in time displayed on the screen. Dave tried to avoid remembering, as well as looking, by dropping his head, this time, into his hands; a slight difference of time, but the same old story...

...Roc *looked about his new tribe, and at his new mate.*

No longer chieftain, having woefully lost his bid to take on the leader of the neighbouring tribe, but satisfied to have at least won places for himself and the few survivors who had made it the hundreds of miles to the nearest cave settlement.

Roc had thought that they would at least swell the numbers of this new tribe that he had fought so hard to be part of, with strong warriors, and fecund females, but while they were still nursing injuries from the battle into the tribe, members of the new tribe had started to sicken with the same illness that had wiped out most of his own people.

Several warriors were already gone to the gods, and the females were falling ill and weakening too.

Roc did not understand what was happening.

Sheltering in the entrance of the new cave network he now called home, Roc, one of the last surviving members of what could have been the most dominant species ever to live on Earth, felt a sick shiver start up somewhere deep within his broad bulk, and sweat break out on the surface of his hirsute form, as he peered fearfully out from beneath his heavy brow, as lightning ripped across the sky.

Chapter Nineteen

Dave shook himself, more dog-like, he would have realised, if he had known about dogs, than man-like,

Who would have thought such a little bit of...social interaction... in the name of research, could have had such an effect? Bizarre!

But then he marshalled his thoughts, and re-directed his attention to the solution he had come up with to redress the issues caused by his small …lapse in protocol.

He was always much happier reminiscing on the brilliant solutions to the problems he created, than remembering the problems themselves.

He had had that wonderful idea involving the almost parallel civilization developing on Satis-et-Satis, he remembered, which wouldn't have even *been* there at all if it wasn't for him... but maybe that was another memory best left ...*un*-analysed, he decided.

Anyway, he had fixed it, so all's well that ended well, etc, etc.

And he was sure that once this new female subject adjusted to being alone, he would be able to observe typical human behaviour on planet Earth, as it stood 45,000 years after his last contact!

Then Earth could once again be one of his favourite planets, he thought hopefully, as it had been, before it became tarnished for him, with associations of his downfall!

Well, one of his downfalls, he corrected himself wryly.

Dave flicked the screen to his new favourite planet, a moon, actually, Satis-et-Satis, belonging to the fifth planet orbiting a distant sun that the humans had christened Tau Ceti.

It bore a remarkable similarity to Earth, barring for a slight gravitational discrepancy.

Colourful images, this time, in high definition, and with surround sound auditory support, slid across the screen, to accompany Dave's reminiscences of the solution he had created, and for added clarity, for anyone who was interested, a Title Screen!

Satis-et-Satis: Second moon of the Fifth Planet of Tau Ceti 45,000 years ago….

And then... Earth: Third planet of Sol 45,000 years ago…

…Blood pounded in the young warrior's ears, as he raced to stay abreast of the gigantean beast that would feed many mouths for days to come.

One spear already embedded in its flank, the tall lean hunter sought to avoid becoming entangled in six pounding legs as he attempted to lean into it, and steer it towards his tribesmen, who were pulling in from the other side.

He could not afford to back off now, or the enraged animal would turn on her attacker, and he would no longer be the hunter. The exhausted beast was starting to weaken with blood-loss and panic, as it veered this way and that, trying to shake off its tormentors.

The hard body he was pushing in to suddenly evaporated beneath his own brawny shoulder, and his legs seemed to be pumping momentarily against thin air, and then he was suddenly running and falling to his knees on strange sandy ground.

He threw out his hands to prevent himself from being further ploughed into the ground of the suddenly alien landscape that surrounded him.

The primitive hunter jumped to his feet, reaching for the shard dagger he kept tucked in the top of his tarik-skin boot, looking quickly to the left, then the right of him, trying to work out what was happening.

He stood stock still as another of his tribe literally popped into existence in front of him, running to his knees, and then rolling over into a ball, before scrambling to his feet, and looking around himself in amazement.

He turned this way and that, as more and more of his hunting party materialised in front of his eyes, then briefly the tarik they had been hunting joined the fray, looking as disorientated as any of the tall hunters, then just as quickly as it had appeared, it disappeared, leaving the hunters standing open mouthed staring at each other.

None among them had had time to gather their scattered wits before a dust-filled cloud of panicking mammoth charged towards them, then through and over them, leaving little evidence of the universe's first intergalactic pre-historic hunting party, and a loud tut of chagrin could have been heard across the skies if anyone had been left to hear it.

The skies had then echoed with a short, exasperated sigh...

Dave took advantage of having a head, and eyes, to glance furtively over his shoulder, to ensure that John was not around, or at least not watching the screen, as

Dave realised that he was re-living a log of his first, *failed* attempt, at re-colonising Earth!

His later, more successful efforts, had resulted in the population on his erstwhile favourite planet flourishing to a phenomenal degree!

Another piece of stellar work that Dave did not feel he got as much credit for as he deserved, as it had only ever been acknowledged as *partially* redressing the balance!

The similarities between the civilizations of Earth, and Satis-et-Satis had been immensely helpful during the whole Neanderthal episode, Dave remembered, as had been the almost parallel evolution of the dominant species.

Which, as far as anyone else knew, was pure co-incidence!

And that would continue to be the case, unless, that is, anyone scoured the ancient annals of a certain individual who would one day become known as Dave, and checked the diligence, or lack thereof, of adherence to policies on cross-contamination of virgin planetoids!

Although the slight difference in heights of species of equal proportions, due to the gravitational difference, had almost caused a problem, he thought he had got away with it!

Most developing civilizations enjoy a bit of a mystery anyway, he knew, and early archaeologists on Earth had had a merry old time trying to understand why the Neanderthals had such a big brain, and Cro-Magnon, apparently the next evolutionary step up, taller and more upright, had a significantly smaller brain!

They had all sorts of theories going on about that one!

Missing links indeed!

How would that have even worked? What did they think the missing link would have looked like? A hominid, taller than Neanderthal, shorter than Cro-Magnon... and with an *elastic* skull to hold that huge burgeoning Neanderthal brain?

Dave gazed lovingly at Satis-et-Satis's amber and cerulean landscape on the screen in front of him, languidly analysing the population projections of the current dominant species.

At his last analysis of the world currently decorating his screen, he had projected that in another ten thousand years or so, the rapidly proliferating population would have multiplied to such an exponential degree that they could potentially present a threat to his own people.

If they started moving skyward, to accommodate their numbers, as they developed their scientific abilities, his own immortal people could be greatly inconvenienced by their through-traffic!

The projection had also predicted that the dominant species were likely to wipe out many of the *sub*-species on the planet, having a massive negative impact on their own well- being, if they had but understood that!

Dave used the well-practiced shaking of his head, and tutting, at the memory of this poor inferior species' lack of insight!

His own options had not been clear cut.

His responsibility to his own people demanded he do *something*, of course, and steering his own non-corporeal species to an alternative dimension would have been quite a massive feat of accomplishment, and therefore would indeed have gained him great merit.

He could have totally cleared his Neanderthal slate! And it may even have led to him being promoted back up to Middling of Middle Sector Analyst* Significantly Senior! (MoMSA*SS)

He had instead taken the magnanimous option of tinkering with the dominant species fertility rates, thereby selflessly depriving himself of these opportunities!

A relatively simple DNA adjustment, would almost imperceptibly slow down societal expansion, he had calculated, thereby keeping the population more or less static.

At least until the end of his duty period.

That this was by far the easier option was inconsequential, at best, and purely serendipitous, at second best, Dave told himself.

He was in the process of enjoying his discovery of a new human sensation, to wit; 'glowing with pride', at the memory, when he almost swivelled right off his chair, as he suddenly registered the prediction that the numbers in front of his eyes were forecasting!

Not again!

Well not again, again...

Chapter Twenty

Cece's next find on the beach elicited an even stronger response from her than that of the ammonite.

Flip-flopping back and forth in the shallows, floundering on the beach like, well, a beached flounder, and although somewhat worse for wear, but apparently still zipped and holding contents, her own waxed cavalier bag!

Cece dropped down beside the bag, pulling it on to her lap, then hugging it to her chest, like a rescued toddler.

"I don't know how any of this is happening," Cece whispered under her breath, and even though she had never been in the habit of believing in anything, or anyone, other than herself, but as is often the case with desperate people, or sometimes just grateful people, she looked skyward, and said, "but thank-you, thank-you, thank-you."

And then, to cover all eventualities, she scanned the treeline, and repeated her gratitude.

"Thank-you, thank-you, thank-you".

Trying to remember what she had packed away in the bag, which she was fairly certain she had last seen stowed away safely in one of the small storage holds in her cabin, for use on her days out at the various island visits listed on the cruise itinerary, she allowed herself a moment's fantasising about precisely which precious goodies it might contain.

Having being forewarned of limited storage before she had set sail, Cece knew she had packed up each of the various bags that she had decided to bring, with her few essential holiday odds and ends, to save space.

And she knew she had not really brought along anything on this cruise that she had not thought would be *absolutely* necessary; so whatever was in it was going to be *pretty* darn useful, she was sure.

"Please let there be a first aid box and a water bottle in here," Cece prayed; despite knowing she had never owned a first aid box in her life, and certainly wouldn't have thought to pack one for her all-inclusive cruise holiday even if she had.

Biting her teeth down on both lips simultaneously, bracing herself for both the best and worst of news, she struggled to open the kelp-covered zip.

Finally managing to yank it all the way open, she peered suspiciously inside before venturing in with her hand, fearing a captive crab or jelly fish might be about to make a run for it.

She then nearly stuck her head inside the bag, as she couldn't believe what her eyes were telling her, such was her amazement at the first object that came into view!

Only remembering as she saw it, that she had even brought it along; her little topiary pocket-book, entitled "Artistic Tips for Twigs and Twiglets!"

She vaguely remembered now, that she had thought that she might read up on the topic while she was on her cruise, to give her something to look forward to doing when she got back from holidays, just in case she needed to fend off her usual post-holiday blues.

Although she could not think why she would have gone for that book!

She was no-more likely to start trimming bushes when she got home than she was likely to take up fly-fishing! She yanked the book out of the bag in disgust, and tossed it to one side.

"Well, that's going to be *so* useful Cece! Not!"

The next thing she pulled out of the voluminous bag was no more useful; a mixed cassette tape! '*Love Songs-From Enrico Caruso to Contemporary Hits!*'

She didn't even have anything to play it on!

Actually no, strike that! Nanna's small and ancient portable tape cassette player was also there! For the love of.... what on Earth had she been thinking when she had packed her bags?

She hadn't even listened to this tape, or even checked to see if the cassette player worked for that matter, since she had decided to rescue what she thought of as Nan's treasures, from going to landfill!

The charity shop had already turned down a whole barrage of paraphernalia which her grandmother had asked her to clear out for her, in preparation of downsizing to a bungalow, as Cece, making tentative steps towards independence had applied to university.

But when the old lady had died, parting with any of the clutter she had been hoarding on her behalf seemed even less likely!

Even the so-called 'contemporary' music on there was probably from the 1950s, Cece fumed to herself.

"Topiary for beginners, and Love Songs for old timers!" Cece cursed her own luck, then cursed herself, acknowledging she couldn't really blame anyone else for her packing!

Were there any less useful items in all the world to be your desert island disc luxuries!

Well, yes, as it happened, there were.

The next item she pulled out of the bag was the spare plug to her phone charger.

That would go nicely on an island with no electricity, to go with the waterlogged mobile phone she had found in the messenger bag which had washed up the previous day. There wasn't even a cable lead, which would have least made a good tie, to… well… tie things!

"Really?" She demanded, looking back up at the cloudless sky. "Really??" And then at the treeline, "*Really*???"

With absolutely no expectation now, of having packed away anything which could be of any use at all, in what could have been a godsend of a giftbag, Cece moved a little further away from the water's edge, and up-tipped the remaining contents onto the wet sand.

Her eyes widened as they alighted on the first useful thing she had seen, and she heard herself let out a joyous yell as she grabbed up the packet of unopened (for emergency only, as she had not had one for years) filter-tips, and…a disposable lighter!

Fire!

She had the means to make fire! She could not have felt more gleeful if she had just invented it herself!

"I take it all back" she yelled, clutching the lighter to her breast, and looking up at the sky yet again, and then over to the trees, "it was worth it if just for this!"

On continuing her scrabble through the splayed-out contents, she found another item almost as welcome as the lighter!

"Now that's what I call a desert island luxury!" she squealed, snatching up a tiny bottle of whisky, before adding, as she glanced over her shoulder for any sign of the gift horse, "To start my first aid box off with, obviously."

She had absolutely no recollection of why she would have even stashed the tiny 'wee dram' bottle, a souvenir from the previous year's holiday in the Highlands, on a *semi*-successfully Nessie spotting expedition… she was sure she'd caught a glimpse… but as she had not managed a photo, no-one really believed her.

Clutching the small treasure now, she could only imagine she had had a last-minute panic, at the thought of the possibility of being without access to alcohol for some brief moment on her holiday!

And this being despite being equipped with the knowledge that alcohol was freely available, at all times, as part of the cruise package deal, not only on deck and in all the various bars and lounges, but also could even have been delivered to her cabin, on request!

She thought longingly of the absolute luxury of those few days prior to her present predicament, which she now realised she had not been fully appreciative of at the time!

"Oh, please let me be transported back there, by magic, if that's what's happening here, and I promise I'll really appreciate everything!"

She wondered briefly if she were to stand up and click together none existent glass-heels three times, or something to that effect, whether that wish might also be granted.

"Although they do always say to be careful what you wish for…." she started to have some misgivings, as her current experience certainly seemed to be confirming that theory, to some degree anyway!

Caruso and topiary books indeed!

"But then again, any port in a storm," she thought pragmatically, and allowing all the precious items she had been accumulating in her lap to fall to her feet, Cece stood up resolutely and announced to the world at large,

"I need to be back on the ship! Wherever it is! Now! This instant!"

Cece then stood listening to the universe, with bated breath, waiting to see if the universe had been listening to her, and was going to obey her demands.

Then sudden memories of horror stories about monkey's paws, and images of languishing for all eternity on a ship, which may well now be rotting away on the bottom of the ocean floor, floated into her brain.

She slapped a suddenly cold hand over her mouth, as she scoured the beach for any sign that someone, or something, out there had taken heed of her words.

Something out there *was* listening, and *had* taken heed, but after reporting back, and receiving a somewhat ambiguous response along the lines of, 'mind the subject, but not at the expense of the assignment', had not complied with Cece's heartfelt demand.

Instead, he had carried on with his current task of gathering shells and stones to meet what he perceived to be the last indication of need demonstrated by his study subject.

He had no more, or less, understanding of her elation at her discovery of the ammonite fossil, than he did of her joy at discovering the shoulder-bag he had delivered to the beach for her, or of her mixed emotions on seeing the contents.

He continued his mission, to observe, record, feedback, and where a response came, to comply with that response.

And, as per a more recent amendment to his routines, when his coder was unavailable to respond, to update his own programming, based on how he had previously been instructed to respond to the test subject, so as to be able to meet whatever needs she presented with.

As much relieved as disappointed, Cece realised her latest demand was not to be met, and started to gather the fallen goodies back into her bag, exploring each one as she did so. Some were more useful than others, she mused, but all of them were better than nothing, and had, at the end of the day, cost her nothing other than a walk on the beach.

And a prayer or two.

Among the more welcome treasures she had discovered in the shoulder-bag, zipped up in the lining pocket, she had been gratified to find a small, partially used, tube of something medicinal looking; contents unknown.

From the slightly grubby appearance of the faded tube, it probably came from her supply of lucky-dip creams, she mused; to wit, her assemblage of faded bottles and tubes, labels lost, use by date illegible, but which she hung on to, on the grounds that, 'It's a shame to throw it away when there's some still left in the bottle', or "I'll just hang on to this scrap-end of a tube, until I get a replacement."

Mainly raised by her 'waste not want not' Nanna, under the influence of her 'make do and mend' ingrained great-gran, frugality came as second nature to Cece, even if common sense did not.

That it was difficult to replace something when she did not know what was in it was a step of logic too far for Cece, so she just hung onto the veritable collection of half- used, out of date, and barely recognisable toiletries and medications, in case of emergencies.

Or quite possibly to cause an emergency, if indeed she ever ended up resorting to using half of them!

Screwing up her eyes to aid the scrutinization of the faded small-print, she realised it was impossible to be sure what this particular half-rolled up tube of lucky-dip cream contained, as the words were mainly illegible to Cece; possibly sun faded, possibly written in an unfamiliar language, she could not work out which.

Cece eliminated the potentially most useful candidates; sunscreen unlikely due to there being no discernible sun-factor numbers visible; insect repellent she also thought unlikely, as when she had unscrewed the top and had a good sniff, all she could detect was sea-brine, not the pungent eye-watering smell she usually associated with that particular product!

Ever the wishful thinker, Cece landed on the conclusion that the most likely contenders still left in the running were either after-sun, or after-bite cream, either one of which would be gratifying!

Cece decided to throw caution to the winds, and rub some of the precious supply into the areas most affected by the bites and sunburn, and hope for the best!

Although the cream was a welcome find, even if it was just expired moisturiser, Cece did despondently acknowledge that if it had lost its smell, and the writing had worn off, the likelihood was that it was no longer effective as whatever it had meant to be anyway!

But it was proving to be slightly soothing to skin which was feeling more than a little tender, having been exposed to the incessant beating sun for the second day in a row, and in addition to which, her head was feeling a little light.

She very much wished that she had had the for-sight to have tucked a bit of sunscreen or insect repellent into the bag which had after all, been intended to see her through day trips on sunny isles, but it had obviously not seemed like a priority to her, as instead she had apparently been busy prioritising packing books about how to torture trees into submission, and recordings of deceased singers

With the bag slung across her shoulder, Cece continued along the beach for quite some distance, before her throbbing ankle, and the unrelenting sun, reminded her that she had still to make her way back to her camp site, and she decided that she was not going to find any more bounty on the beach that day.

She had been walking on the beach several hours, with nothing to eat since the morning, and her fluid intake had been limited to what she had had from her fruit.

She realised having her head uncovered was not helping her dizziness, and routing again through the bag to see if there was anything to help that particular problem, settled on the little topiary book.

Hardly ideal, but better than nothing, she thought, as she opened up the pages, and plonked the book on her head, holding it there with one hand, as she made her way back to her shack, her footsteps becoming a little unsteady as she tottered slightly along the beach.

"A hat!" she shouted suddenly, to no-one, "Or something…to put on my head…would be really useful about now!"

Cece almost tripped over an enormous leaf which appeared in front of her feet, drifting along the beach, caught up in a small scurry of wind.

She skirted around it as she continued weaving her way along the beach, clutching the small book to her head.

The next leaf, more massive than the last, that she narrowly avoided tripping over, as it flapped around her feet, eyes half closed against the painful sun, she trod into the sand, as she plodded blindly on.

The shimmering form, imperceptible against the glare of sea and sun, watched for a moment longer.

Then, in imitation of a gesture he had observed Cece to make when she could not fathom what was happening, he stuck both hands out in front of himself, palms up, lifted his shoulders up towards where his ears would be, and gave his head a little shake from side to side, then returned to the task of gathering shells and pebbles.

Chapter Twenty-One

By the time Cece got back to her camp her head was throbbing almost as much as her ankle, and she threw herself gratefully into the relative coolness of her shack, tripping over, and kicking out of the way, what had been an enormous, and neatly stacked pile, of shells, beach pebbles, and other flotsam and jetsam, which she did not remember having been there before.

She illogically assumed that they had been washed up there in her absence, despite the tide currently being several hundred yards down the beach, and being on its way out.

She gave the ruined cairn another savage kick from inside her shack, to ensure she had a good access and egress to her mansion, without breaking her toes on piles of rubble, should she need to pop out for nature calls, during the night.

Cece then suddenly became aware of a random feeling of consternation, for which she could not identify the cause.

It was almost as though the feeling was emanating from someone ... other than herself!

Odd, she thought, before shrugging it off and grabbing a piece of fruit from the stock, which she did not register had been replenished.

Trying to ignore feelings of sun induced nausea, she ate as much of the fruit as she could, guessing that dehydration, as well as the heat, could likely not only account for her pounding head, and dizziness, but also the strange 'otherness' feeling she kept experiencing.

Then, despite feeling that she really ought to be doing more from her Herculean list, gave in to the need to rest, curled up on her makeshift bed, and knew nothing more until waking up rather groggily in darkness, some hours later.

From feeling disorientated and headachy, the sudden sensation that someone was standing behind her, made her start to full wakefulness, her head whipping round to scour the interior of her sanctuary.

Drawing up her knees defensively against her chest, whilst trying to gather her thoughts, as her eyes grew accustomed to the semi-darkness, Cece stared wide eyed around the shack.

No-one was there.

Shivering a little, despite the relative warmth of the evening, and still unable to shake the feeling that someone was watching her, she pushed back the makeshift door of her makeshift shack, and peered out into the gloom of the night.

Cece still saw no-one.

And no-one ... saw Cece!

Not having intended to sleep the rest of the day away, after her earlier sunstruck collapse on to her mattress, waking up to darkness Cece was suddenly more acutely conscious, than at any other time since her unceremonious dumping on the island, of being alone, and defenceless, on the edge of a jungle.

Or more worryingly, *not alone*, on the edge of a jungle!

She remembered that she had not yet even checked to see if the lighter she had been so thrilled to find still worked, let alone finished exploring the contents of her shoulder-bag, and suddenly the need for a fire seemed very important.

Her lighter was quite unlikely to work, she realised, shivering again, having been dredged up from the bottom of the ocean!

She cast a glance over to the pile of now dried out foliage she and her unseen helper had stripped from the branches, and helping herself to a mango to try to quench her constant thirst, she sat in the entrance of her shack, and up-tipped the contents of the waxed bag again, searching for the lighter in the moonlight.

Realizing for the first time that the lighter, along with the rest of the content, was quite dry, she picked up the bag itself, and delved her hand around inside, then slapped her hand to her aching forehead.

Of course! A waxed bag! Water-proof! Not only had it kept the contents dry, but of even greater significance, she now had something with which to collect and store a supply of water!

The bag, potentially containing the means to provide her with both fire and water, she was starting to realise, had been much more of a boon than she had first appreciated!

Her sense of relief went someway to easing her headache, and when she tried the lighter and found it functional, she almost felt like breaking out her tiny tot of whisky to celebrate!

Instead, she shuffled together a small bundle of dry leaves and twigs, and setting them far enough away from her shack to avoid burning the place down, lit herself a small comforting fire.

As it took hold, and she started to feel a bit more confident about being in control of a wild fire, she threw on a few more of the larger branches, and got going a blaze large enough to warm herself against a night which was becoming noticeably cooler.

She felt somewhat safer from the wild animals that she could again hear in the not-too-distant distance, calling to their mates.

Much as she loved wildlife, on the television, she was relieved that so far, surprisingly, to her knowledge at least, she had had no contact with anything larger than a mosquito.

The wildlife was equally surprised at this, but having learned several recent lessons, decided it was for the best.

Cece sat with her arms wrapped tightly around herself, admiring the moon rising over indigo-violet water, which reflected the deepening lavender sky, and seemed to stretch out to infinity, with the stars captured in the rhythmic twinkle of each quietly rolling wave.

She took a moment, really for the first time since landing so abruptly on the island, to appreciate the beauty of her surroundings.

Then, a faint sound from the treeline attracted her attention; some animal passing by, rather hurriedly from the sound of it, she thought.

Peering into the darkness, and seeing nothing, Cece swung her gaze back to the seascape, and caught her breath, dragging in a sharp lungful of salty air.

She had detected no movement, but as though her eyes had taken a second to adjust to a light being switched on, he was suddenly there.

Silhouetted against the inky rocks, he appeared at the same time both darker, and lighter, than the shadows that surrounded him.

He was almost a shadow himself; motionless, barely discernible from the night sky, and barely distinguishable from the sparkling starlit vista that he blocked from her view.

Realizing that she had failed to breathe for several seconds, she started to let out her breath slowly, open mouthed, as if to avoid drawing his attention, which was ridiculous, she thought; he was *all* attention!

And all his attention was on her!

Cece had no idea how long the shadowy form had been there, watching her.

She would have seen someone making their way down from the trees, she was sure; he must have been there all along, while she rifled through her bag, and built her fire!

Getting slowly to her feet, she took a cautious step backwards, edging towards her shack, and to her surprise, the shadow seemed to retreat an equal distance, towards the rocks.

She swallowed, and started to breathe slightly more easily, the increase in distance between the shadowy frame and herself, removing the threat somewhat.

"Please, come out of the shade. I can't see you properly, the starlight and fire are confusing my eyes." She half laughed, trying to lighten the mood, "You're all shadows...."

"Thank you for bringing me the fruit… and twigs… and things," she carried on, when she got no response.

He continued to watch, but did not move.

"Please. Come closer to the fire, I can't see you, and… you're scaring me... a bit…."

Although she could swear there was no movement, Cece was suddenly aware he was no longer there.

She was alone again.

Or maybe she had been alone all along.

The night seemed suddenly darker, and even more full of shadows, but none that shone with starlight.

Chapter Twenty-Two

First checking that John was occupied elsewhere, and not likely to be suddenly hovering over his shoulder, Dave bent down and picked up the bottomless tartan vacuum flask, and poured himself a cup of saucer-temperature tea, which for some unknown reason he had discovered he found strangely comforting in times of crisis.

Shuffling about in his swivel chair, unable for once to get comfortable despite the perfectly tilted seat, Dave settled for perching on the edge, before allowing himself to focus on the figures which had been among the logs transmitted through to him from another less prolific projections program, which he had installed on Satis-et-Satis.

He also started to scan through, and piece together, the various fragments of accompanying narrative that sometimes attached themselves to the transmissions, to try to calculate what had gone wrong.

***...Adi-belle** stood on the porch of the home that she had shared with her half-pair, Adi-beau, for most of her adult life, and looked out over the sea of waving blue and yellow grasses, noting that it was almost time to harvest the ripe* *crop, but for the moment just enjoying the ululation of the grass-crits, chirping, and singing their courtship calls to each other.*

Adi-belle loved this time of year.

The land was bountiful in so many ways; the orchards of deep blue and succulent midwaric fruits, the size of her head, their weight causing them to drag the branches lower and lower, until that weight ripped them from their anchor, plummeting them to the ground, and giving them their common-use name, 'plummet fruit'.

The plummet fruit, in turn, provided fodder for the myriad teaming lifeforms, ripe and fecund, which were deep in the middle of courting rituals; mating, breeding, taking over the planet, it seemed, to Adi-belle, in total contradiction to her own species, which, she was all too aware, seemed to be in a sad decline.

The tall slender figure of the graceful Adi-belle sagged slightly as she placed a hand on her own flat abdomen, which she knew was unlikely now to bring forth new life.

"Belle! Belle!" Adi-beau's voice hailing her from the depths of the dwell, disturbed her reverie, "where did you put the tape? To tape the marmiduk's bill? I can't take her to town snapping and biting at me all the way there! I had left it out ready, and now it's not where I left it!" Adi-beau's voice, tetchy and impatient, momentarily silenced the grass-critts.

"I wish you would leave things where I …oh, it doesn't matter, I've found it. Anyway, I'm just about ready then, and I'll be off in a dot, when I've just found his paddy-claw mitts…." The grass-critts restarted their love songs, as the disturbance of Adi-beau's voice faded out of earshot.

He continued to rootle around the dwell, getting himself ready for the short trip to their neighbour's planting-land, to pair their pet marmiduks, with hopes of new kits before the year was up.

Adi-beau was making the trip, which they usually made together, alone, this once, at Adi-belle's suggestion.

Years of spending too much time together, just the two of them, and finding that they had too little to talk about, when they were finally finished with their various chores about the planting-land, was becoming grating to Adi-belle. She had been consciously trying to make the effort to get them doing things apart from each other when opportunities arose.

The busy life she had expected to lead with Adi-beau, raising their child, teaching him or her how to tend the animals and crops on the planting-land, which had passed down through her family for generations, had not materialised.

It now looked like the planting-land would go to strangers, when she and Adi-beau could no longer take care of it by themselves, as they were unlikely now to create the next generation needed to tend the land.

Of all the years since she had taken Adi-beau's name, hopeful, and expectant of creating a legacy of their love together, it had never hurt as much as it did now, when her dear friends Cas-trelle and Cas-treau had just announced they would be visiting with their new-babe, having successfully hidden Cas-trelle's pregnancy from everyone until the birth!

Adi-belle could understand the younger couple wanting to avoid more communal disappointment, anticipating the probability of another lost life before it had even begun, as had been the case with so many hominid pregnancies on the planet of recent times.

Retracing through the generations, even of Adi-belle's own family, she knew that families used to often yield multiple offspring, going back only as far as her grandmother's days!

And there was record of her great-grandparent having a sister-twin, and two generations before that there was even record of there having been three siblings been born into the same family!

Like a clutch of wild animals, she thought.

Although she wasn't sure if they had all been born at once; the records were not that detailed.

It seemed bizarre to her, that over so few generations the planet had changed so much!

Having been a member of the dominant species, which had once outnumbered almost every other large animal on the planet, she was now part of a species that had fallen into such a decline, that there were even predictions of a total extinction eventuality, within generations, if the trend did not change!

Adi-belle did not believe that of course. It was too absurd!

But still... her and Adi-beau's personal situation did not reflect her confidence in the continuation of the hominid's domination of her beautiful golden and blue planet.

"I've got everything I need, I think, and the marmiduk's taped and tethered. I managed to get his mitts on, by myself, but not before he managed to shred my tunic, mind! So anyway, I'll be off!" Adi-beau's voice floated through to her from somewhere round the other side of the building.

"Alright Beau", Adi-belle answered without looking round, and grimaced as she took another sip from tepid root tea that had transformed, while she had been busy contemplating life and the universe, from being too hot to drink, to congealed and barely drinkable.

Adi-beau's head suddenly materialised around the corner of the dwell

"Unless you wanted to come along, Belle? To get you out of the dwell for a bit?"

Adi-belle sighed, raised her brows, and crinkled the right side of her mouth up towards her ear in exasperation.

It wasn't as though she had not told Adi-beau more times than she could remember, that they needed to spend more time doing things without each other!

And he totally agreed, whenever she said it, so she had no idea why he did not then put the plan into action!

"Oh alright" she sighed, throwing the remnants of her cold drink onto the path. "I might as well."

Chapter Twenty-Three

After tossing and turning fitfully for the first part of the night, frequently half sitting up, and looking about her for signs of her visitor, Cece had at last succumbed to her exhaustion, and sank in to oblivion.

When Cece eventually awoke, to the cacophony of a dawn chorus the likes of which she had never experienced in England, she talked herself into the idea that her midnight visitor had been nothing other than a vision brought on by a combination of sunstroke, de-hydration, exhaustion, and firelight.

His startlingly otherworldly appearance, when she thought about it in the light of day, was to say the least, unlikely!

In any event, she told herself, she needed to access more water today, and maybe start looking for something to eat other than the mangoes which had so far been her only sustenance. Maybe they were hallucinogenic?

There must be other, more substantial fruits that she could find! Maybe nuts, or bananas, or coco-nuts?

She was on a desert island after all! Weren't they mostly made up of banana trees and coco-nut palms… and sand, of course?

Mangoes cannot be the only fruit!

There must be loads of stuff she could eat, she thought, now her ankle was up to wandering a little further into the jungle.

And now she had the means to make a fire she could maybe even catch herself some fish, and make a fish supper!

So, having convinced herself that the strange happenings that had occurred up until that moment were all likely to have been due to heatstroke and hallucinogenic mangoes confusing her senses, and feeling strangely positive, despite being marooned alone on a deserted island, Cece prepared to set off once more along the beach.

As well as needing to go get water, and be able to bring water back in her waxed bag, she decided that she needed to establish how far her territory stretched from either side of her camp, and whether any other bounties may have washed up for her convenience.

Her beach might be the greater part of a tiny island consisting of a couple of miles of sand and a clump of trees, or equally, she realised, might just be the tip of a large island of friendly shack-building locals wondering why she was camping out on their beach without a permit!

The sun was high in the sky by the time she was back at her camp, having walked one way as far as a rugged promontory jutting out into the sea allowed her to go, without swimming out to sea to get round the rocks, in one direction, and then the same in the other direction.

Her basic school swimming certificate, awarded her for perseverance rather than style or stamina, did not, after all, fill her with enough confidence to attempt that!

Having sustained herself so far throughout this trek with the possibly hallucinogenic mangoes, and with nothing yet to drink other than the juice which dribbled down her chin every time she bit into the very ripe fruit, Cece started to think she had possibly done things in the wrong order.

The realization had begun to dawn on Cece as she became aware that her beach stretched further than she had thought it would, and that if she did not set off on her safari soon to gather her water, she would be in danger of still being in the jungle when it started to get dark.

Although, remembering the shadowy figure illuminated in starlight from the previous night, Cece wondered if she should be feeling just as anxious about being on the beach in the dark, as she was about being in the jungle; but strangely, especially in that moment, in the bright sunlight, she didn't.

Cece couldn't even really visualize what she thought she had almost seen silhouetted against the rocks, but she remembered that although she had felt startled at the time, and she had told him he was scaring her, looking back, for some reason, she did not actually remember feeling afraid, as such.

In the hot light of day, what she had seen, could not have been what she thought she had seen anyway, she rationalized; so what was there to be afraid of?

So, after again tipping out the contents of both her waxed cavalier bag, and her messenger bag, and armed only with her stick, which, although she could now manage without, she had decided might come in useful in the event of an animal attack, Cece felt prepared to tackle the jungle.

Then, after a little more deliberation, Cece decided to also take the tiny nail scissors, which might be useful in the event of a very *small* animal attack; she cross-slung the bags over her shoulders, and started out in search of water and supplies.

With the route seeming almost familiar, the trek to the water-source had seemed even shorter this time than the previous two trips.

The occasional feeling of being watched had become so familiar that Cece had not only stopped looking over her shoulder, but sometimes even found herself adjusting the tone of her endless self-chatter, to accommodate the needs and understanding of any potential audience who might not have been privy to her life history.

"Lost in a bloody jungle, searching for water, with a buggered-up ankle, and a sore toe, bitten to death, just another typical bloody Cece week!

"Well maybe not exactly a typical Cece week, I wouldn't want...anyone... to think I do this all the time! To be honest, it is a fair old run of bad luck, even for me..." intermittently nodding and shaking her head to her own musings, Cece continued to weave her way through the trees.

Her unseen companion kept pace both with her stumbling gait and her bumbling monologue, and even shook or nodded his head occasionally as if in agreement.

He still routinely reported back, but as he was getting fewer and fewer responses to his reports, the avatar often found himself just managing his own analyses, and offering appropriate responses to the developing situation as needed; as per the remit of his updated program.

At one point during Cece's trek to the waterflow she found herself whistling quietly under her breath, and then stopped suddenly in her tracks as she heard the same tuneless whistle bouncing back to her from the trees.

"Oh!" she said surprised, "Parrots! Or more probably, in this part of the world, Minah birds!" showing off her lack of knowledge to anyone who cared to listen; or record and transmit, as the case may be.

Chapter Twenty-Four

With night almost closing in around her, Cece still felt strangely buoyant, as, rehydrated, and furnished with a waxed bag full of water, a messenger bag full of possibly edible berries, and a bunch of green bananas under her arm, and feeling as though she had earned a safari merit badge, she emerged onto the beach, to what she was quickly adapting to the idea of being her home, albeit, hopefully a very temporary one.

She was, however, startled out of her near nonchalance, as she threw herself and her bags down, in the doorway of the shack, to find herself looking directly into the starry face of a midnight-blue, darkly-lit, man-shape; the substance of which, seemed to the starstruck Cece, to be nothing more than fluid starlight!

The figure had thrown himself down a few feet away from the shack's entrance, mirroring the cross-legged pose she herself had collapsed into, in an almost companiable reflection of the astonished Cece.

Chapter Twenty-Five

"Did *you* bring me the food?"

After having scrambled to her feet, and staggered backwards a couple of steps, into what suddenly felt like an extremely flimsy shack, she had stood in gobsmacked silence, trying to process what she was seeing for so long that even her reflection was starting to look uncomfortable.

Cece had become worried that she may be appearing rude, and not usually one to be short of something to say, had decided she had better say *something* to the apparently… alien… being, hovering mere feet away from the remnants of last night's camp fire, and had opted for mundane.

Although he had jumped to his feet when Cece had, there was no obvious sign that her visitor had understood, or even heard her, or indeed, even had anything other than the outline of ears, with which to hear her, so she reverted to mime.

She put her fingers to her mouth, in an eating gesture, and repeated her attempt at an opening gambit, "Did you bring me the food? The fruit?" She pointed vaguely in the direction of her fruit store.

"And the wood, and... stuff?" and then trying what she felt was an even more direct approach, "Did *you* weave my walls?"

"Ok," she continued under her breath, taking a small step forward, but still feeling semi- sheltered, just inside her wicker den, and facing the figure she now knew had been her midnight visitant, "starting with neighbourly trivia is not working as much of an ice breaker. So…getting straight to the fundamentals..." She lifted the pitch of her voice then, in case her visitor was in any doubt as to who she was addressing, "*What on Earth are you*?"

Although Cece could detect no apparent reaction from her guest to her questioning, behind the swirling plethora of stars which currently served as a face for the avatar in front of her, he was transmitting for further instructions from his programmer, concerning a possible calculation and planned response error.

Observing and analysing the subject, and having the subject observe and analyse you back, he calculated, involved a whole different skill-set, which, he transmitted, he had not had the programming, previous experience, or instruction, to anticipate!

And although the concepts of worry, and panic, were as alien to the entity as were, well, everything else in this newly created existence he was functioning within, he did send his latest queries on an increased priority code.

A *significantly* increased priority code!

Unaware of this response to her chatter, the mesmerising starlight which swam within his dark frame drew her in, and Cece watched in fascination, as not only stars, but whole galaxies, seemed to chase each other through the depths of his face, and momentarily, she felt herself to be drowning in those depths.

They stood looking at each other for what seemed to her like a lifetime, to him… something between an instant and an eternity; she… trying to make sense of him; he… observing, analysing, recording, transmitting.

Cece felt as though she was staring into oblivion, and suddenly afraid that she was going to faint, sank back to the floor, cross-legged again, in front of him, firelight separating them and bringing some warmth to her suddenly chilled limbs.

The dark-lit man also sank to the floor, again mimicking her cross-legged pose, and Cece's attention was momentarily distracted by the fire, now crackling away, where, when she'd dropped to the floor, only ashes had been.

She had hardly even been aware of the evening darkening.

"And …I believe ...you just lit my fire...?"

Giving her head a little shake to try and bring some clarity to her thoughts, Cece decided to try again, with a different approach, and leaning forward she swept the sand smooth between them.

"So, maybe I need to go all Robinson Crusoe on your ass?"

He leaned forward and watched as she drew several wavy lines.

"The sea" she said. "That's the sea," and pointed out towards the crashing waves rolling up the beach.

She then drew a conical shape poking out from the wavy lines.

"This island," she said, gesturing expansively around and behind herself to help illustrate her point.

She then quickly added a couple of approximations of palm trees sticking out of the top of the island, and then giggled out loud at her own crude efforts.

"Sorry, I failed Art and Design!" she told him, with another short giggle. His head tilted from her drawing to her face, then back to the drawing.

Stretching as far away from herself as she could reach, to indicate distance, she hoped, she drew a long curvy line to the side of her island.

"Land," she explained, pointing off out to sea. "Far, far away! That's where I'm from."

Aware that as far as detailed information went, her descriptions were not really giving her visitor much to go on.

But the fact that he at least appeared to be listening, and *trying* to understand, motivated her to carry on.

She made a dot in the middle of the land mass that she'd created.

"Me!" she said poking her finger further into the dot. "That's me! At home! In England! A long, *long* way away, from here."

She made another dot on her picture, this time on the island, "Me, again. Here! On the island!"

She looked at him for a response; it did not come.

She made another dot next to the first, "And you. You are here too, aren't you? On the island?

"But I don't think you belong here anymore than I do, do you?" She took in the now cobalt-blue figure, the sprinkling of luminescence playing across his face, "Well, *less* than I do, really…"

She drew in a deep breath, then let it out slowly through her nose, her mouth clamped shut.

"*Where* are you from? Out there?" she asked, pointing out towards the sea again. The shape of his head turned to look towards the direction she indicated, but he took no other action, nothing to confirm or deny her comments.

"Or are you from here?" She asked, pointing inland towards the trees.

Again, the shape of the head swivelled, as he appeared to peer into the jungle she was indicating.

"Or are you from…?" she paused, then slowly directed her hand up towards the sky, and steeled herself to ask the more obvious, yet somehow more terrifying question, "are you from somewhere ...else?"

Again, the figure seemed to follow her indicating finger with his gaze, then slowly he bent slightly forward, his arm reaching out in an arc, star-trail following his movement.

Cece automatically leaned back, in response to his leaning forward, and he paused for a moment, but then his arm continued its arc, as he smoothed out the sand between them.

And then, in the absence of further direction, he began to draw.

Chapter Twenty-Six

Dave put down his drink on the console in front of him, so that he could thread his fingers together, twisting his hands inside out, and stretching out his fingers, until the joints made strangely satisfying popping sounds.

Although Dave felt he had well-nigh straightened out the little bliplette, on Satis-et-Satis, he thought he probably ought to continue to monitor the situation just until he was sure it was fully resolved, before he needed to tell John about it.

But then again, if it was totally sorted, he probably didn't need to tell him at all; he was such a tittle-tattle!

But then again…again…as he was making such a good job of resolving the issue, it would be nice to *share* that with John.

Dave then went through the motions of twiddling with a non-functional dial or two, to help him tune into the right mind-set, to monitor the goings on in an apartment, somewhere on the far side of the planet from where he was studying Cece… by proxy.

Glancing briefly across at the rapidly flashing orange light bulb at the front of the console, Dave chose not to register the fact that the flashes seemed significantly closer together than they had been; he had not after all broadened the avatar's remit in dealing with new situations to have to deal with every little change in circumstance himself!

He then picked up his tea again, and he settled down to watch what he had named, if only to himself, **'Dave's Satis-et-Satis Rescue Plan!'**

***Pale** from lack of sleep, exhausted beyond belief, the young first-time mother slammed down her mug of cold coffee on the marble-effect kitchen counter, then inhaled to the count of seven, and slowly exhaled to the count of ten, thinking to herself as she went a bit lightheaded, "I don't think I'm doing that right!"*

Hot tears suddenly spilled onto her face. She loved her daughter. She really did! So much!

But she had certainly not planned to be a mother at this early stage in her life!

A careless tryst fuelled by lust and vodka shots had had more far-reaching consequences than she had anticipated in the moment, and her life had turned suddenly upside down, when she had surprised even herself by deciding to go ahead with the resultant pregnancy.

She felt little more than a child herself.

She loved every tiny finger and every tiny toe of the beautiful tiny lifeform she had managed to produce, and every tiny bit of rapidly plumping flesh in between!

But if this beautiful baby girl did not soon start to sleep through for more than an hour at a time, the exhausted teen felt she would be seriously justified in dropping her off at a well-being centre and not leaving her taxi fare home!

She settled instead for turning her face skyward, when the continuous wail became too much for her to bear, and uttering vague pledges, about how she would be a better person, and try to do...well...everything... better, if only someone, anyone, would just take the little screaming scrap of humanity away somewhere, anywhere, just so that she could sleep!

Taking another deep breath, and flipping the switch on the kettle to warm up yet another cup of coffee that had gone cold before she had had chance to drink it, she headed through to the other room in her tiny flat to calm down her steadily bawling baby.

Before the kettle had come to the boil, she felt herself sag with relief when she realised that her baby's strenuous crying had stopped.

"Eventually worn herself out, thank God!" she muttered to herself.

"Please be asleep please be asleep please be asleep" she chanted under her breath as she took her freshened drink through to the little room that served her as lounge, bedroom, and nursery, wondering if she ought to leave well enough alone and not even approach the cot while the baby was quiet.

But she did so love to watch her baby sleeping peacefully, which did happen sometimes, although all too rarely for her liking.

She loved to watch the furious tiny red face calm to a warm pink, as the anxiety and frustrations of her little life receded, and she drifted off into brief slumbers, exhausted by her own efforts.

The young mother's eyes flicked briefly to the window, as she caught the tail end of a flash of lightning out of the corner of her eye, and she gave into temptation, and tiptoed over to the silent cot, thinking that the thunder she could hear rumbling in the distance was probably going to waken her momentarily quiet little daughter anyway.

For a split second, she stared uncomprehendingly into the empty cot, then her mug fell to the floor, coffee staining the multi-toned beige and brown carpet, a heart-breaking cry erupting from her soul!

...But before she had had time to drag in air for a second wail, a panicked Dave, having realised his mistake, had hastily returned the tiny bundle to its mother, bemoaning his lack of understanding of these contrary earthlings, and returned himself to the drawing board to consider plan B!

...And so the trembling young mother was left rubbing her eyes, and silently adding exhaustion-induced hallucinations to the list of grudges she was holding against her innocent, star-travelled babe!

'Anyhow,' Dave thought irritably, 'it's not even as if it's any of John's damned business!'

Chapter Twenty-Seven

Cece absorbed another slow, steadying breath, letting it out gradually through pursed lips, then craned her neck forward to see what the figure, illuminated by darkness, was drawing.

Several wavy lines, to start with.

"The sea," she said.

He made no gesture to confirm or deny her interpretation, seemed to hesitate, then leant forward again, and added a dot below the wavy lines, as Cece herself had done during her own demonstration.

Cece frowned, trying to fathom the meaning. The figure placed a twinkling hand on his star-filled chest, again mirroring Cece's earlier gesture.

"The dot's you?" she asked. "Under the sea?"

A thought suddenly occurred to her, gazing at the starry form in front of her, which made way more sense, "Or are you drawing the waves from *my* perspective, not yours? Is that dot meant to be *above* the wavy lines? Are you saying you are from *above* the waves? From the sky?"

Cece felt her jaw drop open as she watched his gestures, the tip of her tongue pressed up against the roof of her mouth, her fingers splayed against her throat, as she sought to quieten her breathing, afraid the sound of her intake of the extra oxygen she suddenly felt the need to gulp down, would spoil the moment.

But seemingly unconcerned by her increasingly agitated state, he continued to enhance his artwork, with another dot, this time above the wavy sea-lines.

Again, the star-filled hand went to his swirling chest.

"And that's you again, is it? In the sky? *And* below the sea? I don't really understand what you are telling me. You're from the sky? *And* from under the sea?"

This time the star-filled arm swept out further, trailing stardust in an even more expansive gesture than the one Cece had made earlier, when trying to impress upon him the distance of her own origins.

"You're from …out… there?" Her teeth bit down into the end of her tongue, so desperate was she not to let out the harsh panting she was increasingly feeling she needed to give in to, and was so terrified would break the spell.

This star-filled midnight-blue man was rocking her understanding of everything she thought she knew; his very existence; his presence here with her; the sheer fact of his communicating with her, let alone whatever it was he was trying to communicate to her, Cece felt was in danger of blowing her mind!

"You are from ….out *there*?" She repeated herself, pointing up in to the night sky. She looked back at his illustration.

She pointed at the first dot he had made.

"You said that was you? Beneath the sea? Are you from...under... the sea? Or ..." indicating the second dot, "the sky? Out… there?" she gestured towards the sky. "I don't understand!" she repeated.

After a pause, he repeated the gesture, first pointing out to sea, and then the slowly star-trailing hand swept upwards, towards the sky, then trailed back down to the skyline.

This time, the gesture seemed all encompassing to Cece, the stream of stardust that followed his every gesture trailed out from his finger-tips, illuminating the growing darkness inside Cece's shack.

Cece shook her head, and rubbed at her eyes, trying to follow the stardust coursing in front of them.

"You're from the sea.... and the sky? You're from .... everywhere?"

His hand dropped back into his star-filled lap.

Cece allowed herself a huge lungful of air, the tip of her tongue now pressing up into the top of her front teeth, as she stared at him in consternation.

"What *are* you?" quietly, almost to herself, her head tilting slightly in her awestruck wonderment.

And then, as a whisper, as the being's head tilted ever so slightly in response, she queried, "*Who* are you?"

"*Who are you*?" barely audible, the words came back to her.

She started backwards, pushing herself to her feet again, almost dowsing the fire with sand in her haste to scramble away from him.

"You speak?" Cece gasped incredulously. "You speak *English*?"

This time the figure did not react to her hurried retreat by moving back himself, but neither did he move closer, and as she did not think her legs were going to continue to support her for much longer, she took a couple more quick inhalations of air, then chanced sinking back on to her knees.

"Did you ...?" Doubting her own senses, not to mention her sanity, Cece tried again, "Did you just ... speak to me? Did you just ask me who *I* am?"

Continuing to stare at her visitor, gape-mouthed again, trying to take in as much oxygen as possible, with as little fuss as possible, Cece was no longer too worried about whether she was appearing rude.

She had decided that it was fairly unlikely that there was precedence on etiquette for this situation.

But she closed her mouth anyway, so that she could clamp her lips tightly shut, as she blew the breath back out slowly through her nose, trying to ground herself.

"I'm Cece," she managed at last. "I guess I should have started with that really, shouldn't I?"

Putting her hand to her chest. "Cece. Well, Narcece actually, Narcece Fontaine. I'm from Yorkshire…in England? You know, 'the faraway land' I just told you about?" she laughed a little, pointing off into the distance, in the direction she vaguely hoped her homeland lay.

"I fell off a ship."

She laughed again then, at her own summary of herself and her life... My name is Cece Fontaine … I fell off a ship!

"Out there", she added, pointing out to sea.

Again, his gaze seemed to follow her indicating digit.

She drew another quick breath as a thought occurred to her.

"*Oh*! Is that what you meant? Did you fall off your ship, as well? Only…from out of the sky? *Into* the sea? Are you a …space-man? A space …castaway?"

She looked at the blue-black figure whose starlight was suddenly filling the den behind her.

"Or, more like… a star-man? A man…made of stars..." then, trying to comprehend the whirling entity before her, "...*and* space? And you fell out of the sky? And landed here! On my island!"

She had not noticed him change position, but suddenly realised that he was now also on his knees, and as she sank back on to her heels, suddenly exhausted by all the revelations, he sank back too.

They sat facing each other for another small eternity, Cece trying to make sense of her own emotions… and wondering what he might be thinking about her, and he… continuing to observe, analyse, record, and transmit.

As silence continued to emanate from the figure, now mirroring the cross-legged position she had re-settled herself into, Cece started to question what she had heard.

"So…. can you really speak? Did you speak? Earlier? Or did I just…."

Cece decided to try again, more slowly, placing her hand on her chest.

"I am Cece."

During another lifelong pause, Cece watched in fascination, as not only stars, but whole galaxies, seemed to chase each other through the depths of his face.

She felt she was gazing into the face of infinity.

And then, again mimicking the action of the being facing him, placing his own starry hand on his cosmos-filled chest, a deep rumbling voice emanated from somewhere in the vicinity of the shimmering form.

"I am Heracles!"

Chapter Twenty-Eight

Dave perched ever more tentatively on the edge of his swivel chair, his tepid tea stagnating by the console, as he glanced furtively about the deck to check John was not around, before he tuned in to watch 'Dave's Satis-et-Satis Rescue Plan- Plan G'.

***Baby** number seventeen listlessly observed the flea-bitten tabby, which, despite being shooed out of the nursery several times already that day, had returned to perch on its usual window-ledge, the slightly annoyed flicking of its mangy tail the only distraction available to the infant in the otherwise barren clinical nursery ward.*

Old enough to be able to focus his large brown eyes all the way over to the fly-screened door, and old enough to have learned that no amount of crying was going to bring any sort of comforting presence, he lay listening to the squalling of younger, and more hopeful, nursery mates, the discomfort of the hot moist air, intensified by the occasional irritating insect, landing on his defenceless little face.

The nursery-maid who tended the ward, and shared his discomfort, flapped a hand at her own face, briefly providing herself with a slight breeze, and momentary relief, from the constant irritation of buzzing mosquitos.

On her way to deliver the round of warmed formulae to the crying babies, the young woman was stopped in her tracks by the rumbling of approaching thunder.

Catching the sight of sharp white light, illuminating the sky, she abandoned the trolley of glistening glass bottles, to scurry outside and bring in the lines of identical faded nappies, before the heavens opened on her recently pegged out washing.

The cloudless blue sky that met her outside, however, had her turning on her heel, grumbling to herself about the unpredictable nature of weather, as she returned to the feeding schedule

She came to another sharp stop, when she re-entered the room which moments before had housed a couple of dozen whimpering babies, to find it devoid of life, except for a window-ledge-full of fleas, dispossessed of their home by the sudden departure of the cat!

Chapter Twenty-Nine

Cece had thought that she could not raise her level of astonishment any higher, her mouth, now used to gaping open, did its thing, no prompting.

"So… you're …Heracles? And you do understand me? And can speak to me? So, *what* are you then? I'm sorry! That sounded so rude! I meant to say... well... what *in hell's name are you*? I'm sorry, I realise that was even worse…it's just that I can't think of a better way of saying... well, what…on Earth… are you?"

Cece attempted to gather her wits to try again, "I'm sorry! I know that was even...! But where are you *from*? Oh, I know you've fallen from your ship, into the sea, like me, and all that, but where are you *from*? Originally, I mean? And I know I'm just sounding ruder and ruder; my Nanna would be *cringing* if…"

Cece's inane rambling eventually faltered to a stop, as Heracles remained silent, and she watched with fascination, as the swirling stars making up the magnificent form in front of her seemed to be gathering momentum, as Heracles transmitted, and transmitted again, as no response came; and no response kept on coming.

Eventually Cece stretched behind herself to grab a handful of sticks from the pile inside the doorway of her shack, to build up the fire, wondering if she could try to expand on the illustrations they had started to design earlier.

"We could go back to pictures in the sand if that works better for you...?" she started as she turned back round with the sticks, but realised she was addressing thin air, as the space the star-filled man had occupied, was simply... space.

Chapter Thirty

Never had Cece felt so alone or bereft as she did in that moment, as she realised that Heracles was no longer there; almost as shocked by the sudden lack of his presence, in fact, as she had been by his appearance.

The space he had occupied until a few minutes ago, so empty that it seemed almost like a vacuum.

Feeling suddenly drained, she grabbed a mango from her replenished pile, then collapsed onto her leafy mattress to eat it, gazing at the roof of her shack, illuminated, she wrongly assumed, by the firelight still crackling away outside the hut.

"What on Earth are you, my midnight-blue man?" Cece mused quietly to herself, taking a huge bite out of the over-ripe mango, and wiping the juice away with her upper-arm as it started to dribble down her chin.

"*What* are you, and *where* did you come from? A *space*-alien? The *boogieman*, that haunts *everyone's* darkest dreams ... or maybe even a Christmas spirit, or sprite?

"Or did I just make you up in my head? A…manifestation…of my *own*…whimsy?

"When I was little, my Nanna used to say that I had 'a touch of the whimsies' about me. She had a shedload of daft sayings, bless her.

"But I wonder if that's what you are, though? Some sort of whimsical being, created from my own imagination, I mean? Are you a …whimsy? Or a '*Whimsy*' even… capital W!"

Cece took another bite out of her mango, as she considered that one for a moment.

"She also used to say that imagination is a powerful thing, and that I had too much for my own good!

"She said my imagination was so lively that if it had legs it would get up and run away with itself!"

Cece let out a little giggle at the thought of her imagination gaining legs and running away with itself.

"So if imagination is a powerful thing… I wonder how powerful a *Whimsy* is?" Cece took another bite out of her mango.

"But seriously? Is that it? Did I just conjure you up for company? To stop myself from going mad?

"And have I made you 'run away with yourself'? Would you still be here now," Cece frowned suddenly, as she considered her own role in the situation, "if I hadn't done my usual trick of trying too hard, and scaring you off?"

Cece then started to really laugh out loud at her own summary of events, causing herself to choke, and inelegantly cough up a bit of mango peel.

"My usual trick! Yes, I do this every time I meet a spaceman! And is it even possible to scare off a figment of your own imagination?

"Anyway," Cece sighed, continuing to munch on her mango, "I think the ship has already sailed on the trying to keep my sanity thing! I'm laying here cackling to myself, and talking to a creature that I'm debating with myself as to whether it is an 'ali-being' or a 'whimsy- being,' created by my own imagination, and *still* actually worrying about whether or not I might have upset it!"

With her arm tucked behind her head, Cece hitched one leg up to her bottom, and threw the other leg over it, and lay watching the shadows cast across the shack wall created by her jiggling, tapping foot.

Exhaustion took over from the adrenalin which had until so recently been coursing through her body, and still deliberating her questions, she drifted off into a patchy sleep, oblivious to the fact that the shadow was not being cast from the direction of the firelight, but from the gently glowing figure standing silently at the back of the shack, sending transmissions, on a constant loop, requesting input.

Priority one!

Chapter Thirty-One

Feeling slightly less agitated, as his plan was at last coming together, Dave casually tapped the light on his console, which had started to transmit a continuous orange tone, until it stopped flashing altogether…obviously a mechanical blip… he noted with some satisfaction, then relaxed enough to top up his tea between flipping screens depicting the two planets, to watch his plan play out…

Although *the fleas were too small to come to the attention of the nursery-maid as they wandered around the cat ledge looking for their home, if she had hung around a moment longer, she would have been startled to see the cat suddenly re-appear, with a range of emotions playing across its face; surprise at its double interspatial trip, relief at finding itself, for the first time in its mangy life, without fleas, then... disappointment... as he was once again reunited with said fleas!*

But then, only seconds later, when Dave had had time to not only fine tune his transporting skills, but also, due to a momentary, and uncharacteristic, consideration of the repercussions of his actions on another life form, and with a twinge of slightly *more characteristic compassion…as he had never been one to* consciously *harm another individual... decided to permanently relieve the cat of its irritating house-guests.*

And so Dave, not only chose to bring the cat back to earth, but having witnessed, and been moved by, the brief relief the cat expressed at being without the nuisance of the fleas, made the monumental decision to send the fleas to Satis-et-Satis, instead.

One grateful feline, therefore, was relieved of a lifelong irritation!

And one small, but rapidly breeding, population of pests, were inflicted instead upon the somewhat less grateful, previously flea devoid, Satis-et-Satis!

The nursery-maid, however, was oblivious to this secondary drama, as, with another panicked cry gathered in her throat, she had already fled the room, almost tripping over the thin air, where two minutes previously she had planted a trolley full of shiny glass bottles full of cooling formula.

Chapter Thirty-Two

Cece was as oblivious to either of these unfolding dramas as she was to the continued presence of the starry sentinel, standing guard over her bed, until the uneasy and dream-filled slumber to which she had eventually succumbed, was interrupted by the onset of the jungle dawn concerto.

Raising bent arms so that her elbows met, she arched her stiff and aching back in a long and languorous stretch, and rolled over to find herself staring straight into the twinkling visage of infinity!

"Heracles!" she gasped, springing to her feet, and straightening up the wraparound dress, which had managed to wriggle itself up and wrap around her waist, during her brief and restless sleep.

Sudden pain had shot through her ankle as she had jumped to her feet, forgetting to not put her full weight on it in her agitation at awakening to find herself not alone. "And, ouch, by the way," Cece winced.

"And I guess I'm not going to be using my dress as a bandage again anytime soon," she added, dragging the hem down over her knees.

The idea that walking round in her underwear was no worse than walking round in her bikini seemed somehow ludicrous under the all-encompassing starlit gaze.

"It's a shame I don't have another half-dozen of these hanging around somewhere," she lamented half to herself, smoothing the wrinkled material down, and shifting her weight to her good foot.

Cece stood contemplating her guest, unsure as to how to proceed.

The guest stood surveying Cece.

"Thanks for staying, and ...watching ...me!"

Then, bethinking herself, "And I didn't mean to make that sound anything like as …creepy… as it did! It's just…I thought you'd gone! Actually... I'm glad you hadn't."

Slightly more awake now, and recovering from the shock of realizing that she had had company all night, Cece's loquacious nature was taking over.

"Did I even properly say thank-you, by the way? Yesterday? For the fruit, and the help… with the shack, and ...everything?"

Cece stepped out of the shack as she chattered on, feeling strangely self-conscious about being in the confines of her 'bedroom' with a strange...well… with a stranger. As she stepped over the remaining pebbles that she had not managed to kick out of the way the day before, another thought occurred.

"And do you know, I never even noticed these yesterday, this big pile of…stones …and shells you collected for me! How very… kind! Strange! But kind! Is it a custom among your people to give each other rocks and things?"

Looking about her for something with which to reciprocate the gesture, Cece's eyes alighted upon the ammonite, which, unbeknownst to Cece, had instigated the gathering of the avalanche of shingle and other sea detritus which had been mounted high in front of her shack.

"Here, from me," she said, suddenly shy, holding it out. "For you!" she continued, in case it had not been clear.

As she reached out a hand towards him, he mirrored the movement until their fingertips would have met, except she drew back her hand at the last second, as she suddenly lost her nerve before her fingertips touched the stars that made up his own star- trailing digits.

Instead, she made to drop the ammonite into his hand, and although he did not catch it, neither did he draw back his hand when she withdrew hers, and suddenly the fossil seemed to hover over his hand; an amazing piece of architecture, ancient but newly discovered, cupped in the palm of another.

Garnering her courage, Cece reached out and traced the sharp edges of the spiralled fossilised creature hovering over his hand with her fingertip. As she withdrew her hand and looked into his face, he copied the movement, slowly and carefully tracing the delicate lines.

Then cast his eyeless gaze directly into her eyes.

"What a beauty." The words were so quiet as to be hardly audible, but Cece caught them, and gasped, and felt her stomach tighten into a knot, as a dark flush swept up her face.

"Oh!" She squeaked, then "Oh!" again, then she fluttered a giggle at him, and then got to her feet and started examining the pile of rocks and pebbles and shells as though her life depended on it.

She chose a particularly colourful pebble, red, veined through with green, to study for a moment, until she could feel her flushed face start to calm down.

"This one's pretty", she said, and then picking up a large shell, "and I am sure I can use this one for something. In fact, I collected a big shell like this myself, which I thought would be nice to use as a cup, if only I had something to drink from it!"

She knew she was wittering again to cover her embarrassment at the unexpected compliment, from the strange star-full of a man, but chatter was her usual go to response in uncomfortable situations.

And comfortable situations.

Any situation, really.

"Actually, I *do* have something to drink now!" she remembered, and having drank nothing herself since waking, eagerly grabbed up her waxed cavalier bag, full of water.

Suddenly remembering her manners, and always eager to try to impress, she poured a small amount into the shell, offering it first to her guest.

After an almost imperceptible pause he reached out and took the shell from her hand.

And held it, awaiting further instructions.

"Drink," she said, miming the action by tilting her hand to her own lips. "It's water. It's all I've got, I'm afraid." He copied her action, tilting the water to the area of his face where a mouth would be, then copying her gesture, dropped his hand as he finished the motion, as she had done, resulting in the small amount of water she had allocated him slopping to the ground.

"Well!" she gasped, snippily. "If you don't want it, don't waste it! I walked miles to get that!" then felt immediately contrite at having chastened her wonderful visitor, guiltily remembering all the things he had done for her, not least of which, calling her a beauty!

"Ooh, I know!" she said, suddenly feeling reckless, "I *do* have something else you might prefer!"

She started routing through the pile of goodies that she had tipped out of the wax bag, and dug out the tiny bottle of whisky. She looked at it longingly for a moment, thinking guiltily of the half- promise to save it for medicinal purposes, that she had made to herself, and to whoever else she had thought she was making pacts with, and having half a thought that she may well be needing it to see in the new year, before splitting it between two large shells, having first wiped them out on her filthy dress, then held out one to Heracles.

He reached out and took the shell, and observed Cece.

Despite her eagerness for the prize, momentary wariness of the effect the seashell might have on the wonderful contents of the bottle, Cece daintily stuck out the tip of her pink tongue and touched it into the shell.

"Mmmm..." she said, "A fine single malt whisky!" she licked at her lips somewhat noisily, assessing the flavour, "Or blended maybe... with a hint of prawn." She then watched with interest as a small starburst of a protuberance manifested from somewhere near the centre of Heracles face, which he in his turn daintily dipped into his shell of whisky, as he analysed the content.

"To you and yours!" she toasted, holding the shell up in the air between them, and tipping the fiery content down her throat in one, then almost choked on it, as Heracles echoed her words,

"You and yours," as he emptied the liquid into the swirling black hole which had replaced the protuberance.

Not even recognising the echo of her own actions, the lip-smacking sound which followed seemed incongruous to Cece for so many reasons, not least of which was Heracles lack of lips... and mouth. And yet... he had materialised a tongue when he had need of one, Cece considered, contemplatively.

"Mmmm, I wish there was another hundred where that came from!" she said, more to keep her mind from wandering, than any real desire for more whisky.

Her mind not entirely on the alcohol, she swiped her finger round the inside of the shell, and slowly licked the remnants of the vaguely fishy whisky from her finger.

As Cece watched the milling and weaving stars wash around his face, and indeed his entire body, as Heracles analysed the content of the liquid he had absorbed, she realised that the tiny tot of whisky had been more than enough, and suddenly found she was struggling to keep her eyes open.

And in the presence of not only the most unbelievably fascinating phenomena she had ever seen, but the most exciting ... man... she had ever met, Cece found herself yawning, and apologising.

"I am so sorry Heracles; I am not used to drinking whisky on an empty stomach... or for breakfast for that matter…or maybe it's the excitement, I mean... exhaustion... I hardly slept a wink last night. Well, it is still last night really, isn't it? It's hardly even light. I'm sorry. I know I'm going on a bit…and you don't have to listen to my constant chatter just to be polite you know, if I'm boring you."

Cece noticed the gaping hole opening in the centre of her guest's face before she noticed the one opening in her own as she gave another massive yawn, and her hand, half raised to cover her mouth, changed direction of its own accord, and covered her eyes instead, feeling suddenly light-headed.

The twinkling visage in front of her seemed slightly blurred and out of focus when she drew her hand away from her eyes.

"When I'm tired, I just come out with…rubbish… verbal diarrhoea...please just ignore me when I'm doing that...in fact, I think I really am going to have to close my eyes for a tad…." and before she was even conscious of doing just that, overcome by exhaustion, emotion, and whisky, she swayed forward, asleep.

This time, Heracles did not mimic her movement, but instead caught the collapsing figure before she hit the ground, and laid her atop of the pile of leaves and twigs, before turning his attention to the cooling remnants of the night's camp fire.

Without awaiting further instruction he built a roaring blaze, to ensure his study subject maintained optimal body temperature, while she continued to sleep the morning away.

Chapter Thirty-Three

Bright light streamed in through the many gaps in her wicker shack, as Cece allowed her mind to dwell for a moment on the strange night's dreams of alien encounters with fossil- loving star-men, before forcing open gritty eyes to face the realities of the day.

Cece shaded her face with her hand, in anticipation of the blinding sunlight she knew awaited her outside the shack, before pushing open the wicker door and stepping out ...right into the first of a long row of water filled shells, stretching as far as her eye could see.

One hundred in all if she would have bothered to count, and alongside each one another shell, full of brown brackish looking liquid.

Not knowing whether to first rub her eyes or her poor beleaguered foot, which she had just crunched into the first sharp-edged shell, she tried to do both at once, resulting in her toppling over, right on to the row of shells, scattering the contents of the first half-dozen into the sand.

"Bugger!" her initial reaction, which then gave way to a few seconds of eye- rubbing, and treating her foot to a cursory massage, before she finally reached out and picked up one of the water-filled shells.

Dipping her finger in first, and touching it to her tongue, wary of taking another mouthful of brine, she found it was indeed fresh, clean-ish water.

It did not taste as though it had been washed in by the sea at any rate, she thought, as she chugged back the lot.

So even if her midnight...and then early morning... visitor, had indeed been a dream, or an hallucination, and she instead had actually only been visited by a friendly local or two, he, or they, had at least left her an ample supply of fresh -ish drinking water!

And possibly a row of guzunders, she thought, contemplating the second row of shells, brimming with a dubious looking amber liquid.

Although she certainly had no recollection of filling any of those during the night!

She then tentatively picked up one of the shells containing the slightly less savoury looking liquid and held it first to her nose, before even risking her finger in it.

She withdrew her nose quickly, as the strong earthy smell was not what she expected, it smelled almost like....

Cece dipped her finger into the pooled content of the shell, and tentatively touched the end of her tongue to her fingertip.

Then dipped her tongue into the shallow shell.

Then took a sip, then, after glancing at the long row of shells laid out in front of her, she knocked the whole thing back in one, resulting in a coughing fit that included her snorting a bit of the content back down her nose.

Ok. So the locals had access to a whisky distillery.

Who was she trying to kid?

Cece picked up a shell of water and knocked that back too, as apparently, she was no longer on rations, then, muttering, "What the hell!" she picked up another shell of whisky and sat sipping it as she stared down the line of the best open-bar set-up she had ever seen in her life!

Pondering upon what she realised she was going to have to start and acknowledge had been a genuine, out-of-this-world, encounter, and not to mention, a strange and wonderful night, she looked round towards the treeline, where she had come to the conclusion that he must live.

"Wherefore art thou, Heracles?" she whispered so quietly that she wasn't even sure if she had said it aloud.

But as if magically summoned by the call, she suddenly became aware, even without turning her head, that Heracles was standing behind her.

And she knew without seeing him, that he would be softly emanating that beautiful starlight glow.

What *on Earth* was he?

Cece's audibly rumbling stomach suddenly brought another thought to the forefront of her mind.

"I think I need to eat something with all this whisky, Heracles," she commented hopefully, "or I'll be asleep again!"

Heracles's starry hand suddenly came from somewhere behind her, holding out one of the riper, sweeter mangoes, from her pile of stores.

"Oh! Thank-you Heracles, she said, trying to keep the disappointment out of her voice, as she sank her teeth into it. Food was food after all. "Erm, this fruit's …delicious," she said through a mouthful of mango.

"Mmmm, lovely!" she added, not wanting to sound ungrateful, then, "It's really kind of you, to keep picking them for me," as she took another bite, "but... I was wondering… well, I think I'm going to need something a bit more ...substantial... at some stage. Especially if you're going to keep plying me with alcohol!" She giggled a flirty little giggle, just so that he knew he was not really being told off.

His other hand appeared from behind her from the other side, holding another mango.

"Ah!" she said taking it from him, "Right. Thank-you", and letting out a deep sigh, carried on munching on the mango.

Standing up and wiping the mango juice from her chin, and then from her hands down the front of her already very grubby dress, Cece started to made her way round the back of the shack, to find a quiet place to go do private things.

Then she stopped in her tracks, as it suddenly occurred to her to wonder if she could in fact consider anywhere private to go and do her personal business, now that she had realised that it was likely that Heracles was never far away.

But then it also occurred to her that he may have been around every time she had taken herself off to the proverbial bushes ever since she had been on the island! As her bladder felt as though it was on the point of bursting, and as he was not actually currently in sight, she decided she would just have to get over it!

Or maybe find some bigger bushes!

However, continuing around the back of her shack, the needs of her bladder were again put temporarily on hold, by yet another odd sight which met her eyes!

Squinting against the sun, Cece tried to make out what it was that she could see, hanging from the various trees and bushes in the treeline nearest to her shack.

"Are they... pieces of sail from the ship?" she wondered out loud.

The fact that her cruise ship, even if it had sunk, would have been no more likely to have spewed up *sails* in its death throws than ...well... than she would, did not occur to Cece, in her eagerness to believe she had found evidence of some*thing* else, if not some*one* else, to have finally found its way on to her island.

"Well, the trees are in the same direction as the big bushes anyway," she thought, as she set off at a trot towards the pieces of dappled cloth flapping against the trees.

When close enough to examine the fluttering 'sails', Cece found that she had still not yet quite gotten to the stage where she could no longer be surprised, as she identified that she was looking at at least half a dozen dresses, not dis-similar to the grey and dingy excuse of a dress which currently clung to her own lanky frame.

Actually, make that *exactly* half a dozen dresses, just 'hanging around'! And on closer inspection, they were not 'not dis-similar', or even similar, to her own now somewhat tatty wrap-around dress, but identical!

Down to the last stain!

Well, almost the last stain!

The most recent mango juice stains she had created, those being the ones since she had unknowingly put her order in, were unique to the one she was wearing, she would have discovered, if she had had a mind to examine the dresses more closely.

But her bladder was making itself known again, so she did not take the time to examine them *that* closely.

After having availed herself of the bushes, and so feeling better able to concentrate, Cece dragged the dresses down from the various trees and bits of shrubs that they seemed to have draped themselves around.

Her acceptance of Heracles's presence on the island, and in her life, meant there was no need for her to concoct stories about how an unwanted shipment of pre-loved clothing may have washed up on her island and conveniently hung themselves up, in full view of Cece's camp, and at her arm's reach.

All she really had to work out, she decided, was what were the magic words she had to say, to help him make his little gifts more... appropriate!

He really was trying, bless him, she thought, what with the fruit baskets... the beverages... and now gifts of clothing!

And of course, he wouldn't have a clue as to ladies' fashions, she reasoned, the dress she was wearing was probably the only ladies' clothing he had ever seen.

She thought about his sparkling...naked...physique.

Probably the *only* clothing he had ever seen, she corrected herself!

And he probably didn't have much of an idea about hygiene either, she thought ruefully, as she waved one of the dresses under her nose, arm-pit first, and turned her face away quickly.

Although he himself didn't look like the sort to sweat!

She allowed herself a moment to contemplate that one as well.

She trailed thoughtfully back to her camp with the filthy clothing hanging over her arms, and as there was no sign of Heracles, she carried on down to the water's edge, to try to bash some of the grime and sour sweat out of the dresses.

Dresses, she was beginning to realise, which could also double up, as bandages!

And sheets!

And maybe she could even construct herself some sort of privacy screen!

Actually, they might serve her as any number of things!

"Clever Heracles!" She suddenly credited him out loud. "You are so thoughtful! And actually a bit of a genius, really!"

Chapter Thirty-Four

Dave was starting to feel more relaxed, and able to appreciate the perfectly tilted swivel on his chair again, as he settled down to review the latest feedback reports from his Satis-et-Satis projections program, and accompanying floating narratives.

He made a point of searching out the subjects he had first looked in on, when the not-so -natural disaster had first come to his attention.

He had even provided himself with a small plate of biscuits to accompany the endless cups of cool tea that his flask kept doling out for him.

Cas-trelle *proudly thrust her new baby daughter into Adi-belle's arms, her pride slightly tinged with concern, being mindful that Adi-belle's reluctance to visit with her since she had announced the new arrival, was probably an indicator that Adi-belle might be struggling with her best friend having managed, at last, to accomplish what she herself had not.*

Cas-trelle had experienced the same disappointment, year after year, trying to fill her own empty nest, and she too had settled herself to the idea that she and Cas-treau would be each other's everything.

She and Cas-treau were younger than Adi-belle and Adi-beau, and the trend for a family to be a couple without the expectation that there would be offspring was becoming more established by the time Cas-trelle had stood up to take Cas-treau's name, many years before.

"She is beautiful Cas-trelle! Absolutely beautiful!" Adi-belle cooed over the baby, her heart aching with love for the little creature that was not her own, laying warm and solid in her arms.

"Hello little Pica-trice! I am your Detty Adi-belle! And you are one beautiful little baby!"

The rush of emotions which flooded over her as the tiny child nestled into her breast almost masked the slight twinge of concern that she had for her friend, and the child, as she gently lifted her away from her body to get a better look at her sweet little face, and noted how extremely tiny she was.

"Did she come to you early Cas-trelle? You were not even showing at Mar-teau and Mar-telle's naming day, and she is so...small!"

Cas-trelle snatched back her baby from Adi-belle's arms, pretending not to notice Adabel's obvious reluctance to give her up to her mother.

"Of course she's small! She's a baby! But yes, she was a little... unexpected!" Cas-trelle's tinkling laughter washed away any hint of awkwardness her action may have caused, but Adi-belle's lingering concerns were not so easily assuaged, especially when the tiny dot started to cry to feed, and instead of taking her to her breast, Cas-trelle took out a strange shiny glass bottle, of what appeared to be milk, and started to feed the baby from that.

Adi-belle looked quizzically at Cas-trelle, and noticed the girl's cheeks colour.

"The strangest thing!" Cas-trelle laughed again, "For some reason she wouldn't feed from me! I was in a panic! Then I remembered an old wives' tale about babies who would not feed from their mothers being fed with the milk of a marmiduk who had recently calved! So I thought I'd give it a go, and she took to it like, well like a marmiduk to a plummet grove! She's thriving on it! "

'I don't know about thriving,' thought Adi-belle, looking at the tiny form, but looking from her friend's happy face, to the flushed one of the tiny Pica-trice, making sweet little sounds of contentment, as she sucked at the glass bottle, her emotions again took over any reasoning thoughts. Except...

"Where did you get that strange bottle, you've put the marmiduk milk in? I've never seen such a thing before. Well not being used like that anyway!"

Cas-trelle's countenance darkened.

"Belle! What's with all the questions! Just enjoy her! That's what we are doing!" She swung her shoulders slightly away from Adi-belle and pulled the edge of the baby blanket round Pica-trice's chin, partially hiding her from Adi-belle, so that she could not see her feeding from the strange glass bottle that was generating so much interest.

"She's beautiful! And she's all mine! All mine!" Cas-trelle crooned, as she swung little Pica-trice from side to side.

"I'm sorry Cas-trelle!" Adi-belle was immediately contrite, but puzzled by Cas-trelle's strange response to her question. She found herself hugging the pot cloth she had picked up to fill the space in her arms where the baby had been, and unconsciously cuddled and rocked the damp rag, in time with Cas-trelle's swaying of her baby, back and forth.

"I didn't mean anything by it. I just... is she ok? Are you ok? "

"We are fine! Everything is absolutely fine now!" She was looking down into the baby's face and didn't see the tears well

up in her friend's eyes, as she crooned to the baby, "We are among the lucky ones aren't we Pic-ty? Yes, we are! Yes, we are!"

The tears spilled, but had been quickly absorbed by the already damp pot-towel, before Cas-trelle smiled back up at her friend.

Dave finished his biscuits and wondered why his face seemed to be frowning. Everything was going according to plan, and he didn't understand why he didn't feel happier about it.

Something about the little scene he had just monitored did not feel as satisfying as he had expected it to, but he was not sure why.

Part Two
Rescue Party!
Chapter One

"Food!" Cece said out loud, both to herself and to her shining shadow, feeling almost as hollow as her companion looked.

She wondered how he could look so hollow and, at the same time, so full of... well, everything!

Cece felt as though she had divided her time and energies, over the last few days, in almost equal proportions, between the two major issues which seemed to dominate her every thought.

Firstly, trying to communicate with, and further her knowledge and understanding of, the mystical being, who seemed now to be her constant shadow, except, well, when he wasn't!

And secondly, but by no means of any less importance, trying to work out how to get her new found friend to understand that she needed to access food, other than the ubiquitous mangos!

Mangos had now slid some significant way down her list of most delicious fruits in the world.

Cece had adapted surprisingly quickly, to the starry figure appearing when she addressed him, but then disappearing in the middle of her speaking to him, only to re-appear some distance down the beach, having been occupying himself with his apparent love of collecting stones and shells.

Or suddenly coming out of the trees, arms loaded with firewood.

He did seem to love a campfire!

Her adaptability to the situation may, or may not, have been something to do with her now apparently unlimited access to, what could only be described as, questionable, sea-tainted whisky at her beachside shack!

Alcohol might not be a cure for all that ails you, Cece had decided, but it certainly took the edge off!

"If I eat another mango, I'll barf!" she declared dramatically to Heracles, who, registering the new word, and potential new activity, as something which may be worthy of a report, stood by, on full alert.

Having devoured three of the fairly green bananas that she had brought back from one of her early sorties into the jungle, and suffered terrible gut pain for several hours afterwards, had decided not to try them again, despite large bunches of similar fruit having joined the original bunch that she herself had retrieved from the jungle.

She wondered if, rather than bananas, they may have actually been something she had read about, called plantains, and if they may have been easier to digest if she had cooked them first.

Or maybe even waited for them to ripen?

But they had seemed fairly palatable at the time, washed down with a couple of shells of whisky, as she had again tried to engage Heracles in sand picture creations. He seemed to have lost interest in their art sessions however, after his initial attempts to explain to her where he was from.

She supposed the gut ache she had experienced on the day she ate the questionable bananas could possibly have been due to having whisky on an empty stomach... and for breakfast... or the even more questionable water she had been drinking.

Or maybe the handful of berries she had brought back with the bananas were to blame.

Or the several more shells-full of whisky she had tried later, in an attempt to settle her stomach ache.

"I'm erring on the side of caution," she had explained sagely to Heracles, as she had thrown the remainder of the soft ruby berries away, after the initial onset of her gut ache. "Because you can never be too careful with berries. I think we all know that, anyway."

Cece had seen way too many wild-cookery programmes to get caught out with that one, she nodded wisely along to her own thoughts. A handful of the wrong berries could kill you! Just as well she had only eaten a few, Cece thought virtuously.

And Heracles, detecting the change in Cece's tone, and noting that she had changed her stance so that she could ensure that he was observing her as she made this proclamation, dutifully made note of the information, and passed on the intelligence, with a suitable priority ranking.

Chapter Two

"So, what's this now? About dangerous berries?" John asked, looking over Dave's shoulder at the screen, which was currently set to visually display Heracles's incoming transmissions.

"Oh, it's nothing to worry about." Dave tried out what he hoped was a reassuring tone, with a nonchalant expression on his face to match.

He flipped the screen to the window which showed life-sized images of the beautiful sea-life surrounding the little vessel, and which he hoped would distract his colleague from yet another trouble, which his increasingly unruly avatar seemed to have deemed significant enough to have brought to his attention.

"Just an extra bit of research he seems to... I mean *I* seem to... I mean I *am* doing, on fruits, and other dangerous earth entities, you know, which may present a future threat to our species, just to sort of... bulk out... the initial projection analysis that I am very legitimately engaged in.

"And obviously we all know the potential of fruits... to be...erm ...dangerous...anyway." Dave chattered on, Cece like, whilst practicing the newly discovered skill of 'fingers whizzing across a keyboard', as he frantically tried to identify what potential danger berries may one day present to his own immortal-kind.

He also searched through the infinite virtual data bases that he had limitless access to, when he was not trying to be part of the immersive human experience.

"Oh yes, of course, the well-known danger of... berries...that we all obviously know about," agreed John, somewhat distantly, momentarily mesmerised by the shifting light bouncing off the shoal of dancing herrings, darting back and forth in their endless mission to fool their more predatory neighbours, before diverting to his own internal data base, to do a bit of private research of his own

Chapter Three

"Yes, almost definitely the berries," Cece concluded to herself, as she sipped on another shellful of fishy whisky. Or the bananas. Or plantains. Or the numerous ripe, and not so ripe, and totally unripe mangoes she had eaten over the last few days.

"Mmmm ...Prawn-suffused whisky!" She mused, taking another sip.

"My new favourite thing! Who'd have thunk it? I've had worse! In fact I've had worse Christmases, if I'm honest!"

That thought brought Cece up short for a moment.

She had totally lost track of how long she had been on the island, and could not even work out whether or not Christmas may have already been and gone!

The irrelevant thought slipped out of her mind as easily and quickly as it had slipped in.

"And I'm really going to have to patent this when I get home!"

Throwing the empty shell on to the growing mound that she was accumulating, and getting a little unsteadily to her feet, she weaved her way back up to the tree-line, where she had draped the slightly cleaner looking, and significantly fresher smelling, dresses to dry.

"So that's the washing done. Warr-els did I 'ave to do?" Her words starting to slur slightly even to her own ears, reminded her.

"Oh yes. Eat. I need something...other than mangos... to soak up the prawni-sky! The prawnsky! I really am going to have to patent it now! I've made a name up for it!"

The prawn- whisky-suffused Cece found her own ramblings hilarious, bending over double with laughter!

"And it would go lovely with prawn cocktail crisps! Or crab sticks! Or any sort of food that isn't a mango, actually!"

"But how do I make you understand I need some proper food? And how do I know what you can get me?" She continued to think out loud.

The avatar tuned into these last questions, detecting the slightly querulous tone which he identified as being among the sounds she made when she was making a deliberate attempt at communication, as opposed to the various other sounds his study subject tended to constantly emit.

He filtered out what he now recognized to be the regular rhythm of her circulatory system, the gentle susurration of her respiration, and the somewhat more irregular gurglings and other noises produced by her digestive system; not to mention the verbal diarrhoea, which she had instructed him to ignore.

He filed quite a lot of her utterances under this category, and consequently filtered them out of his transmissions.

He concentrated on transmitting various requests for information, and advised the entity now transmitting as Dave, that he would even settle for confirmation of his own conclusions, then waited patiently for further input, from Dave, or even from the subject now known to him as Cece.

Or from anybody, really.

Chapter Four

Walking along the shoreline, using her stick now more as an aid to poke things with, than a staff, Cece had a new mission in mind.

Heracles's understanding of the English, or maybe, the human, language, seemed somewhat erratic to Cece.

He was taciturn, to say the least, she had decided; communications with her were… selective, and when he did speak, had no discernible accent.

Unless possibly, if she had had to put her finger on it, and as improbable as it seemed to Cece, maybe he had a slight… Yorkshire inflection? Similar to her own, in fact!

But there seemed to be something ...wanting... in his understanding of what she was trying to communicate to him.

She felt that he was desperately trying to understand her, and was obviously trying to help her out, in whatever ways he could, but he seemed so lacking in understanding as to what she actually needed, unless she had some way of making it blindingly obvious.

She realised that wherever he was from, was likely to be so different to her reality, that he could not be expected to anticipate what her needs might be!

If the situation was reversed, she thought, how on Earth would she even start to try to make sure that *he* was ok?

She would not have a clue where to start! So, coming at it from that perspective, he was doing remarkably well, she realised! Cece suddenly felt incredibly insensitive and ungrateful, and terribly guilty!

She had not even made any effort to see if *he* was ok, or needed anything! And he also seemed to be marooned here, against his will!

And was probably a *long*, long way from home!

For some reason, she felt unquestioningly safe with him, and after everything she had experienced over the last few days, she did not even count her new found wonder at the universe among today's 'top five top thoughts'!

Her current priorities seemed to be food that wasn't fruit, food that wasn't bad, food that didn't give her stomach ache, food that didn't make her sick, and food that was not likely to kill her, preferably!

In that order.

She thought it highly unlikely that she had the stomach, or heart, to capture, or kill, another living lifeform, even if she hadn't have had the apparently endless supply of mangos to sustain her!

However, increasingly vivid images of barbequed fish steaks, and even what she would previously have thought of as disgusting calamari, were encouraging her to think of alternative dietary solutions.

If she could find a fish that had died of natural causes, such as old age, she reasoned with herself, she might be able to bring herself to do the necessaries with it, in order to prepare it to be cooked.

After all, she did also have her far-from-home companion to think about as well as herself, she thought, as she tried to justify her longings for cooked fish.

He could well be a pescatarian!

"Yes, a dead fish," she said out loud, "preferably one that hasn't died of some unknown disease, or whatever, and then been left rotting in the sun! That's what I need to find!" she started to giggle to herself. "That shouldn't do my constant stomach ache any harm at all!"

She suddenly be-thought herself, and glanced over her shoulder to see if Heracles was listening.

She was relieved to see he was trailing along a good few yards behind her, with a stick similar to her own, which he had picked up somewhere along the way, and which he was dipping in and out of the shallow waves as he trailed through the water, as he had observed Cece to do.

He had no sense for the ironic, and chose the darndest things to understand and take literally, she thought, and did not want to come home to a pile of dead and rotting fish at her camp door!

She had tried to get him to replenish the thee quarter used tube of still unidentified lucky-dip cream, after finding that it had gone some way to easing, if not totally eliminating, both the itchiness from the gnat bites, and soreness from the sunburn, when she had made it stretch as far as it would go, and covered as much of her body as she could reach, with what was left in the tube.

She had attempted every communication method she could think of, starting by trying to help him read the mostly illegible, and probably foreign, small print on the tube, then using mimes and demonstrations, before concluding by trying sheer force of will, and maybe even a little telepathy.

The end result had been a rather disappointing pile of essentially empty tubes, which had appeared outside of the shack the next day, and which she knew not how to dispose of, short of starting her own landfill site.

The upside of the extensive and detailed interaction with Heracles, however, had been that Cece had experienced the most delicious dream that night, of being massaged all over, with a wonderful gnat-repellent-cum-suncream-cum moisturiser-cum-cure-all cream, by a gently glowing, whimsical, and fantastical creature!

It had been so vivid that Cece had found herself blushing when she awoke to the sight of Heracles gathering driftwood outside the shack the next morning.

And she almost fancied that even Heracles's midnight-blue glow seemed to have had taken on more of a crimson hue in the early morning sunlight, but that was probably a reflection of the beautiful sunrise that Cece had felt exhilarated to see washing over the beach that morning!

At least that was what Cece had *hoped* was causing Heracles's pink tinge, and not that he really did have the ability to read her mind!

Or witness her dreams!

She had found her own cheeks soaking up even more of the magnificent sunrise that morning, as that thought had occurred to her!

But to be fair, she thought, she had been a lot less bothered by bites, or the sun, since; the scrap end of cream that had been in the tube which she had used up must have been multi-purpose, and more potent than she had realised!

Dragging her thoughts back to more practical matters, Cece was starting to devise a plan, and carried her waxed shoulder bag with her in readiness.

'Can't kill a fish', she thought, 'Can't eat a dead rotten one. But if I can find a fish, that's *destined* to die of natural causes, caught in the shallows for example, and keep it in my wax bag until it expires...of natural causes...well, that's different!'

She spun out the story of what she felt her conscience, and her stomach, and her heart, could live with, until it seemed to make sense to her.

And so as the tide had started to go down, and small shallows appeared at the bases of some of the larger rocks, Cece poked around until she found a couple of likely candidates.

She found first one tiny fish, and then, a few rocks on, a second even tinier fish, caught in the small rock-pools left behind by the ebbing waters; hardly enough to sustain a mouse, but Cece was starting to understand that quantity was not an issue with Heracles.

"Heracles! Oh *Heracles*!" Having glanced around and not immediately been able to see Heracles, she started to call for him, in her most dulcet tone.

And when that did not result in him stepping out from behind the nearest rock or tree, or even just from somewhere behind her back, as it usually did, she put her hands to her mouth, and losing her aspirates, in favour of gusto, tried once more, with, well, volume.

"'ERACLES! Ohhhh 'ERAcleees! OYE!! 'ERAC.... Oh! There you are!" she cut herself off mid-flow, as he appeared a little way down the beach. "I didn't see you! I thought you'd gone to... wherever you go!"

She plodded over to where Heracles was crouched, dabbling his stick into a rock pool, and showed him her quarry.

He bowed his head, exploring the depths of her handbag, and she looked up into his face, exploring the depths of the universe.

"More of these," she explained, "I need more of these. Or like these. Or similar," she clarified, then turned and retraced her weary steps back to the camp.

She did not really hold out much hope that he would totally understand and fulfil her wishes, but she knew he would try.

It would be interesting just to see what he would come up with, she thought!

However, her anticipation turned to horror, as she approached her camp to see a multitude of flip- flopping fish, gasping for breath, piled high in front of the shack door!

"Heracles! No!" She cried, almost hysterical at the thought of all the poor suffering fish. "This is the total opposite to what I wanted!

"Put them back Heracles! *Please*! Put them back into the sea! They can't *survive* out of water! They can't *breathe*!" she bleated, floods of tears coursing down her face, unable to catch her own breath, her empathy with the poor gasping fishes overwhelming her.

"I mean… I can't eat all *that* many anyway!" Cece sobbed helplessly, trying to justify her upset to Heracles, belatedly, and guiltily, remembering that Heracles had after all only been acting upon her own request.

While Heracles was busy processing, and transmitting, and transmitting some more, the pile of fish started to topple over as something from the bottom of the pile struggled to make its way out.

The octopod, which eventually emerged from the pile of floppety- fish, started creep-crawling its way back down to the water. It had only recently downgraded its outlook on life from vaguely curious, to wary, and was now having to have another rethink!

Unadulterated caution was probably the way to go, moving forward, it concluded.

Cece's mouth, always gape-ready these days, did her justice, not so much at the sight of the octopus making its way unsteadily down the beach, but at how much the sound of suckers against shingle and sand made an almost ... grumbling...chuntering... sound, as it disappeared from view, around a rock.

Redirecting her attention to the poor suffocating fish, and forgetting for a moment that she was speaking to a possibly alien entity, who was probably more powerful than she could begin to imagine, and which had just managed to dredge the ocean bed floor, and dry-landed examples of every species of life sustained by said ocean, and not a cat that had just brought someone's goldfish home, Cece rounded on Heracles.

"*Bad* Heracles! Put them back! This instant! We don't kill fish! We *help* animals! We don't kill *anything*! It isn't... *ethical*! You are usually so *kind* Heracles! And helpful! What have you *done*? What were you *thinking*, Heracles?

Heracles was very busy for the next few minutes, returning the fish back to from whence they came, by creating a small waterspout just large enough to transport the beached fishes safely back to their natural environs, with a few easy calculations and a sweep of his starlit arm, and with a few small breakers thrown in to catch the stragglers.

In addition to that, he was simultaneously transmitting to Dave, requesting information on ethics, and also requesting if Dave could provide additional information, as to 'what had he done', and 'what had he been thinking', whilst concurrently observing Cece, who was continuing to flick away, and swat at, any number of flying, and crawling insects, that she barely registered any more, as she crushed them into none-existence.

And then, at Cece's rather wistful afterthought, once panic had subsided, and hunger taken over, "Unless any have already happened to a have died, as a result of you catching them, 'cause I suppose, if they are already dead, I might as well eat those ones."

Splashing heavily, Heracles plodded back into the sea to fetch back one large expired red mullet.

And then trying again to consult with Dave, who was currently only responding intermittently to transmissions, as Heracles considered adding to the expired mullet, a sea-bass.

It had survived its initial trip to the beach, and also narrowly survived the return trip to the sea, but its vital signs indicated that it was unlikely to survive a third trip.

Dave did not respond to this particular set of transmissions, leaving Heracles to make his own projections and calculations, on effect, and counter effect, of bringing the sea-bass back to Cece.

It would almost certainly be dead by the time Cece saw it, he calculated, which technically seemed to fit the rather confusing criteria she had laid out, which comprised of what she had described as being acceptable, but which seemed to present a juxtaposition against the actions she had actually demonstrated.

But despite having received no clarity on the ethical parameters of the situation from Dave, or any consistency from Cece, Heracles made a calculation that the sea- bass stood a chance of recovery, if left alone, so he decided against bringing it back to the beach, because, to do so just didn't feel ...well…right.

The unadulteratedly cautious octopus missed the water spout ride back to the sea by a sucker's breadth, and, having paused its slip-sliding crawl down to the sea to plop itself into a small pool behind a seaweeded rock to re-moisten, even missed hitching a lift in one of the ensuing small breakers!

He continued to grumble and chunter as he watched his fellow sea-creatures be safely transported over his head, and concluded that 'not being able to even catch a breaker' needed to be added in to his fast-developing philosophy on life.

Chapter Five

Flask at the ready, pop-corn in microwave, (Dave made a note to himself to check the accuracy of his research with John on that one) and settled down to watch...wavy lines clearing to full view screen, and ...action!

"Beau! *Beau! Quick, come here!" The sharp tone bore little resemblance to Adi-belle's normally calm and controlled voice, making Adi-beau drop the tree-cleaver he was yielding out back of the dwell, and go running indoors.*

"What's the matter?" he panted, dashing from room to room. "Where are you?"

"I'm in here, by the bed." Quieter this time, Adi-belle's voice came to him from their sleep-room.

Adi-beau stood stock still in the doorway.

Adi-belle was standing next to the bed, looking down on a tiny figure squirming about on the centre of the soft woven covers.

The wriggling figure suddenly opened its mouth and let out the sort of wail that they had both given up hope of ever hearing.

"We're keeping it!" As though she thought Adi-beau might argue. "We're keeping it!"

Adi-belle swept up the little figure and snuggled it against her chest. Adi-beau stood open mouthed staring from

Adi-belle, fiercely hugging the squalling infant, to the strange glass bottle left lying on the bed from where Adi-belle had just snatched up the baby.

The bottle contained a white milky liquid. He picked it up, and wordlessly held it out to Adi-belle.

For a moment she stared uncomprehendingly at the bottle, and then into the screaming little face, fast turning from red to puce, and with hardly a thought as to what she was doing, offered the shiny glass bottle to the baby, who took the teated end into his rosebud mouth, and started suckling happily away, all suddenly well in his little world.

Dave could still not quite put his finger on why the situation had not 'felt right' before, despite its potential to totally remedy the issue caused by his little miscalculations, or why he had decided to send a child to these particular subjects, just because he was aware of them.

He couldn't pin point where the concept had come from, or even what it meant, really. He'd have to check the transcripts. What had been said about things…feeling…right?

Something that Heracles had said, maybe, he thought.

He stuffed another mouthful of dry fluffy popcorn into his mouth, gagged, washed it down with cold tea, before shoving in another mouthful, then leant back in his chair, enjoying the warm feeling of satisfaction that his humanoid body was experiencing, as he continued to scan for more examples of the good he had done in the universe before he got back down to the business of, well, business.

Chapter Six

Cece threw herself down in front of her brightly burning campfire, feeling she had worked hard enough to justify breaking for dinner, after an exhausting few hours of building up her shack, making it feel more secure.

She had added many extra layers to the panels of her shack, more than needed really, made from bindings cobbled from the shredded leaves, and the more malleable stripped branches.

She was becoming quite adept at using the now tried and tested method of doing a bit, and then walking down to the water's edge, and returning to find Heracles had continued the task.

Cece had discovered that Heracles was a wonderful and tireless worker, as long as she ensured tasks only involved him having to copy whatever task she had started, rather than expecting him to show initiative and take any task to the next step.

The little row of toilet cubicles now turned into a row of hexagonal shacks stood testament to that, all equally well re-enforced and standing to attention, awaiting to be assigned a purpose.

She had decided against allocating herself a shack as a toilet cubicle, despite their apt appearance, as that would have inevitably resulted in her having to devise some method of transferring the contents of whatever she deposited there, to somewhere else, at various intervals!

This was a task that she could manage to avoid, she thought, if she just continued her habit of finding a different bush every time she needed to go!

There were enough bushes and trees around, she considered optimistically, to last her until she got off the island.

She shied away from the thought that she did not want this task to be one that Heracles would almost certainly take over from her!

No, the only reason was that she had plenty of bushes!

Even if she did not know know what else she was going to use the spare shacks for, she thought wryly, it was not as though she was expecting guests!

The denseness of Cece's shack walls may have helped her feel more secure while spending her nights on the edge of a jungle containing who knew what sort of wild animals, but the necessity for safety was actually only in Cece's mind.

If she had but realised it, she was the safest creature on the island, with her own personal bodyguard!

After sitting thinking a moment, Cece got to her feet again and went round the side of her shack and dug until she came to the wet sand, where she had earlier buried the well-travelled red mullet, to keep it out of the heat of the day until she felt ready to tackle it.

Pinching the fish by the tale with her finger tips, whilst holding it at arm's length and pinching her nose with the other hand, Cece brought it back round to the fire, where Heracles had also thrown himself down, and short of knowing what else to do with it, she threw it whole in to the flames and then sat back down hoping for the best.

She looked at Heracles, and a face full of whirlpools and stars looked back at Cece.

"I think I'm meant to have gutted that, or something, but hey ho."

"Hey ho," said Heracles, after a pause which had seemed to require something of him. Despite continuous transmissions to Dave, no further advice had been forthcoming, since the transmission some days ago, which had given the simple, if somewhat ambiguous instruction, "Improvise!"

Ambiguous, or, as far as the avatar was concerned, surprisingly liberating,

"And talking about coincidences," Cece continued, "which, now I think about it, we weren't. Although I have been *thinking* about co-incidences... a lot... lately!

And I was only thinking about Heracles the other day! You know, Heracles the hero, well, the… *other* … hero," she cast a simpering smile his way, his head had already swung in her direction, at the repeated use of his name, "or Hercules. Or whatever he's calling himself these days! With all his labours and trials, and .... tribulations... and all that.

"This whisky's really nice though, in't it? Anyways, I can't remember the exact story, but I know he did have an awful lot of stuff to do, you know… missions …and things, and so have I. Had a lot of stuff to do, I mean, not missions. Or I suppose they might be missions? Not sure what counts as a mission... or a trial, to be fair. Or a tribulation, come to think of it. Do *you* know? What a tribulation is? I mean, who does? Really?" Cece continued to chatter on, and as he seemed to be key to this particular lecture, Heracles took notes.

"And actually, you've done half my trials…or tribulations… for me, anyway, to be fair, haven't you?"

93%, calculated Heracles silently. To be fair.

"And do you know what's another co-incidence, Heracles? You're named after a Greek Hero! Or a Roman hero! Or both, I forget! Anyway, *I* was named after a Greek hero as well! Narcece! I'm named after Narcissus... obsessed with himself, I think, or in love with his own company, or something...even though I usually just get called Cece, as I've told you.

"But…Cece *also* means something in Latin. Blind, or something like.

"My Nanna used to say,

"Cece, oh my Cece!
There are none so blind,
As those who won't see!
See?"

"She said it was a joke, a play on words…or something… 'cause of my name. But I never got it! 'Cause it's not like I'm blind or anything is it?

"And anyway, I mean, who names their child after a narcissist? And then gives them a nickname that's a joke?

"But then, I suppose it was my mam, you know… my mother? She's the one that would have named me, not my Nanna. And it was Nan who did Latin at school, and told me all this stuff, not my mam.

"So my mam wouldn't have known, when she named me, or even my dad. I don't think anyone was being cruel, it's just the way things turned out.

"My Nanna brought me up, you see, from me being little. I didn't even know my dad… but Heracles! I love that name, so heroic!" she tapered off, hoping she had not offended him with her usual fatuous chatter; he did seem to be paying more attention than usual.

"Anyway, 'nuff about me... Heracles! Heracles the Hero! You have been *my* hero anyway! You've probably saved my life at least three times over, since I got washed up on this godforsaken island!

You always seem to be there rescuing me from some scrape or another! And my word! Is it good to have someone to talk to, though!"

"Three times, three times over," calculated a hushed echo.

"What? Did you just say something Heracles?"

And improvising, Heracles shook his head.

Chapter Seven

Despite its singular lack of preparation, after several days of eating nothing but fruit, the red mullet soon began to smell mouth wateringly appetising to Cece, if a little fishy.

She poked it back out of the flames with one of the many spare green stripped branches, and broke it to bits, trying to pick out the bits she recognised as fish flesh, and discard bits that she felt she should probably have discarded before she cooked it.

"You know what this needs, don't you?" she said, springing to her feet again. "Whisky!"

She pottered back into her cabin and came back out balancing several shells full of whisky, along with a couple of shells to serve as plates, and then busied herself sorting out dinner for her guest and herself, feeling almost as though she were entertaining at home.

As was becoming her habit, she again stuck out the tip of her tongue to taste the fish, before deciding that whatever it tasted like, she was going to eat it anyway, and hungrily wolfing down a big piece of, thankfully, adequately cooked, fish.

She was again intrigued to watch the protuberance appear in the middle of Heracles face as he probed the fish also, before throwing it into the dark hole at his centre, washing it down, as Cece did, with whisky.

Having eaten as much of the red mullet as seemed edible, and as much of the whisky as seemed sensible, Cece found herself in a giddy and sharing mood, and found Heracles to be a receptive, even if, unbeknownst to her, captive, audience.

"Do you remember," she reminisced tipsily, as though they had known each other forever, "when you brought me my bag, full of useless paraphernalia, when what I really needed was a first aid bag or something?" She doubled up laughing at what now seemed to her like an hilarious jape, despite it seeming like the end of the world a few days ago.

"Let me get you some of the stuff that was in that bag and show you how ridiculous it was!" she continued, tears rolling down her face, triggering a fresh set of transmissions to Dave.

She staggered to her feet and set about gathering up the foldaway rain-hood, rescued from the first 'bounty-bag', then the topiary book, the mixed tape, and old-fashioned cassette recorder, which she had not yet had inclination to even test out to see if it still worked.

Suddenly assuming an earnest expression, Cece opened out the plastic rain- hat and placed it upon her head.

"Now *this* was really useful. You need to get yourself one of these bad boys!" Cece sat tucking her hair into the hood, and tying the strings into a little bow under her chin, whilst maintaining her serene composure, for a full ten seconds at least, before peering over at Heracles to judge his response to her joke.

Squinting her eyes to bring his image into better focus, against the flickering firelight, to confirm what she was looking at, Cece lost all composure, and nearly her last shellful of whisky, as she burst into uncontrolled hysterical laughter.

Heracles had been sitting looking back at Cece, with an equally serious demeanour, and as earnest an expression on his wonderfully twinkling visage, as a man with no features and starlight for a face can muster, wearing his own spontaneously materialised plastic foldaway rain-hood, on his nebulous noggin, and a bow, tied every bit as prettily as Cece's, beneath his cosmic chin.

As Cece fell about laughing at his mimicry of her, rolling over, and onto the beach, Heracles started to roll about on the sand also, great guffawing laughter erupting from his body, galaxies spiralling round and round his torso, matching Cece's great belly laughs.

He continued to rock, and double up with laughter, until Cece, wiping the streaming tears from her face, eventually managed to recover some self-control.

"Oh Heracles! You are such a…wag! You crease me up! You never cease to surprise me! I don't know where you get this stuff from! You are so funny!"

With lots of deep breaths, and coughing, and nose wipings, Cece, and Heracles, eventually regained their composure, only for Cece to set them both off again, as she continued to spread out the goodies from bounty-bag two, by remarking, "To be fair, this topiary book did come in useful …as a sun hat!" which caused first Cece, then Heracles, to double over again, at what Cece perceived to be her own wittiness.

"And also, to be fairerer, fairer...er," she frowned, then hiccupped, then tried again, "Fairerer...er...I bet you don't even know what topiary is do you? Do you even have topiary where you're from? Do you even have bushes?"

She glanced at the sky, then the sea, then into the jungle, frowning again.

"We didn't actually quite establish where you're from, did we?" She continued innocently, as though it was such an inconsequential thing as establishing from which side of the north-west wash he had originated.

His gaze followed hers from the sky to the sea, then the jungle, then settled on the book she had let drop into her lap.

She looked down at the book.

"*Topiary*," she said as slowly and as clearly as she could manage after a surfeit of prawnisky, as though explaining to a toddler, and then scrambled to her feet, only to then go and throw herself back down next to Heracles, to be better able to show him some of the illustrations.

"It's the fine art of massacring bushes until they don't even look like bushes any more. As opposed to bonsai, that's starving and torturing small trees until they give up the will to grow. That's even more cruel, if you ask me! The poor trees have as much right to grow and live as any other living creature."

She looked off into the wild overflowing jungle, a few yards behind their backs, and thought about all the other living creatures, dwelling so close to her own humble abode, and despite her kindly animal-loving nature, could not help but shudder slightly.

Heracles followed her gaze, looking off into the jungle also, then back at the book.

"At least you can carve bushes into funny shapes," Cece went on, as flicking the pages over, she came to a selection of Disney characters that someone had cleverly, if not very tastefully, created from a row of evergreens, in a magnificent English mansion park-garden.

"Bit tacky, if you ask me," she added, "but you know, everyone to their own, and all that!"

She left Heracles flicking through the pages with his star-twinkling hands, while she prized herself off the floor again, to examine the cassette tape and recorder.

After a bit of fumbling, and the letting loose of a few small curse words, the crackling sounds of the great Italian tenor Caruso suddenly trickled into the air.

"My giddy aunt!" Cece shouted, elated. "It works! I never thought I would be so happy to hear music from the Dark Ages!"

Despite often borrowing her expletives from a similar era, Cece liked to think of herself as a 'modern gal', despite her guilty secret love of all things last generation, including thinking of herself in such terms as a 'modern gal'.

Rocking her head, and swaying, she put the old tape player up against her ear to catch the faint strains.

"Oh Caruso! Oh, how my old Nanna loved you! And how I loved my old Nan!" She was suddenly tearful at memories of herself, as a child, and her grandmother, tissue paper skinned, but twinkle-eyed, hand in hand, prancing around the kitchen floor together, to the fantastic voice of the old lady's hero.

She had almost lost the memory, until she had heard the deep timbre of the beautiful voice again. She tried to sing along to some of the refrains which she neither remembered nor understood, then, quietly, regretfully, "I think the batteries are almost gone! I can hardly hear it."

Then, suddenly hopeful, "I don't suppose you do batteries?" She tentatively offered the machine to Heracles.

Heracles reached out a galaxy and took the old tape machine from Cece, and placed it against his ear, and tilted his head to one side as he had observed Cece doing.

"Can you still hear it? I can't hear it from here. Is it still playing? Or have the batteries given up the ghost?

Caruso! How my nan used to love to hear him sing! 'The voice of an angel', she used to say! I think she really was a little in love with him, or with his voice at any rate.

"We used to dance..." And with her eyes closed as she half drifted off under the influence of several shells of whisky, Cece lifted her arms as though holding the hands of her dear old Nanna, and gently rocked her head from side to side, the memory of the tune still playing in her head.

Then her eyes sprung open, as Enrico Caruso's dulcet tones, along with full orchestral accompaniment, suddenly belted out across the beach.

With her startled eyes wide open, despite her previous alcohol fuelled torpor, Cece's jaw dropped open, almost as wide as her eyes, at the sight of Heracles, standing in front of her, the music and voice somehow emanating from his very being, the tape player no longer in his star-filled hands, which were now held out in front of him, as she had been doing a moment a go; almost, she thought.... inviting her to dance?

Not one to need asking twice, Cece scrambled to her feet, and after almost a second of contemplating the potential folly of touching the heat of a thousand suns, she reached out and touched her fingers to his, and then without even realizing that she was leading, was soon dancing around the moonlit beach, with a man made of stars, to the seductive sounds of a long dead Italian, and the strains of instruments that she did not even know she knew how to appreciate.

Cece and the starlit man, who wasn't a man, drank whisky, and danced and twirled away the night, around the beach, and daintily into the shallows, where, by chance, or possibly by design, a profusion of bio-luminescence of which Cece was barely conscious, such was the magic of the night, added to the canvas against which they performed.

Eventually Cece could dance and drink no more.

She slumped into the starry chest of the celestial figure, and neither cared nor remembered how she ended up snuggled into her leafy mattress, where she lay carefully covered up, and wrapped-around in a wraparound dress, which barring for the odd stain, was very much like the one in which she had danced the night away.

And she knew no more, until the heat of the following day cracked into her dreams.

Chapter Eight

Very few ventilation cracks had survived Heracles repeated duplications of Cece's attempts to re-enforce her shack with smaller and smaller twigs, but still, enough sunlight managed to creep between the tightly woven branches to stir Cece's senses to wakefulness.

A whisky-dry mouth prompted her to immediately start to grope her way out of her shack, in search of the shells of fresh water she knew would be laying outside, even before she had attempted to pry open her heavy eyelids.

She was onto her third shell before she managed to fully open her dry eyes, and was onto her fourth or fifth before she started to believe what she was seeing.

All along the jungle's edge, stretching back as far as she could see, and towering as high as the tallest of the spruce firs, or possibly palm trees… Cece had no clue as to which… which had previously overlooked her private beach, she found herself eyeballing as many twenty-foot-high green Mickey Mice as can be accommodated on a small deserted island.

She pushed herself to her feet, her back to the water, then staggered backwards a few steps, to be able to take in more of the vista, then took a few more steps backwards, just to be sure of what she was seeing.

"Oh Heracles!", she croaked at last, through her still dry throat, "What have you done now?"

Chapter Nine

"And that, Heracles," Cece finished her lecture with a flourish of her pointing stick, which she had used to illustrate her version of the lifecycle of the bird, that she had etched into the wet sand, finishing with an approximation of a worm, wriggling in the open beak of the chick, with its head popping up out of a nest, "is why we don't randomly chop into treetops to make giant Mickey Mouse shapes!"

Cece and Heracles were sitting cross-legged in the sand, on the cusp between where warm dry sand petered off, and smooth wet, teachable sand, began.

Cece had started to feel that she was making some headway into educating her pupil into the rights and wrongs of wildlife preservation.

Which she felt was a bit of a mixed blessing really.

After yesterday's drama of what Cece had started to think of as 'Heracles's first fishing trip', she had to admit she had really enjoyed the resultant barbequed red mullet, and was wondering how she could get him to repeat the performance, without traumatising half the inhabitants of the Pacific Ocean.

As it turned out, it wasn't quite as difficult as she had expected.

"I'm a bit hungry, Heracles," she began, looking up into his twinkling face, "and you look like you might have a bit of a ...hole... to fill," she continued, looking into the swirling mass of galaxies and cosmic confusion where one might expect his stomach to be.

His gaze followed hers, looking down the length of his form, then looking back at Cece, waiting for her to continue.

"We didn't have breakfast yet, did we?" Cece continued, hopeful of triggering some sort of gesture on Heracles's part.

But Heracles continued to wait, whilst transmitting to Dave for instructions, but did not need to wait for a reply from Dave, as Cece decided to take a blunter approach.

"Can you get me a fish to eat, please, Heracles? Like the one you got me yesterday… but without killing anything. If that's possible? But I don't want a live one either," she added hurriedly.

Heracles stood up, then briefly twinkled down at her, before turning on his star-spangled heel and heading back up towards the camp.

Cece followed a short distance behind, with some trepidation, wondering what he had in store for her this time.

Arriving back at the shack, Cece was pleasantly surprised, and more than a little relieved, to find what appeared to her to be almost a duplicate of the previous night's supper, served up on large scallop shells, and accompanied by ten shallow shells, filled with whisky!

"Well, that's lovely, Heracles! Excellent, in fact! Except maybe not with so much whisky! Not for breakfast anyway," she giggled "And it's not like I had *that* many shots last night, at any rate!"

Heracles looked at the row of whisky laden shells he had lined up, calculated, looked back at Cece, then looked back at the whisky, and transmitted Dave, to ask him to check that his program was not malfunctioning.

"Anyways Heracles, for future reference, water for breakfast, whisky for supper. But seeing as you've already got it, maybe just one, you know, the hair of the dog and all that."

Heracles continued transmitting to Dave for information about dogs' hair, and all that.

Chapter Ten

"The thing is, Heracles," Cece explained, sometime later, using her best hushed naturalist tones, as she tiptoed through roots and tree clippings, with Heracles tiptoeing daintily behind her, "you have to be careful in these situations."

Cece tried to explain as delicately as she could, to avoid filling Heracles with the same horror that she was feeling, as she averted her eyes from the remnants of so many bird's nests which lay in shreds at their feet among the clippings.

"You see, what can happen is that the adult birds can either leave the hatchlings to fend for themselves, because the nest has been disturbed, or the little ones throw themselves out of the nest in a panic, before they are ready to fledge."

Her lecture was interrupted mid-flow by the discovery of a small but colourful semi fledged little ball of fluff, which she only avoided treading on by a feather's breadth.

"Oh! Bugger! Look Heracles! Look! A little chick!" Cece squealed in excitement, hushed tones forgotten, at the discovery of the scruffy and pathetic looking little creature at her feet.

"Oh! I don't know what to do now! I only know you are not supposed to touch baby birds, 'cause the parents might be nearby, and you shouldn't do anything to frighten them off, but that's about it really!

"I've never actually seen one in real life, and they only ever really tell you what *not* to do, on the telly, like not getting so close as to scare them, and …"

Cece's voice tapered away as she shaded her eyes so that she could look up at an enormous Mickey Mouse Head, artfully sculpted into a towering cypress tree. "And I think that boat may have already sailed!"

Having made what seemed to be a unanimous decision to adopt the little fledgeling, Cece scooped it up, alongside enough clippings and grass to make a temporary nest, until she could come up with something better, then, holding it safely cupped in both hands, tweeted, and chirped to it all the way back to camp.

"Anyways, we'll have to give you a name now won't we, cheepy? What shall we call him, Heracles?"

Heracles transmitted; Dave did not answer.

Heracles improvised

"Heracles!" said Heracles,

"Well yes…*you* are Heracles," sighed Cece, "and *I* am Cece. But what do we call *the little birdie*? It would be a bit confusing if we called him Heracles as well, wouldn't it?"

Then a thought occurred. "Erm…unless… is it a traditional thing with... your... people? Because you sort of ...orphaned him?"

Cece reddened as the stars that made up his normally affable aspect seemed to almost swirl to the counter-clock, possibly reflecting an inner turmoil, she thought, and suddenly realised how thoughtless her comment had been.

"Not that you meant to...you didn't know. Maybe we could call him Heracles Junior? And just junior for short?"

Cece looked down at the tiny bird nestled in the palm of her hand, half-feathers sticking out at all angles, and her own mouth subconsciously mirrored the gaping beak, and so did not notice that, for once, Heracles attention was not on her, nor even on the small scrap of flesh and feather in her hand, as he searched the surrounding environment, trying to locate matching DNA for the little scrap of feathers in Cece's hand.

"Look at the little thing, Heracles, ugly, but so beautiful at the same time! I wonder what it is? It's starting to get its plumage, look! Can you see? That sort of 'starting', of bits of different colours, in it? It must be a parrot or something, I think. With all those colours in it. It seems to have hints of all the colours of the rainbow in it!"

Heracles bowed his head then, over the tiny feathered scrap, then looked back into Cece's excited face, waiting.

"Ah! Heracles! I know what we can call it!"

She beamed up at him. "It has all the colours of the ...*rainbow*... in it!"

He waited.

"So, what could we call him, Heracles? It has all the colours of the ... *rainbow ...in it*!". Cece raised her voice, for emphasis.

"*In it*!" Heracles boomed suddenly, echoing her excitement! "*In it*!!"

"Oh!" Cece hesitated, "That's not exactly what I had in… oh what the heck, yes, why not. In-it it is. Hello little In-it!"

She paused, not quite ready to quit the battle. "But maybe, as a sort of pet name, we could still call him...?"

"Bugger?" interrupted Heracles, improvising for all he was worth.

"Well, I'd been going to go with Rainbow, or even Junior, but I guess he's your bird," Cece conceded weakly.

"Anyways, you go find your little In-it some food, Heracles, and I'll keep him warm."

Cece tucked her head over In-it, leaving Heracles to do his thing. But a few minutes later, when she smelled barbequed red mullet, and whisky, she looked up.

"Tell you what," she said," change of plan. You keep him warm, instead. This one's on me."

Cece set off, quite pragmatically, to dig in the wet sand, until she found half a dozen wriggly sand worms.

With the life of the newly adopted In-it at stake, she had felt she would have to compromise her principals, and sacrifice the poor worms, even if it meant trying to do it with her eyes closed!

She was saved from having to carry out the distasteful task of feeding live worms into the orange gaping beak by an unlikely event.

Half way into performing the task, her eyes were startled open by the shock of suddenly finding her wrist being gently but firmly grasped, by the starry hand which was not currently nestling the bird.

She paused, and the worm, squirming frantically between her thumb and forefinger, also momentarily paused its wriggling, as Cece looked up in surprise into Heracles twinkling face.

And Heracles twinkling face looked back, first at Cece, then at the worm.

Cece looked from Heracles to the suddenly still worm, which seemed to be waiting with baited breath. She remembered the lecture she had given him about not harming living creatures, and cursed herself for showing herself up as a hypocrite.

"Heracles, you're right of course, but…he's a bird! And birds eat worms! Unless it's a seagull, I suppose?

Then maybe you were right ... with the fish? Although, you probably didn't need to grill it first!"

She looked down then, at little In-it.

"No," she murmured. "Definitely not a seagull!"

"But this little chick does have to eat, Heracles! Oh, I don't know what to do!" she cried, wretchedly. "You are right, of course, I can't pick and choose which animals to save and which to sacrifice, can I?"

Heracles's gaze dropped briefly as he noted Cece slap a small midge into inexistence as she spoke, then looked back at her face.

"But I can't let him starve either! I really don't know what to do now! You do put me to shame!

"Shame," echoed Heracles.

"Well yes, it would be a shame if he died now. But birds eat worms, and insects... and... seeds! I think. Oh... yes! Of course! They eat seeds! I think. I'm sure I've seen that! Keep that bird warm Heracles! I'll be right back."

Throwing a half-dozen startled but relieved worms back to wriggle their way down into the wet sand, and rubbing worm-slimed hands down her dress, Cece jumped to her feet again, and headed back up to the tree line, with Heracles, carefully cradling In-it, following.

Chapter Eleven

One evening, some days after the adoption of In-it, and after yet another fish supper, Cece decided to broach the repetitive nature of the bill of fare.

She thought she'd start with the drink's menu, because although she had been initially thrilled with the addition of whisky to the nightly feast, once the novelty had worn off, of having alcohol back in her diet, she had to acknowledge that she had never actually liked whisky all that much, and prawnisky even less, and was much more of a prosecco drinker, given the choice.

"You don't have access to any wine, by any chance do you Heracles?"

Heracles looked at Cece, and transmitted to Dave for instructions.

"*Wine*, Heracles!" she enunciated more clearly, wondering if the three whiskies they had already sampled that night might be interfering with their communication, "Wine!"

Heracles continued to look at Cece, and transmit to Dave, then, suddenly Cece became aware of a high-pitched wailing tone coming at her, it seemed, simultaneously, from multiple directions.

"All my days!" Cece complained, cramming her fingers into her ears! "What on earth is that awful noise?"

The high pitch wine stopped abruptly, and Heracles sat silently, looking innocent, and transmitted to Dave again.

"It doesn't matter," Cece said taking one finger experimentally out of her ear, and listening to the usual sounds of the jungle to which she had become accustomed, and which were gradually starting up again, after it too had paused, to listen.

"It's stopped now," she reassured Heracles, "It must have been a bit of tinnitus, 'cause I seemed to have gone a bit deaf for a minute there as well… couldn't even hear the birds or anything. I can't even remember what we were talking about now, can you? It doesn't matter, anyway…!"

"Dave, it doesn't matter." transmitted Heracles.

Chapter Twelve

The ongoing chores involved in feeding and nurturing little In-it had distracted Cece somewhat from her task of staying alive, which, she had to admit, had become significantly easier since realizing she could take Heracles's presence, and help, for granted.

The tweezers from her manicure set were proving ideal for dropping little seeds into In-its increasingly large gaping mouth, and Heracles had proven himself to be a natural at performing that delicate little job, having once watched Cece perform it, to the extent that the two of them almost ended up fighting for the privilege of performing the task.

Cece had almost decided to forgo the seemingly insurmountable challenge of getting Heracles to vary her fish diet from red mullet, when something happened which lead to an almost miraculous, as far as Cece was concerned, addition to their diet.

Cece had decided not to worry about from where he was getting the seemingly endless supply of tasty fish, as long as she did not have to see it being caught and slain.

However, as wherever he was getting it from did not seem to be presenting Heracles with a moral dilemma, she started to wonder about the nature of Heracles ability to be able to duplicate things that they already had, seemingly from nowhere, and with nothing, and doing no harm to anyone, or any thing.

And if necessity is the mother of invention, sweet-teeth and hormonal fluxes are the grandmother, and possibly great-aunt, of inspiration!

So, whilst sorting again through the contents of her two shoulder bags to make really, *really* sure she had not missed anything interesting, she came across the screwed-up chocolate wrapper, which she had so diligently collected from the beach, having thrown it down in disgust at the salt-addled taste of the contents, she had an idea.

"The contents of this chocolate bar was *disgusting*," she told Heracles, waving the offending wrapper in front of his nose, "because it was soaked in sea water.

"Can you, by any remote chance, get me, say, half a dozen, no, a dozen, of these? *Not* soaked in sea water, though? Just...you know... if you can?" Then suddenly remembering her manners, which for once, she had mislaid, somewhere between her eagerness and her greed. "Please?"

Cece had dropped the wrapper into the swirl of stars which Heracles held out, her salivary glands already starting to kick in, in anticipation, but as she had not demonstrated consuming the imagined contents, and there was no content to duplicate, Heracles's first offering was, unsurprisingly, somewhat disappointing.

The foil wrappers, when applied to her bon-fire that night, did nonetheless provide a beautiful display of violet and purple flames, almost dazzling enough to compete with In-it's vibrant emerging rainbow tones!

Not one to give up at the first hurdle, however, and certainly not with so much at stake, Cece had tried again.

This time she pointed out the small print, including ingredients, on the wrapper, and, for added clarity, demonstrated enjoying eating a massive chocolate bar, with relish, which Heracles observed, intently.

Cece could have cried, and hugged him, and then cried some more, when Heracles drew her attention, somewhat hesitantly, after the unexpected response to the dozen foil wrappers he had presented her with earlier, to the enormous block of caramel chocolate which he had placed in the doorway of her shack for her.

In addition to what now seemed like an endless supply of caramel flavoured chocolate, the novelty of which was not likely to wear off quite as quickly as the novelty of red mullet, or prawn flavoured whisky, Cece had also been able to broaden the nutritional repertoire of their diet more extensively, and somewhat more conventionally.

They had started to sample many delicious and filling fruits and berries on their many foraging trips into the jungle, since Cece had decided to trust Heracles's judgement on what was, and was not, edible.

This was after having observed his methodology of carefully pondering each new piece of fruit for quite some significant time, with each taste test that he performed, with the tongue-like protrusion, and which she had noted, not without interest, he seemed to be able to manifest at will.

He then either handed the approved fruit or berry to Cece, for their meal later, or if it did not pass inspection, he carefully replaced it, seemingly as was, back on the bush or tree from whence it came

Cece found that her baked caramel chocolate covered plantain, which, after a little practise, she had perfected, and which with no practise at all, Heracles could re-produce, tasted divine!

At one stage Cece wondered whether it was worth risking confusing Heracles, by trying to get him to reproduce the foil chocolate wrapper again, but maybe in larger pieces, so that she could use it as baking foil.

However, after some consideration, and a one-sided conversation with Heracles about litter, pollution, and global warming, Cece decided she could manage quite well by baking things in banana leaves.

She left Heracles to analyse the relevance, not to mention accuracy, of the vast amount of information she had just poured in to him, whilst stripping bare a banana tree to bake supper.

Even In-it's endless supply of sunflower seed, once discovered by Cece, and accepted by In-it, were in a plentiful supply each morning, alongside the bounty of different fruits which now appeared in one of the spare huts, and which Cece had indicated to Heracles was now the store room.

She had also once pointed out one of the shelters, at a modest distance from her own, and explained to Heracles that that was *his* hut.

She had then walked over to her own hut, and clarified that this one was *her* hut, then pointed again to the one she had allocated to Heracles.

"Heracles's hut."

"Heracles's hut," he had eventually repeated dutifully, understanding from her direct stare, that something was expected of him.

But that night, after their supper of fish, chocolate caramel bananas, and whisky, snuggled down on her mattress of fresh leaves, and only the greenest, and bendiest, of twiglets, which she had eventually convinced Heracles made better sleeping companions than the sturdier ones he had favoured for her in the early days, she had still had that strange, but reassuring feeling, of his presence being around her, and did not mention the hut that she allocated to him again.

Chapter Thirteen

No longer believing her survival to be dependent on sea-drift, Cece knew she did not really need to spend so much time wandering along the water's edge, but she did it anyway.

Despite being an unwilling visitor to the island, she was starting to love the whisper of the tide, pulling back over the fine white sand, almost as much as she used to love the clatter of the cold English sea rattling on shingle; she was more able to appreciate the beauty of the silver sands, and azure sea, as the horror of her experience of almost being gobbled up by it was starting to fade.

Heracles wandered along behind Cece, trailing a stick through the shallows, her constant shadow, and with In-it now eating and flying independently, though not yet having exactly flown his metaphorical nest, never far away from the pair.

"Oh, my giddy, giddy aunt! Another fossil! I'm finding nearly as many fossils here as I did at home! And our British coasts are famous for fossils! We have more than anywhere else on Earth!" Cece blithely mis-informed Heracles, as she savoured the tactile sensation of the smooth black finger-length of rock between her palms, before holding it out for him to examine.

"It's only a belemnite, sort of a prehistoric squid-type thing, I think," she told him, as he peered into her hand.

"Mind you, I didn't exactly get chance to wander along the shore, day in day out, at home.

"And this is nothing, of course, compared to what I used to find at home. I used to love finding an ammonite still encased in rock, and when you broke it open you knew that yours were the first human eyes ever to have seen that ammonite! You know, they are hundreds of millions of years old! Can you even imagine that?"

Heracles lack of imagination did not present him with as much of a problem with Cece's narrative as it might have done, so he felt no need to go to Dave with that one.

"And once, I found a piece of an ichthyosaur! They were amongst the biggest marine animals to have ever lived! In fact I think they may have been among some of the biggest creatures to have ever existed! Maybe even as big as the blue whale, which is the biggest animal on the planet today!"

Heracles starry face was twinkling in that intense way it did when he appeared to be most interested in what she had to say, Cece was gratified to see, with comets shooting across galaxies, and black holes creating microscopic cosmic collapses. And so, having found a theme which not only seemed to have captivated him, but was also one which Cece was genuinely enamoured with, she rootled round in her memory, to add more meat to the pot.

"They might even have been *ancestors* of the blue whale! Which are massive! But totally harmless! They just eat plankton, which is just mostly like... sea-weed and stuff," added Cece, dismissing the daily sacrifice of a trillion krill.

"So ichthyosaurs were probably not dangerous either, 'cause they looked a bit like dolphins. I'm not a hundred percent though, when I think about it, 'cause whales evolved from some sort of ... hippo... I think... anyways...."

Despite Cece's longstanding intention to familiarise herself with a deep and meaningful understanding of the natural history of her own planet, her life had never, so far, insofar as she was aware, simultaneously afforded her both time, and opportunity, to meet that particular ambition.

However, what Cece lacked in actual facts was well compensated for by totally misunderstood facts, and half-forgotten memories, which she felt usually sufficed, and so, given that she did have a more than willing audience, she carried on.

"They started off living in the water, I know that much, and evolved on to land, then evolved back into the sea...although I might be getting a bit mixed up there again… it does sound a bit odd..." Cece's brow furrowed as she tried to make the random bits of memory make sense before she fed it to her eager pupil.

"Well...the thing is…" Cece's natural honesty forced her to admit, "I know lots of stuff, but I can't always remember it *all, exactly* right...but I know the ichthyosaurs varied in size a lot though… I think… but anyway, I do know one thing for sure, I would absolutely *love* to come across a complete one of those! Even a small one!" Cece finished more confidently, back in what she believed to be safer territory.

And Heracles also calculated that he was on safe territory, as gleaning information on the natural evolution of a variety of species on this planet, to enable a better prediction of how it was going to continue to evolve, was definitely part of his remit.

He was therefore able to comply promptly with the request, seeking only minimal clarity from Dave, who, tuning in to his favourite avatar, was relieved to be finally getting more than basic information from the study subject.

For once, he wasted no time in responding to Heracles, confirming that he should continue along the line of developing a further understanding of any other creatures on planet Earth, which may one day evolve along the lines of becoming a stellar traveller.

Any animal related to the blue whale definitely came into that criterion, as even their concepts of thought travel might one day interfere with the thought travel of his own non-corporeal species.

Cece had her head down, still pouring over the four-inches of ancient belemnite that she was so thrilled to have scooped up from the incoming waves, so did not see the sudden drama starting to unfurl just on the edge of what would have been her peripheral vision, if she had looked up.

To the north of her horizon, almost a dozen spinner dolphins chose that moment to vacate the vicinity, at great speed, breaching the water in dazzling synchronicity, and pirouetting to maximise the volume of the warning signals sent out as they hit the water, in what would have been a beauty to the beholder, if anyone had beholden it.

And to the south of the vista, making a similar breach, a large humpback whale, travelling as fast as it's calf could be expected to keep up, breaching only infrequently, and totally giving the pirouetting a miss.

The speeding humpbacks were closely followed by a small pod of orcas, who had been stealthily sneaking up on the young calf, and its mother, and who did not bother to add to the scenery by breaching at all; they just swam as fast as they could, overtaking the whales, and then the dolphins, to regroup, and discuss what they had just seen, and what this new threat in the ocean meant to their previously self- assured life-styles!

Chapter Fourteen

Still oblivious to the unfolding theatre happening mere miles from where her toes enjoyed the warm tropical water, Cece continued to prattle on.

"When I think about it, I think it might actually have been the largest sea *predator* that ever lived, so maybe a tad more dangerous than a dolphin!"

But Heracles had momentarily filtered out what he reckoned must broadly be considered to be an episode of verbal diarrhoea, as he had bigger fish to fry...and only filtered back in to her chatter in time to catch...

"Or was that the megalodon? You know, the sort of, giant, prehistoric shark thing? I'm not sure. I think one was bigger, but the other had a bigger mouth, or something. I would just love to come across either! What a find that would be!"

...And so the drama out at sea continued into act two.

The sea bubbled hotly, at the energy being dragged from ...local resources...to bring into existence the second largest marine animal to have ever existed, its giant jaws giving it the advantage over a rival that was never meant to inhabit the same ocean, at the same time.

And two much smaller individuals, in their current guise, at any rate, only slightly open-mouthed, watched a view screen, which had suddenly been filled by the relatively distant display, of the two behemoths who were putting on a show the likes of which had never before been seen on this small blue planet.

"Erm...what are we watching?" John asked, initially only slightly bemused, but growing increasingly concerned, as the desperate pursuit turned in their direction, and as the ichthyosaur sped past their tiny vessel, the giant gape of the gargantuan megalodon headed straight towards them...

If Cece had chosen that moment to look up from her find, she might have seen a small flying saucer emerge at great speed from the sea, and not only being followed by, but suddenly engulfed by, the enormous voracious maw of the monstrous megalodon which came flying out of the water after it.

Heracles did observe the show, and juggled several conflicting instructions to his programming, not least of which was his ever-evolving moral code, which seemed now to include not killing any creature, or allowing anything to die, and helping out others, wherever reasonably practical, and practicable...as long as it did not inconvenience the primary instruction givers *too* much.

Serendipitously, Cece chose that moment to relieve the pressure on Heracles's embryonic ethical values, by declaring,

"I think we can all thank our lucky stars that there isn't anything like that out there *alive* anymore! I would *not* want to come across one of those in the flesh! I think they died out for a good reason!"

Cece did not expound on her theory as to the good reason for their extinction, but that did not get in the way of the batch of *very* lucky stars, currently masquerading in the form of an entity named Heracles, being able to resolve his dilemma.

He set about returning the matter that he had so effortlessly used, to recreate two of the world's most deadly ever predators, back into the benign creatures that had almost, unknowingly, just exchanged their existences, for very different lifestyles.

And an octopus, among others, who had of recent times been living an unadulteratedly cautious life, had for a fleeting episode in its once humdrum existence, felt like the king of the sea.

It was now wondering where its feelings of self-confidence had disappeared to, or maybe more pertinently, where they had briefly come from.

It was also wondering why they had felt so familiar!

Chapter Fifteen

"What... just... happened?" Bafflement was starting to become almost second nature to John, he realised, the more time he spent with Dave.

"What? Oh that? Nothing. I just thought I'd give the old engines a spin, you know to stop the...er ... brakes ... seizing up, and what-not."

"Erm, yes, I know about the... brakes, and the erm... what-nots, seizing up. I meant more the...de-materialising, just after the big ...gaping mouth thing...?"

"Big gaping mouth thing?" Dave could not have looked more innocent.

He really couldn't.

He knew this for a fact, as he had been practicing in front of a mirrored view screen, for just such a situation.

"Have you been over doing it... old chap? Why don't you go lie down a bit?"

John, ever suggestible, and suddenly feeling surprisingly tired, found himself acceding to Dave's recommendation.

"Well maybe just for a little while. I have been doing rather a lot lately."

Dave maintained the sympathetic expression, which he had also recently perfected, until John disappeared through the automatic door, with a swish-swish effect, and turned back to the view screen.

"Heracles," he transmitted. "We need to talk! NOW!"

Heracles was also becoming familiar with the occasional use of an innocent expression, although it would perhaps have been quite difficult for him to mimic, let alone perfect, having no eyes, as such, to widen, and no understanding, as such, as to the necessity.

"I really enjoyed today, Heracles," Cece continued her almost constant chatter, as they sat around the camp fire, and glancing first at Heracles, then, innocently, and then, more pointedly, at the fire, she waited until Heracles had built it up with more branches, before she carried on.

"Finding that fossil, and being able to tell you all about my love of all things pre-historic! It felt almost like being back home with ... a ...friend."

The excitement of her day led Cece to drink rather more of the shellish-whiskies than she was in the habit of doing.

And what with Heracles's busy, and allegedly, 'almost *catastrophically* disastrous' day, he had met her alcohol consumption shell for shell.

"I have always loved the ocean, you know, the salty smell, the sunshine shimmering off the surface of the sea, the sibilant...is it... susurration...? You know, the sound of sand and shells being shoved up and down the shore, and such!" Cece continued her lyrical waxing.

"I love dolphins! And whales! So much so, that I wanted to be a dolphin, when I was little! Well, when I was not so little, really!" She giggled at her younger self, snorting shelly- whisky down her nose, and dabbing it up daintily, with her multi-flecked dress.

"When I was *little*, I wanted to be a mermaid! But then I realised that they weren't real, so I decided that I wanted to be a dolphin!

"I bet you can't imagine me as a mermaid, can you? Or maybe you can, you naughty...thing... you!"

Cece snorted more whisky down her nose, and down the front of the dress, trying to catch it with the back of her hand, and look coquettishly at Heracles, at the same time.

"I don't know why I swapped my mermaid fantasy for a dolphin fantasy when I realised mermaids didn't exist! It's not like I could ever be a dolphin any more than being a mermaid! I guess I was trying to keep my goals within reason. I have never been one to set the bar too high!"

Cece set herself off into another fit of the giggles, unobserved by Heracles, who was calculating whether he needed to check with Dave before granting any more 'almost *catastrophically* disastrous' requests.

His attention was drawn back to Cece as he noted a direct question.

"Talking of childhoods, Heracles, what were you like when you were young? What did you think you would do...or be like... when you were older?"

The galaxy of celestial bodies that was currently occupying Heracles's face region swirled at an accelerated rate, as Cece's last question had generated such a vast volume of information, as well as a whole deluge of queries directed at Dave.

Observing what she took for emotion, on the swirling visage of her companion, Cece checked herself, and back-tracked somewhat on her line of questioning, to a tack she felt was more neutral.

"What about nick-names? Did you have any nick-names when you were little? Or now, even? Do you have any pet names? You know, something that only your family, or ...friends, call you? Like, I've told you my full name is Narcece, but people call me Cece. And In-it, his name is well... In-it...but you said you'd like for him to have the nick- name … 'Bugger'…"

She paused to knock back another whisky, and Heracles paused his transmissions, to do the same.

"So do people ever call you anything other than Heracles?"

After a pause, Heracles offered, "'ERACLEES?"

"Indoor voice please, Heracles. Yes, I know your name is Heracles... and a lovely name it is too. I really like it. But it's a bit of a mouthful sometimes, isn't it? So I just wondered if anyone called you anything else? Ever? Something for short, or a nickname?"

After a barely perceptible pause, but long enough for a quick scan of his back-logs, Heracles tried again. "ERAC?"

"Eric! Well now, that's nice! And you look like an Eric... sort of!

"So is that your first name? Or a kind of ...pet name? Is that maybe what your ... significant other... calls you, for example?" Cece felt her whisky suffused face flush even pinker. "I can imagine it is the sort of name a significant other might call you..."

Then, realizing he was not going to answer, she had another shot of fishy-courage, and ploughed on, "Am I being a bit impertinent?" She looked up at him through her lashes.

"I wasn't meaning to pry, and, I mean, *I* don't mind telling *you*... *I* don't have a significant other... currently... you know, I'm single.... But you don't have to tell me ...if you don't want to. I mean, your ...people... might not even have... significant others," she trailed off somewhat forlornly at Heracles continued silence, feeling suddenly very tired, as the excitement seemed to drain out of the evening.

"Anyway, I think I'm going to bed. It's been a long day."

And still caught up in the perpetual background noise that was Cece's chatter, Heracles signed off his transmission to Dave, as Eric.

Dave sat pinching on his bottom lip, he knew not why, as he swayed gently back and forth on his adequately tilted swivel seat, and wondered briefly whether he should be worried that Heracles was asking for clarity as to whether he should be considered 'single'.

Heracles was one of the least 'single' entities in existence, Dave thought, given that he was comprised of almost innumerable particles of matter, and the early elements of a goodly number of solar systems.

You are definitely not single Heracles!

And... Eric???

Cece's head had barely touched her leaves when Heracles terminated his communication with Dave, but she lifted her head slightly from her bedding, as she thought she had caught a quiet echo, so distant that she couldn't work out if it came from Heracles, or if she had imagined it.

"Not single..."

Not wanting to hear any more, she bundled into her ears one of the dresses she had taken to using as a sheet-come-pillow-case, but the faint words which Cece had thought she had heard still echoed round her head, despite her makeshift earplugs, "Not Single! Not single!

Chapter Sixteen

Cece laughed in exhilaration, as she sped through the starlit sea, bursting out from the water to pirouette again and again, before continuing her journey, surfing along the breakers.

Coasting along on the white horses, then diving down again, well below the waves, speeding through the clear blue depths until, thinking her lungs would burst, she surfaced again, blasting water out of her blow-hole, before dragging in massive quantities of oxygen, so that she could sink back down into the inviting depths.

Suddenly she was swimming along with other sleek, laughing figures, cetaceans, like herself, dancing and circling round her, asking her questions that needed no answers, welcoming her.

She hurtled through the night, catching and eating, without qualm, any small silver darting fish not fast enough to dodge out of the way of Cece and her new companions.

She had no conscious thoughts in her mind, but seemed to know, and understand everything! But that understanding seemed so unimportant, compared with the pure joy of just ...being!

She had never felt so free, so beautiful, or so alive, as she swam so effortlessly through salty nutrient filled water.

The experience seemed to be outside of time, she wasn't aware of it starting, or finishing, she was just aware that she was exactly where she should be, had always been there, and would always be there.

A crack of sunlight crept in through the crevices of Cece's shack, and fell across her tired face. She flung her hand across her eyes to block it out.

"I really need to take more water with it," she croaked groggily.

She suddenly remembered that she had gone to bed with a heavy heart, after Heracles had somehow imparted the knowledge to her, that he was neither available to her nor, apparently, interested in her.

Due to the excessive amounts of shellfish whisky, Cece could not even remember the method by which she had come to these conclusions, but come the morning light, found herself to be strangely accepting of the information, perhaps even slightly liberated by it!

'You were getting yourself a bit of a crush there Cece,' she told herself, 'And I think it is safe to say, it would *not* have worked out! Differences attract, and all that, but there are limits!'

Then, out loud, and without even feeling the need to check if he was there, "You know what, Heracles? I'm even tireder now than when I went to bed!"

Then squinting up at him, his light hurting her eyes, "But I had the most wonderful dream! I dreamt I was a dolphin! Fantastic! So real!"

Dragging her fingers through her hair, to pull away what she thought were a few stray whisps of hair that were tormenting her face, she paused to grimace, and sit up.

"Ugh!" she exclaimed, wrinkling her nose, and curling her top lip up over her teeth, in disgust.

"How did I manage to go to sleep with all this seaweed in my hair, without noticing!" Cece wailed, picking up the comb that she had shown Heracles how to carve out of a clam shell, by demonstrating carving out one shelly tooth with her teeny tiny scissors, then letting him do the rest.

"And you didn't even tell me, Heracles! In future would you *please* take a bit more notice! And tell me if something doesn't seem right with my looks! Please!"

Heracles took more notice of Cece's looks, noted the starfish still hanging on to her dress, and after only a small hesitation, he gently peeled it from her hem, then carefully walked it back down to the sea.

Bemused, Cece watched his departing figure wander down to the sea, leaving a faint trail of footprints in the sand.

Chapter Seventeen

Cece had established that her beach only stretched so far around her island, before it turned into rough and rocky terrain, which she had so far not troubled herself to try and tackle.

She had a fair old stretch of about three miles of beautiful, mostly white-sanded beach, to beach-comb, she reckoned, but so far had not found anything washed up more remarkable than her own two shoulder bags, which either the sea, or Heracles, had provided her with, in the first couple of days of her arrival on the island, as well, of course, as several very ancient fossils.

Cece had walked the several miles backwards and forwards over her stretch of beach enough times to recognise all the familiar landmarks, with Heracles her almost constant shadow.

She also found venturing more deeply into the jungle from various entry points from the beach, not nearly as scary with Heracles by her side.

Although she never crossed paths with any of the larger, or more deadly animals that she occasionally heard or saw evidence of, at least not to her knowledge, she remained a little wary of what might be lurking around the next tree.

And what was lurking around the next tree, remained wary of what was usually lurking behind Cece, so her sorties continued to be mostly uneventful.

One day, several weeks after their arrival on the island, Cece got as far as the rocky terrain and consulted Heracles on a thought.

"We ought to try to climb up here a bit, didn't we? To see how far it goes up? And to see how much island there is at the other side?

"I don't really know whether our bit of beach covers most of the circumference of the island, or whether there is another half an island round there somewhere.

"There might be a whole population round the other side of this ridge, for all we know! Or if we could just get past this bit, we may be right back at the other side of our beach! It's difficult to tell, isn't it?

"I suppose it might be easier for *you* than me, to maybe just pop up this bit of a cliffy thing, and have a look?" Cece was sitting flopped on a rocky outcrop one hot morning after trailing the length of her little world.

She shielded her eyes from the sun and looked up at Heracles. He shielded his starry eyes as he looked back at her.

"Maybe you could...just pop up?" she tried again.

She looked up to the top of the crags wending their way up from the beach. Heracles followed her gaze, looking up at the crags, then looked back at Cece.

"Maybe... just ... pop...?" This time she accompanied the vague words with a vague waving gesture of her arms in the direction of the rocks.

Heracles followed the gesture with starry eyes, then gave a similar wave of his starry arms, but his twinkling toes made no such gesture; they remained firmly planted on the rocks next to Cece.

"Bugger!" she sighed exasperatedly under her breath. He was a love, she thought, but he couldn't half be slow on the uptake, sometimes.

"Ok," she said resignedly scrambling to her feet. "Come on."

The heat on her back seemed magnified as Cece started to scramble up the rocks, with Heracles two feet behind her.

How come the sun was millions of miles away, yet whenever you went a few feet nearer to it, it seemed hotter, she thought irritably, and you were more likely to get burned?

And how come Heracles always followed at a respectful distance behind her, when if he walked an equally respectful distance in front of her, he could be offering her a helping hand and pulling her up?

She felt even more irritated as she contemplated that one, oblivious to the gentle breeze that followed her for the duration of the climb, keeping the heat bearable, and helping to propel her over the trickier crags.

She was just considering what else she could grumble to herself about, when she realised that she had almost reached the top of the rocky outcrop, and hoped that if she could get to the top of that bit, it might at least give her a view of whatever else her island might have to offer.

As she reached the top of the rock formation, her eyes on her feet, which were precariously straddling the topmost rock, rather than what was ahead of her, with her hands outstretched to keep her balance, she risked looking up to survey the view.

What she saw startled her so much that she immediately lost her tentative footing, and went careering back down the last dozen or so feet she had climbed, bouncing off various rocky edges as she fell, and eventually landing on her back, looking up into a midnight-blue starry face, which, in turn, looked down into her red and sweaty one.

"Bugger?" suggested Heracles.

Chapter Eighteen

Bouncing back from her fall quicker than she would have imagined possible, but knowing she would probably pay for it later, Cece had soon scrambled back to her feet, and regained the last several yards climb.

This time, being more familiar with the rock's layout, she had managed to get herself into a safer position, to be able to survey the scene that had startled her off of her perch a few moments ago.

Her beach, she now realised, was obviously just one half, or less, of the island. The rugged cliff she had just climbed separated her beach from another significant amount of island, boasting an equally beautiful beach, which bordered on an equally lush jungle.

The main difference to her own beach, and the cause of her ungainly toppling, was what else the other half of the island currently boasted: that being, several large luxurious tents!

Shielding her eyes from the blinding sun, and looking further afield, or rather further a-sea, Cece could see a ship, anchored half a mile out to sea, and several smaller boats, pulled up onto the beach, obviously having been used to bring the party ashore!

"All my days! My sainted, giddy Aunt!" Cece had taken to using less profane profanities these days, due to Heracles tendency to repeat her, as hearing obscenities coming out of Heracles did not seem somehow... right.

"I'm saved, Heracles! I'm saved! They are here for me! It's my rescue party!" Cece had started to do as much of a jig and a dance as was possible to do on the top of a cliff face.

Then she started to try to dash about randomly; a step or two this way, a step or two that, undecided as to which way to go.

She wanted to try to head further towards the party on the beach, even though she knew she had already navigated her way about as far along the rocky path as was possible, but her initial instinct was still to carry on heading that way towards ... people!

But looking about her she realised the path had tapered off, and the road ahead was not really passable.

Half of her also wanted to run back to her camp to fetch ...

Fetch what…? What did she need to go back for?

What did she have on the island that she really needed?

What, of any importance, did she have on the island other than... Heracles!

That thought brought a halt to her frantic activities.

Heracles stood motionless, observing the scene play out.

He looked down at the party on the beach, then looked back at Cece, and recorded the new behaviours that Cece was displaying, then started transmitting to Dave.

Chapter Nineteen

"Well, you have really only gone and done it this time haven't you? John exploded. "You've only gone and created...."

"No!" Dave tried to interrupt him before John could put his own fears into words. "And stop reading over my shoulder! It's rude! And no! I haven't! I haven't created... what you were going to say....at least... I don't think I have..." he trailed off.

"You have! It's *thinking* for itself! Its responding to her needs! It's ..." John slapped what was fast becoming a metaphorical hand over what had already become the memory of a mouth, as his never too solid corporeality lost cohesion in his panic, but was too late to stop the last word escaping "... *feeling*!"

"How *dare* you? It is NOT *feeling*! It is *functioning* exactly how I programmed it to function! It's just evolving through as many stages as it needs to, in order to complete the GIRT-AP directive- Gather Information, Record and Transmit- Analyse, Project, (respond), repeat."

But in his great agitation, the entity who has come to be known as John, began to bounce wildly around the area currently serving as command control, manifesting at great speed, into every gods-fearing and gods-forsaken creature he had ever encountered (of which there were many!)

One half-formed creature after another briefly popped into existence, and then morphed into the next, before it had even had time to attempt to slap another... whatever might be serving as a hand, over... whatever was serving as its communication piece.

Dave's own heightened state of anxiety, greatly enhanced by his colleague's temporary loss of control, briefly propelled him into the same state, but not without him fortuitously managing to materialise a hand, simultaneously with John's serendipitously materialised face; the resulting satisfying *thwack* could be translated in any language as 'a show stopper'.

The slap brought both beings up short, and John managed something like an embarrassed cough, in the last instant that he was still possessed of a throat, and Dave was able to briefly put something like a tentacle on what turned out, in the moment, to be something reminiscent of the fluorescent carapace of a Gallimedian sludge-beetle, before they transformed back into the transiently-corporeal states known as John and Dave.

"Sorry," said John. "Panicked!"

"'S'alright. Understandable. But don't do it again. Erm...what *exactly* are *you* panicking about?" Dave tried for an air of nonchalance.

He did not pull it off.

"You said, 'Gather Information, Record and Transmit, Analyse, Project, (*respond*) repeat' Didn't you? Because if you did say (*respond*) there, and I mean, to be fair, you did say it in brackets, so that's why I'm just *checking*... that you haven't actually initiated a protocol, off *your* own back, that allows a projected avatar, created by yourself, to *respond*, off *its* own back, to the subject? Without any intervention from you?"

Dave started to experience a faint itchy feeling at the back of where he usually kept his head.

"Erm… Yes…? But I don't think it's as bad as you think. I think there is a perfectly reasonable explanation for the way my projection is behaving. I think I have it …sussed!" But even Dave could hear the slightly hollow quality to his words, despite the re-embodiment of his corporeal form.

"And, just to be clear, you gave it permission to *evolve* through as many stages as necessary…?" John had managed to grow brows in time to raise them through a hairline that was still doing its best to catch up.

"Of course not! I didn't *say* that! Well, not exactly that. Did I say that…? Well, actually, yes, I might have. But that's not what I meant! And obviously, I didn't tell *him* that!"

The itchy feeling was becoming more pronounced, and if Dave was in the habit of sweating, or indeed was used to having the body of someone who sweated, there would have been a slick gleam on the skin that wasn't really there, as Dave tried to remember the actual words he had used to Heracles!

The damned avatar tended to be so literal! That's why, at their last exchange after the whole being eaten by a prehistoric creature escapade, he had testily told him to 'grow-up…'

John, unfamiliar with recognising discomfiture, but very familiar with lecturing his oft-berated colleague, continued down the familiar route, unaware of Dave's growing realization of what he may have done.

"So tell me, *Dave*, since when do we ask avatars to *respond* to a subject's *feelings*? You have asked it to *respond* to feelings.... and given it permission to ...*evolve*...in order to be able to do that? So now it seems to understand... and *experience* feelings?" John had left his raised brows on high alert.

It seemed appropriate.

"I mean, really! And while we are on the subject, since when have we even *created* avatars to do our work for us? And using random, and, might I add, extremely *volatile* and probably *unpredictable* cosmic matter? And... did you just refer to the avatar as *him*?" The brows went even higher, if possible, as he continued his rant.

"You do remember what happened the last time you didn't stick exactly to the rules don't you?

"You do remember the whole Neanderthal fiasco? We all had to attend the subsequent 'Missing Link' lecture...!"

Dave's eyebrows were starting to form what he might have described as a glower, if he had been familiar with the term. He wasn't, but it was seeming to be coming naturally to his brows nonetheless.

"Also," John continued his pontificating, "I seem to remember another lecture on using spare cosmic matter, when I think about it! Because it has been established that no-one knows whether it's spare or not, till we reach the Outcome, and see whether or not it was needed!

"So, explain to me... Dave...just how you managed to not only create a ...life-form ..." John looked away from Dave's wounded expression as he eventually put both their worst fears into words, "which I have to point out, goes way beyond an activity that will be... 'frowned upon'..." still mastering eyebrows, John struggled with this new concept, "by you know who, when he gets to hear about it...!"

"*If*!" Dave interjected, his panic almost triggering another morphing competition. "*If* you know who gets to hear about it! You said you would hear me out before making any decisions! And as I keep *trying* to explain, he is not a *life-* form!

"He's barely even a life-form shaped avatar! He doesn't even have a *face*!" Dave expostulated, desperation failing to lend much credence to his argument, but giving him ample opportunity to demonstrate the impressive array of expressions that he had been working on applying to his own countenance.

"As I was saying," John continued, trying to ignore, but being secretly impressed by, Dave's range of expressions, "you not only managed to create a *lifeform*, but a life-form, who can actually create *other lifeforms*! You've broken every rule laid down by the Higher High council!"

"He *isn't* a life form!" Dave insisted. "And he can't *create* anything!

"All he can do is *re*-create! Copy! Duplicate! Mimic! Or to use one of their own analogies, *parrot*, what he has seen or heard!"

Dave was in full swing now, realizing that he had to convince John of his innocence, before John chose to come over all, well, *John*, and follow one rule too many, and get him decommissioned... permanently!

Dave and John originated from a society where the state of being immortal was only as permanent as the metaphorical small print in your contract said it was!

"He was only able to re-create the things that he re-created because they have already existed, somewhere, at some time, so he had a blueprint to go on!" Dave expounded on his theory, desperately.

"He couldn't do the mermaid request, for example, because no such thing has ever existed! Therefore he couldn't *re*-create, what has not yet been created!

"Believe me John, he has not got an original thought in his head!

"I know how it looked there, for a while, and even I have worried, at times, that maybe I had let things get a little out of hand, and I thought he had started to develop a… personality! But he hasn't! It's all just been a matter of timing, or the way that the timing of things made things appear, really!

"When I have been back and checked the logs, all that he has *actually* done, is to follow *my instructions*! He's an avatar! A projection!! A *program*!!!"

Dave finished his speech with as dramatic a flourish as his own continued misgivings allowed him to muster, only to be brought up short by John's sharp rejoinder.

"He's *calling* himself *Heracles*! And, by the way, mermaids? Real! If he couldn't find a blue print, it's only because the earthlings whose data bases he searched for his information do not yet know they exist, as they have not yet found evidence.

"So therefore, they 'know' they don't exist, and they will continue to 'know' they don't exist, right up until they find evidence that they do! Then they will 'know' something different!

"They are very sure about absolutely everything they 'know', right up until they know they were wrong, then the *next* bit they've learned is the 'definitive' truth!

"It's a human thing, apparently! You're not the only one who has been working on private projects!" John suddenly somehow seemed taller to Dave, as, chest puffed out, John continued expostulating with his own theories.

"If the avatar…and are we expected to call it Heracles now? …had searched the whale's memories, rather than limiting itself to human logs, it would have got an entirely different story about the mermaids!

'I *wish* we were *only* expected to call him Heracles now!' thought Dave unhappily, painfully conscious of the fact, that in Heracles's most recent communications, he was now not only signing himself off as *Eric*, but for some reason, he had also started addressing Dave as 'D'!

'And what's that all about?' worried Dave, finding that frowning was starting to become second nature to him these days, and wondering where John had gotten all the mermaid info from?

He found himself wondering who John might have been in communication with.

Surely not someone at Head Office? Dave felt an uncomfortable twitching behind his eyeballs at that thought.

Or even another operative? Not that there were any within, well shouting distance. Although…he vaguely recalled the legend of a former colleague who had been assigned to this quadrant, who had mysteriously disappeared.

The originator of the 'immersive research technique', who some thought had been so deep under-cover for so long he had lost sight of his identity!

Others thought he had simply spread himself so thin, trying to cover such a large area that he simply lost cognitive cohesion.

His disappearance had resulted in the previously immortal beings now only thinking of themselves as 'almost' immortal! And reduced the amount of cosmos for which each entity now had responsibility for, to a more manageable perimeter, so, all good there, as far as Dave was concerned.

'And thank goodness then, that *fortunately* I didn't put him on to the whales', Dave continued to cogitate to himself, 'or I would now probably be looking at a whole different set of problems!'

But perhaps *unfortunate* that he had not put him on to the octopuses, some might argue.

Chapter Twenty

"Heracles! Oh! Heracles! You don't know what's happening, do you?

"It's people! *My* people! Someone must have sent a search party out for me! "They've come for me...."

Realizing the impact that these new events might have on her constant companion of the last few weeks, as she watched a vision of constellations chasing each other at speed across the star-man's twinkling visage, the excitement suddenly drained out of the moment.

"Do you think anyone will be ...coming... for *you*?" She asked hesitantly, guiltily.

"I mean...I'm just thinking...I'm going to have to go, you know, with ...*them*." She waved in the general direction of the beach party, out of her line of vision now that she had scrambled back down from the pinnacle from where she had first espied them.

"They've come an awful long way, to take me back to where I came from... from where I belong... people will be missing me. Someone must have sent them... and I'll have to go... back... with them".

She bit her lip, realizing the implications of what she was saying; trying to judge how the news was effecting Heracles.

"I mean, it's what we've been hoping for all along, isn't it? To be rescued? At least... it's what *I* have been hoping for... and you... won't really be able to come...with me."

Cece became aware that the salty breeze which had playfully buffeted her all the way up the craggy climb, had dropped, and she felt the weight of her words as they hung heavily in the air, the atmosphere suddenly thick, and cloying,

She carried on looking uncertainly at Heracles, wondering how he was taking this new turn of events.

Heracles remained unfathomable, and forever sparing with his speech.

And, she also started to ask herself, *when* had *she* actually last wished, or even hoped, to be rescued?

It had been a constant little prayer in the back of her mind when she first landed on the island; but recently, she conceded, not so much.

How could that permanent mantra, keeping time to everything she did, have stopped without her feeling it?

Actually, she realised, she *did* know when it had stopped...

Heracles was motionless.

He was busy transmitting to Dave, 'D... for short'... not only on the increased animations of the Cece subject, but also on the party on the beach, which he had also started recording, and transmitting on.

Heracles was requesting immediate instructions from Dave, as to whether to incorporate the activities of the new party, as there were many more dynamics to observe among the larger group, which would provide a significantly richer pool of information as to the inner workings of the human species, than the one that the Cece subject was providing them with.

Cece and Heracles were both spared from making a decision on how to move on from what had become a difficult moment, by In-it suddenly flying out of the trees behind Heracles, and echoing Cece's last words, "With me! With me!"

"Oh listen!" Cece was thrilled, for the moment, her current dilemma forgotten.

"In-it's finally copying *me*, and not just you! I thought he was never going to say my words!"

In-it landed on Heracles starry head, his claws firmly grasping into all manner of matter, that wasn't there.

"With me," In-it parroted again, "With me."

Receiving a response from Dave, Heracles suddenly turned on his heel, startling In-it into flight, but he compensated for the little bird's loss of a perch, by holding out a starry hand and forefinger, providing an alternative resting place for In-it, who immediately resettled himself on his new perch.

As Heracles turned his back on Cece and headed back down the steep cliff, with In-It perched firmly on his finger, but without Cece, she thought she heard Heracles reassuring In-It, by quietly uttering the pet-name he had given the little bird, as it alighted on his hand.

"Bugger", she thought she had faintly heard him say.

Then a further plaintive echo of her words barely reached her ears, as he turned a corner and disappeared from sight, and she was not even sure whether it was In-It, or Heracles, who, turning that corner, had uttered, "With me! With me!"

Chapter Twenty-One

"**And** your explanations do not excuse the fact that he has done everything that she has asked!" Dave came out of his own musings to the realization that John was still listing his and Heracles's transgressions, "including manifesting a 60-foot sea monster that you have only now finally seen fit to tell me, did, however briefly... *EAT ME*!"

"Well we would have re-materialised later, anyway... probably... but he hasn't actually done *everything* she asked him to!"

"Well, just about everything but the mermaid! And what do you mean we would have *probably re*-materialised?"

"Not just the mermaid thing!" countered Dave, ignoring the more complicated issue, raised by the somewhat flimsy science, of the survival chances of an *almost* immortal entity, after being consumed by a creature, that had been *manifested* by another entity, which he was trying his hardest to convince himself, as well as John, did not exist!

But without putting said entity down, if possible.

Because, after all, it had feelings!

Apparently!

At least, thought Dave, finding *something* in the shambles to be temporarily relieved about, if John had not seen the last message from Heracles, signing himself off as Eric, then neither must he have caught the end of the accompanying message.

Heracles's response to Dave's instruction to *switch* observations to the new party, was a *request*, from Heracles, to continue to study Cece, as well as the new party!

His reasoning for this, Heracles had explained, was because he *felt* she was ...significant!

Dave suddenly felt the need to clasp hands to the head that seemed too small to contain all the contradictions waging wars within it.

"The subject also asked to be put back on the ship that she was washed off, at one stage, and he didn't do that!" Dave was grasping at straws, but in his eagerness to disprove Heracles's existence as a lifeform, started grabbing at all the wrong straws.

"And also, at the start of the assignment, I suggested creating a small freak wave, you know, just large enough to wreck a vessel, and *he* chose to just wash the one subject over, so...."

"You do realise that you are supposed to be demonstrating that he is *not* a thinking functioning entity here, don't you Dave? Because you are not doing a very good job of it, you know. And you are not exactly putting yourself in a good light either! You gave the avatar the option of creating a tidal wave *big enough to wipe out the ship*, and the *avatar* decided against it?"

"My *point* is, he went for the more *energy efficient*, and ecological option, as I had originally *instructed* him, and he just so happened to extrapolate that there was more than an even chance that causing a tsunami would also wipe out a small community of island dwellers in the process, so he thought, maybe not..."

"He thought *maybe not*? *He* thought maybe not? He *thought*.... Honestly Dave I don't know where to start!"

Dave hardly had time to start to put a relieved look on his face before John continued, "But I'll give it a go!"

"Ok," Dave interrupted sullenly, "admittedly, he misunderstands the remit of his instructions sometimes. And then I got caught up in something..."

"Listen to yourself Dave! You have not only created a life-form, an immensely *powerful* lifeform, but one who *doesn't quite understand* his own remit! Or his own *boundaries*! And does not always even do as he is asked!

"You had better tell me just exactly what it was that got you so 'caught up' that you left Heracles, I mean the avatar, to his own devices!"

"I don't think you're in the right frame of mind to listen now!" Dave said petulantly.

But then seeing John start to manifest into something from a distant place Dave did not even remember visiting, and which was quivering with what Dave could only imagine was mounting rage, he capitulated somewhat.

"Obviously the plan was always for me to continue to monitor and advise the projections avatar, based on the information that it gathered for me, not just let it continue to evolve and update itself indefinitely, but I got a bit distracted, and well, you know how it is.

"We have a lot of projects going on at the minute! I took my eye off the ball, Ok? Like you have never made a mistake? But then, I don't suppose *you* have!"

"Dave, I can't tell you on how many levels what you have said is wrong! So *so* wrong! I mean, really! I wouldn't know where to start!"

Dave was feeling too chastened to even get his hopes up this time.

Clearly John *always* knew where to start.

He did not, however, know where to stop!

"Firstly," John puffed out his chest as he ploughed into a soliloquy, "we are, just about, immortal beings, with the capacity, nay, the *obligation*, to simultaneously monitor the minutiae of a million species on a myriad galaxies, to gather information, assess trends, analyse patterns, and feed-back billions of *projections*, to assist the Highest of High, his most Elevated of Elevations, He Who Knows It All, in understanding the purpose of The Beginning, and therefore, be able to forecast The Outcome!"

"All we have to do is observe, analyse, and feed-back! So what was it that was so absorbing, complicated, or distracting about that, that you managed to take your eye off this particular ball long enough for one of your own projection avatars to tootle off and start developing a personality?

"And another thing, you don't even have eyes to take off balls! You don't even have any…"

Dave interrupted him angrily, "There is no point in us taking on the forms of the subjects we're studying, and communicating in their language, if you don't at least try to fully *immerse* yourself in the experience!

"We both agreed to do it like this, didn't we? Mix it up a bit, we said. *Didn't we?* A few millennia or so ago? But you pop in and out of your corporeal forms as quickly and frequently as a mating Phobus transport-flea, whenever it suits you!"

"I *totally* fully immersed us in this one!" John countered, totally fully immersing himself in anger.

"I imagined and designed this whole ship we are on, and immersed it at the bottom of the ocean! What more did you want?"

"Well not so much imagined and designed, as researched and duplicated!" Dave came back at John, "And when I say researched, I mean you tuned into one old Earth 'science fiction' programme, and when I say duplicated, I mean created a very sketchy reproduction.

"Half of these controls don't even work!" Dave tapped a few of the key pads on the shiny work station in front of his swivel chair.

"And as to being immersed, you are *way* too literal John, I didn't mean immersed as in, *at the bottom of the sea!*"

"I tuned into *more than one* old Earth science fiction programme!" John's voice retorted crossly from somewhere across the other side of the saucer, having lost all interest in maintaining his corporeal form, such was his high dudgeon.

"And they *did* immerse their ships... sometimes", the petulant voice continued to berate Dave even though his physical presence had de-materialised.

"And" the voice now just came to Dave as if a thought on a breeze, "*None* of *their* control panels really worked! *Ever!*"

Chapter Twenty-Two

Heracles having disappeared from view, Cece started to make her way back down the cliffs by herself.

She found climbing down, alone, strangely more taxing than the climb up, with Heracles bringing up the rear.

Probably because her legs were already being tired from the climb up, she supposed. And in addition to that, she thought, having used up all her adrenalin during her euphoric episode at the top of the cliffs wouldn't have helped.

The initial excitement at discovering the rescue party had been all but extinguished, at the realization that not only would she have to leave Heracles behind, but that he clearly was not happy about it!

Over the last few weeks, since he had made it clear that he was not available to her, in any way other than a companion... and total saviour... she had tried to not think of him in any other terms.

But it only now occurred to her, that maybe *he* thought of *her* in terms other than a companion, but was just being honourable, to whoever he had left at home, wherever home was!

And even if he didn't think of her as anything other than a companion, losing your one and only companion, when you are stranded on a desert island, was obviously a big thing, for anyone, she thought desolately.

She tried to imagine how she would feel if Heracles was the one who was getting rescued!

Probably something similar to how she was feeling now, she conceded, having seen neither star nor comet of him all the way down the rocky descent.

Except at least he had In-it for company, she thought peevishly!

She also wondered, if it had been Heracles that was getting 'picked up', rather than herself, whether he would offer to take her with him?

Or at least drop her off somewhere!

He probably would, she thought morosely.

He always seemed to do the right thing.

When he could work out what was the right thing to do, that is!

She could not really imagine him just leaving her behind! But *she* had just dismissed out of hand, the idea of taking *him* with her!

As she arrived at the less steep, and easier to navigate, lower section of the cliff, Cece found she did not need to concentrate so much on where she placed her feet, and so her mind started to wander, and she found herself fantasising about taking him back with her, to England.

She imagined introducing his sparkling, twirling form to her friends at the Little Chickadees.

"How did we meet? Well it's a funny story! Is he from round here? Not...*really*. He doesn't speak much, no, but his Enrico Caruso impersonation is ... out of this world! And he does a red mullet in whisky and caramel sauce to die for! And lordy... you should see him dance!"

The thought of Heracles waltzing her around the nightclub brought the fantasy…whereby she had almost started to wonder if there might be a way…. to a close, as images of Heracles spinning her round a dance pole, were suddenly replaced by ones of the crowds running and screaming out of the turn-style exits, as portrayed in so many old black and white B Movies.

She let out a heavy sigh, as she tried to re-focus her attention on not twisting her ankle at her hurried descent on the rugged path.

When there was still no sight of Heracles by the time Cece's feet were back on firm sand, and feeling exhausted and dispirited, she felt at a loss as to what to do.

After giving her jelly legs, weak from the strain of the climb, a minute to stop shaking, she briefly reverted to the frantic state that she had been in at the top of the cliff, when she had spotted her rescue party.

She oscillated, for a few minutes, between just running back and forth, at the water's edge, where she thought she would be more visible when they came round the island looking for her, in case they sailed away again without her, and running towards her shacks, more to catch up with Heracles than to fetch any of her possessions, which she now realised, would not really be fit to ever see the light of day again, once she got off the island.

Common sense prevailed, as it occurred to Cece that a rescue party would not come thousands of miles searching for her, then not bother to do a full circuit of the island! So she decided not to worry about that one!

She was, however, worried about Heracles, and his reaction to the rescue party!

So, having already walked three miles across the beach, climbed up and down a cliff, and run around in numerous pointless circles, she decided to stop running around like a headless chicken, and make her way at speed, or at least, as fast as the heat of the day allowed, back to the shacks.

Back to Heracles.

Chapter Twenty-Three

"I don't see the point of any of this," the thin voice for some reason triggered a memory log in Heracles, which he had filed away under 'wine'.

"I agree," said an even thinner voice, "This so-called 'paradise island' is covered in midges, and the heat is just *ruining* my hair! And where is the so-called scenery that we've come all this way for? It's all just sea, and sand, and trees! Why can't we just film it on a set, somewhere?"

Another voice, the tone of which sounded familiar to Heracles, but to which he would not have known to identify as 'long-suffering', joined in at that point.

"Well let's just give it one more night, shall we? And then we can do a few more shoots in the morning, when it is a little cooler? Do a quick scoot around the island, make sure we're not missing out on anything spectacular round the other side, and maybe get a little bit more footage of the scenery. Then, if you are all still feeling the same, we can probably do the rest back at the studio."

"People queue for days just to get a glimpse of me! And consider it a privilege! And now look at me! Covered in midge bites! My hair full of sand!!" The thin voice wined on, regardless as to whether anyone was listening.

"You don't get skin like this by exposing it to real sun you know! And remember! If I wrinkle, I sue!"

From his privileged position in the trees, Heracles observed the new party, and even if his tendency towards invisibility was not as pronounced as it once was, it is unlikely he would have been observed by the inward-looking crowd.

The interactions continued, but did not really vary, so after observing, and transmitting, for what he felt was adequate to meet the task, he set off back round the other side of the island. Back to Cece.

Chapter Twenty-Four

Having brought the Satis-et-Satis situation to a satisfactory conclusion, and being more than a little concerned about the way the avatar was acting, Dave had decided to monitor his transmissions a little more closely, before deciding whether or not he needed to give John a more fulsome apprisal of the Heracles and Cece situation.

What he had just read was not helping to put his mind at rest.

The sun was just starting to set when Cece eventually got back to her camp, and the fact that it was empty only came as half a surprise to her.

During the long walk back from the cliff edge, she had had plenty of time to think about Heracles reaction to the news that she would be leaving, and also to analyse her own feelings about the situation.

He was bound to be upset, she berated herself, ashamed of how unbelievably callous and thoughtless she had been, not even considering how her imminent departure was going to affect him; they had been inseparable practically since they first met!

She had obviously been a good distraction for him, from whoever, or whatever, he had been separated, she decided; wherever he came from.

Or maybe he did have a ...little … crush... on her, as she had had on him, at one point, she conceded.

But hopefully he would come back before the rescue party found her. She would be devastated if she had to leave him, without saying goodbye!

Which was probably nothing, she thought guiltily, compared to how he would feel!

But what else was she supposed to do?

She couldn't very well say to a lot of strangers, and possibly one dear friend, or maybe some distant relative, or even a potted plant... because she could not for the life in her decide who might have launched the search party...'Can you just hang around a while so I can say goodbye to the alien I've been living with here on the island?'

They would have her off the island and into the tropical diseases hospital before she had finished the sentence!

This particular aspect of Cece's dilemma however, resolved itself.

By the time she had strewn several wraparound dresses atop of the various shacks that made up her camp, to ensure it was as visible as possible when they came to look for her tomorrow, and thrown herself down in the doorway of the shack she slept in, and considered home, Heracles was there, sitting cross-legged beside the small fire he had already built, in anticipation of the cooling night ahead.

Chapter Twenty-Five

"I have a dilemma, John."

Having finally worked himself up to confide some of his escapades to his colleague, Dave was a little taken aback by John's dismissive response.

"Don't we all. I'm sure that whatever it is, you'll work it out."

"Right, well...erm... thank-you?"

John was not known for unpredictability.

Not only in his 'John' form, but throughout the millennia of working together, Dave thought he had always been able to accurately predict John's responses to most situations.

He did, after all, have a lot of experience in predicting responses, and forecasting outcomes.

Also, he had presented John with enough situations, to establish a precedence for most circumstances!

"The thing is, you know how we were wondering if Heracles was developing a bit more of a personality than I had maybe hoped he would? Well…"

"I am afraid that is a problem of your own making, Dave, and as it happens, I have other problems of my own to deal with at the moment"

John's response stopped in its tracks, the nervous pivoting in the swivel chair, that Dave had been attempting.

"You've got...? Sorry? *What?*"

"I have problems of my own. My wife is leaving me!"

Dave swivelled completely off of his chair, landing painfully on his tartan flask, and John strode over him, as he marched dramatically across to a viewing screen at the other side of the bridge, to stare out at a passing shoal of herring.

"And she's taking the children!"

Chapter Twenty-Six

"**The** thing is… Eric… I can't stay here with you. Much as I have loved spending time with you, we both knew it would not last forever!" Cece paced up and down between Heracles and the fire, wringing her hands.

"It isn't anything you've done wrong… Oh god, now I sound like 'it's not you, it's me', don't I? But this really *is* me! I'm weak! I need other people! I need physical *contact*, human *touch*, and you're, well, you're just not…. *human*, are you?" The cruelty of her words stabbed deep into Cece's own heart as she tried to avoid acknowledging to herself, how they must be effecting him.

She had come to a halt in front of Heracles, her hand clutching at a handful of dress, held close to her chest.

She looked down at the twinkling face tilted up at her, and then became distracted and she let her eyes drop for a moment, as she became caught up in studying a rare astral confluence, which seemed to be developing somewhere deep within his cosmic chest.

Heracles dropped his own gaze, looking down at his own galactic form, and raised his hand also, as though to touch the unfamiliar starburst which seemed to be erupting somewhere round about where his heart should be.

"I can't stay here alone with you forever, and you *really* can't come back with me. To say you would not fit in with my friends, would be a bit of an understatement."

The image of him swirling her round the dance floor at Little Chickadees, more Swayze than Caruso, briefly skittered across her mind again, but she hurriedly dismissed it, and went back to trying to defend her position to Heracles, "I have a life to get back to, after all, *I* didn't just .... drop from the ... stars...!"

Cece faltered to a stop, her thoughts tripping her up, as she simultaneously realised that she had yet again been incredibly tactless, just as it also occurred to her that she had been avoiding looking at some very disquieting thoughts, ever since she had been on the island.

Cece forced herself, for a moment, to look at the life that she had to 'get back to'. 'Let go', by her employer. *Replaced*, by her boyfriend. And her payday prosecco pals! The ones who had let her come on the cruise alone! And none of whom were close enough to her, to compete with a potted plant when trying to identify the likely contender to have sent out the rescue party!

Cece then found herself examining uncomfortable memories of her preparation for her cruise, the details of which she had been hiding, even from herself, as she started to face the fact that maybe she wasn't the people person that she liked to make herself out to be.

She had indeed pictured herself basking on a towelled deckchair, people milling around her, enjoying the sun, like herself, but she, with her topiary book placed defensively on her knee...to dissuade casual approaches from other holiday makers, who spotting a singleton might be tempted to enfold her into their merry-making.

Add to that image the old-fashioned clunky headphones of her Nanna's old cassette player, enhancing the impression of a person being too occupied... or singular... to be disturbed; the cigarettes completing the aloof image.

She had introduced herself to enough people to ensure she had an outlet for her constant chatter, whenever she needed one.

But also, she now acknowledged, enough to ensure that she did not have to get to know any of them any better than she wanted to.

Heracles now sat with one hand clasped around his knees, holding a shell of whisky in the other, and leant towards Cece, in perfect symmetry of her own pose, as he observed the emotions flit across her face.

"I am so thankful for your company, and all the fantastic things you've done for me, Eric, and the stuff you've got for me, and made for me, but sooner or later there will be things I need, that you *can't* provide me with."

Heracles tilted his head a little to one side, a mannerism he had observed so many times in Cece, and which he had learned, when he copied it, led to her elaborating on her stories.

"I guess really, I'm talking about ...love! And all the stuff that goes with it!"

On cue, a little bird which should have already settled to roost, appeared from no-where, as Heracles extended a starry arm, and perched on one twinkling finger. Cece paused a moment, to stretch out her own, less starry arm, for In-it to hop between the two; then she spent a moment chirruping reassuringly to the little bird who had been disturbed from his sleep.

Chapter Twenty-Seven

Dave picked himself up off the deck, and checked that his flask hadn't broken, before pouring himself another cup of tea, and re-arranging himself back onto his swivel chair.

"Do you want to run that one by me again, crew-man?"

He had been familiarising himself with human mannerisms and lingo, using John's tried and tested study method of tuning into random airwaves, and had been feeling that he was knocking the metaphorical spots off of his hitherto conformist colleague.

The effect of John's dramatic pose, back of hand against forehead, sailed over Dave's head, as it wasn't one that he had learned. The implication of his words however, did not.

"Did *you* miss the lecture on the whole *Neanderthal* thing? It wasn't *just* aimed at me you know John! Did you learn *nothing* from my mistakes, I mean, experiences? It might seem like fun at the time, John, but believe you me, when you find out that that fun has started the decimation a whole civilisation, because a minute particle of something quite harmless to us turns out to be lethal to them and highly virulent ..."

"Oh no Dave! It isn't anything like that! That isn't even *allowed*! Is it? That's not what you...?"

"Erm...No?" Dave interjected, confused. "Well what have you been up to then? A wife? Children?"

"Yes, three little ones. All gone!" John resumed the dramatic pose.

"I am sorry John, but you are either going to have to explain or let me get back to other business, there are ...other things going on that need my attention."

Things that needed my attention before, by the look of it, thought Dave.

Even almost immortal beings, with almost infinite capacity to multi-task, can be prone to having too many balls in the air to be able to juggle successfully, it would seem.

John let out a practised sigh, perching himself on the previously untouched second swivel chair, "Well, where shall I begin..."

And Dave let out an even bigger sigh, no practise needed.

Chapter Twenty-Eight

"How do I explain love to you?"

Heracles tilted his head to the other side, as though contemplating Cece's rhetorical question, noting that her eyes glistened as she spoke.

"I suppose it's that... *safe...* feeling you feel when you see someone, and the pain, in the pit of your stomach, when you don't." Cece looked at him through wet lashes, trying to gauge the impact of her words.

"It's the feeling of being home, no matter where you are, as long as they are with you!" She paused to take a sip of whisky.

"It's someone who makes you feel good about yourself, and lets *you* know the best things about *yourself*!" Another pause, a bigger sip.

"And makes you feel ok to be ...in your own skin! 'Cause you know that someone else loves your skin, and everything that's wrapped up in it!"

Heracles emptied his shell of whisky, as Cece emptied hers, and replaced both their shells, prompted by nothing but the sight of Cece's empty shell.

"So," Cece continued, as she took the shell from him, without even acknowledging the action, struggling to put her muddled thoughts into words, "it's like… what you' got... wrapped up in your skin, must be worth having... sort of thing."

"And if there's someone you love, their skin, and everything they' got wrapped up in their skin, is, you know, worth its weight in gold!

"And there's nothing like having someone in your life, who you know you are their world, because, suddenly, that means that that is what you are worth! You are worth the world!

"But that's all a matter of perspective... I guess", she gave a little half laugh, and took another sip from her fresh drink.

Heracles looked down at the not insignificant representative sample of the universe, contained within his own sparkling form, and then considered the contents of Cece's skin, and then added to the transcript that he was sending to Dave, 'define significance of *perspectives*'.

This time Cece half -laughed, half sobbed, as she took a bigger swig from her shell.

Memories of dancing and laughter lit her face, which for a moment took on a reflective starlit quality that could have competed with Heracles's own shimmering countenance, before again clouding over.

Half-memories also tugged at her tipsy unconscious, dreams of an electrifying massage, which she had unsuccessfully tried to re-invoke on more than one occasion, and swimming the night away with the dolphins.

"But if that person chooses to leave you, you are worth nothing!"

Cece suddenly choked, and the midnight-blue figure watched the tears fall from Cece's eyes for a moment, waiting for her to continue.

"You *become* worthless, or, it's more that... you realise you were never really worth anything anyway, you just thought you were…" her voice sounded different, to the starlit man, when she started to speak again, thicker, but more… *hollow*, as though her words were coming from a cavern that was buried deep inside the subject he knew as Cece.

She wiped her nose with the back of her hand, then wiped the back of her hand down the side of her dress, and when Heracles, unbidden, held out one of her spare dresses, she took it, and unself-consciously gave her nose a good hard blow.

Heracles added it to his list of Cece noises.

"Love is being with someone you can be yourself with, no matter what", Cece continued, handing the soggy dress back to Heracles, "but it's ... lots of other things as well though," she eventually continued, "you know, it's ...having somebody... *solid*... you can *lean on*... somebody that, you know, won't... *blow away*... when life gets messy."

She snuffled into the dress, her voice, like her heart, cracking a little as she carried on.

"Somebody that you can *hide behind* when you're not feeling brave enough to be out on show, on your own!

"It's lots of things really, and I know you have looked after me, and fed me, and kept me safe, and oh my god, I could talk to you till the cows come home! And you listen! You *really* listen! And not just 'cause you got to! But because you're interested! In me!

"Because we seem to have so much in common, don't we Heracles? What with the topiary…and… beach combing… and wildlife conservation! We even like the same food! And everything! Sometimes I think you are more like me than, well ... than *I* am! We share so many interests, and I know all that is important, it is, it really *really* is, but…."

She paused, at a loss for words at last, and he waited… and waited…and then, concluding that she had come to the end of her transmission, started analysing, but then she carried on.

"But there's …other stuff, too! Physical… stuff. Things I can't really explain to you, or make you understand. Like… the electric touch on your skin, when a certain someone brushes up against you! That doesn't happen when just *anyone* touches you!"

Again, half-memories flitted through her head, without quite catching hold, of a delicious dream massage, and the hair standing up on her arms, telling her he is around, even when she can't see him.

"It must be a chemical reaction, or something, 'cause they call it having chemistry, when two people fit together right, and it only happens when you're with the right person! Well, maybe they're the wrong person…but sometimes it feels right, at the time!" She paused to draw a long juddering breath.

"I can't describe some bits, the feelings and stuff, it's almost… out of this world… and *you* could not possibly comprehend… well… actually…" she paused, looking at the man, who wasn't really a man, made of starlight, and definitely not of *this* world, sitting in front of her, and laughed, "look who I'm telling!"

She laughed again, "So maybe you would, but either way, I wouldn't know how to tell it, so we won't go there!"

Cece paused to scrape a bit of prawn-grit from her tongue, and casting her silent companion a sidelong glance through still wet lashes to see how he was reacting to her words, caught a glimpse of him mirroring the action, giving her a second pause, for thought.

"Those bits of prawn shell certainly do get ev-ery-where, don't they?" she commented to Heracles, bringing up her arm to scrape her tongue down the back of her forearm, partly to remove any remaining shell, but mainly to test out a theory.

'Okay…' to herself, as Heracles again mimicked the action. 'Question asked and answered! That's definitely a thought worth coming back to on another day, Scarlett'

And never having excelled at multi-tasking, even when sober, Cece shook her head a little to clear her thoughts, and bring her focus back to the matter in hand.

"I really am *so* grateful that you have been here, while I have been on the island, but it's time for me to go back to my own kind now. And it's time for you to go back to your own kind too, if you can... wherever that may be... and whatever 'your kind' is!

"Because I need... I just need... to be able to not only *talk* to somebody, I need *somebody*, who can *talk back to me*! Not all the time, just sometimes, and I know it can be hard to get a word in edgeways with me anyway, some-times, I've been told... but I need more than *you* can give me Heracles!

"You couldn't possibly understand!

"Understand," echoed Heracles.

"I do hope you do," Cece sniffed. "And I know that you've given me *so* much, Heracles! And I'm so *sorry*… that *it is not… enough*!"

"Not …enough." came quietly from Heracles's side of the fire, and then, as Cece lifted her head to catch his quiet words, again, "…enough!"

"I am so sorry if you don't want to hear this Heracles, but I have to say it…I have to explain why I can't stay here with you.

"You could never give me what I need, because... because..." She hid her face in her hands, her drunken words garbled by sudden wracking sobs, which seemed to swirl around her, reverberating from the walls.

"It's not just that I need human warmth… and *touch*…I need someone to…*love me*!" she wailed, wiping her streaming face on her dress. "I've *always* wanted someone …to...love me…please, Heracles, try to understand!

"If I stay here, with you, I will *never* have anyone looking at me and saying "I love you! Not and *meaning* it anyway!"

Looking up, still sobbing, she was startled to find Heracles no longer there, but that the huge sobs which had been spilling out of Cece, seemed to be being met by sobs rolling in from the sea, the sky, the stars.

"Oh, Heracles, *Eric*, I didn't mean to hurt you! I am so sorry!" Cece sobbed anew, her face awash with tears; she felt her heart breaking. "I am so *so* sorry!"

"*Love you*!" bounced back at her from the walls, "*Love you*!", from the skies, the sea, the stars, but Cece's sobs drown out everything but her own distress, as she rocked, and cradled herself, immersed in her own misery and despair.

And what could have been the first signs of a tropical storm gathering momentum, a lavender streak lighting up the vast sky, a precursor to thunder rolling in behind crashing waves, totally drown out the final words that were trying to echo across the sky,

"Love *me*… love *me*… *please*!"

Chapter Twenty-Nine

"So, just to be clear, you have had absolutely no physical contact with this human, I mean, woman? You never actually met her? And the ...erm...I am using your words here John, *relationship*, happened...on-a-line? And the offspring are hers? And hers alone? And you have never met *them* either?"

"Well I don't think the offspring are *entirely* hers alone. I think that is a human impossibility, but I did not get that far with the research, it's something about being blended, I think, she said *we* would be a *blended* family anyway, but you don't need to be so snitty about it," John practised a hurt look, in the reflection on one of the viewing screens.

"You are the one who kept saying I didn't take enough risks, or vary my research methods enough".

"But that's just it though John! You still haven't done *either* of those things really, have you?"

"I did! *You* don't know, because you haven't done it! It's a human thing! They have these sorts of relationships all the time! From one side of the planet to the other, make lifelong commitments, without ever having met, and, well... life can mean different things apparently... and another interesting factoid there, actually…

"My darling wife, my significant other, is currently 'serving' life! In some sort of …institution… apparently, so she wouldn't have been available to meet in the flesh, so to speak, even if I had been.

"But I *have* learned all sorts about what being a good human being means! Well, what a good parent means, which I can only assume is the same thing!

"She has told me that she is a good parent, because she has 'set her children up' *for life*, before she went to do the serving life thing, that she is doing

"Not *quite* sure of the details, but it all seemed to be connected, somehow.

"I didn't really understand it *all*, to be honest, but now," John paused for dramatic effect at this point, and even managed to produce a tear, "I never will…. because she has ...left me!"

Dave interrupted again before John indulged himself in more theatricals, "Well, well done then, I suppose, but back to more pressing issues, dry your... tear...as I was trying to tell you, I think you were right about Heracles."

"I was right about *what* about Heracles?" spontaneously coming out of the well-versed high dudgeon.

The dramatic response to the possibility of his colleague having possibly defied every rule in their society's rule book, and likely dragging him along for the ride, which Dave was anticipating, was nowhere near as pronounced as the multi-morphing exhibition he had made of himself the last time he had had to confront that possibility.

This was partly as John felt it did not flatter his new more mature character, that of a recently married, *and deserted*, individual, but mainly it was just because he did *so* love to be right.

Chapter Thirty

Sick to her stomach from exhaustion, whisky, and misery, Cece curled up into a tight ball on the scant grass mattress, the pain of her fingernails piercing the palms of her hands, a woefully inadequate distraction from the icicles stabbing her stomach, and the tight bands around her chest.

The thought of having hurt Heracles, was unbearable, and the thought of leaving him behind, alone, on the island, unthinkable.

Almost as unthinkable as ...taking him with her…

But how could she stay here with a man, that wasn't a man?

Never again to be held, touched, or even, really, *spoken* to!

Never to have *human* companionship again!

Heracles did not, *could* not, expect that of her! Surely?

Accepting the sudden chill that had started to seep in to her shack, as a natural part of her misery, Cece was unaware of other indications that the weather was starting to change.

She neither heard the low rumbles of thunder, over her own snivellings and sniffles, nor saw the approaching flashes of lightning, with her eyes screwed up, to avoid looking at a room devoid of Heracles. She was oblivious to the white horses being whipped into a frenzy, somewhere not too far off her beach.

Trying to block out the misery of the dilemma as to what to do about Heracles, Cece put her mind to concentrating on looking forward to her rescue party arriving, and all that she had to go back to.

When she tried to picture the faces of the people she had been longing to see, whether they might be part of the rescue party, or just the people behind sending it, she found she could only envisage Heracles starry countenance.

The beautiful face, that wasn't a face. The eyes that weren't there, that nonetheless saw everything, and seemed to look into infinity, and into her soul.

As she curled into an even tighter ball, as the thunder rolled in over the shore, and the white horses rode ever further up Cece's beach, she started to wonder what she had done.

She had been so intent on ticking boxes, as to what she thought she wanted from life, that she had not stopped to consider what was happening in her life right now, in this moment, and the fact that she was happier, she realised, and more content, settled, and fulfilled, than she had ever been in her life.

And obviously it was all down to one...being.

Becoming aware of dazzling light trying to creep between her clenched lids, and without even attempting to open her heavy tear-gummed eyes, Cece's tears started afresh, this time with relief, as she cried, "Heracles! Oh Heracles! Thank God you have come back! I thought I had driven you away for good this time!

"I have been such a fool! I love you! Of course I love you! And I hope you love me too! But even if you don't, or don't even understand what it is, it doesn't matter! I love you enough for both of us! It has just taken me thinking we were going to be parted to realise it!"

Eyes still closed, Cece sat up, crying into her hands, rocking to comfort herself, and to give herself strength to say what she needed to say to Heracles.

"*You* are worth the world to me! *And* the stars, *and* the universe, and *everything between*! *You* are my everything! I am not... whole ...without you! You're not just like my ...other half...you are like my... *me*!

"I wouldn't be *me*, without you in my life! I really wouldn't! I was only half alive, only half a person, before I met you! Pretending to be happy, pretending to be something I wasn't!

"I can look at who I am, now that I've got you with me! I *love* who *we are* together...!"

Aware that she could go on forever, with her declarations of love, before Heracles was likely to interrupt her, and her voice hoarse ad cracking from her crying, Cece eventually forced her eyes open, expecting to see Heracles's quizzical look beaming down at her.

Cece gasped at finding the shack was not lit by Heracles's starry light at all, but by flash, after flash, after flash, of blinding lightning.

Chapter Thirty-One

"Well, if you ask me, which you haven't," the thin voice whined, "I don't see the point of hanging around here another day, with this storm looking like it's settling in for the duration, just to get more footage of the same! Why can't we just leave now!"

"Well, I'd rather be on the island than out on the boat right now, wouldn't you? I don't even know where this has blown in from, there was nothing about it on the forecast! It will probably blow over as quick as it blew in, and then we'll likely have another gorgeous day by tomorrow!" a slightly less petulant voice, trying to make the best of a situation, joined in.

"And I don't want to miss the opportunity to get extra footage, if there's anything worth shooting, while we are here. I don't suppose there will be enough budget to come back, or if we would even find the same island again, if there is anything we don't get on this trip. We only landed upon it by chance this time! It wasn't even on the map!" a voice that was trying to sound like it was in charge added to the conversation.

"If you want to come back here again, you can get yourself another star!" the thin voice sniped.

"You're using the word *star* figuratively, I assume!" the producer snapped back, his patience stretched to the limits, and at the end of his tether.

He was not looking forward to having to spend the night in the miniscule tent he had been re-allocated, due to the storm having already made half the tents uninhabitable.

It was less than a quarter of the size of the one that his so-called star-lead had insisted on having to herself, despite the rest of the cast and crew agreeing to double and triple up.

"We'll see what the day brings tomorrow, shall we?" he said a little more sympathetically, as he saw a slight indication of her eyes widening, as the thunder rumbling ever nearer sounded like it was building up to be quite something.

There was a chance she was feeling genuinely anxious, he thought wearily, although her frozen features made it difficult to be sure.

"I suggest we all turn in and try to get some sleep, if we can, amid all this noise!"

Chapter Thirty-Two

So, to summarise," John was back on lecture mode, strutting up and down the saucer bridge, finger-tips of both hands steepled together in front of him, forefingers digging into his chin, "you *have* created a life-form, and you have made him out of volatile matter, and random pieces of ...galaxies?"

"*Pre*-formed, and *undeveloped*, galaxies...yes." Dave kept pace with John's strutting, but keeping a respectful distance behind, only two aware that he may be reliant on his colleague's good will to survive this latest predicament.

"So... stars, the most powerful, not to mention unpredictable, energy sources available to us..."

"More star *remnants* really...."

"The most powerful, not to mention *unpredictable*, sources available to us," John repeated, ignoring the interruption, "and you gave him power, equal to your own, then told him to *develop* it, and to *grow up*...and then told him to *use his own initiative*, and *improvise*."

"Well it sounds bad when you put it like that!" Dave squirmed, but John carried on regardless.

"And he has developed the ability to create..." Dave's hand shot up to protest, but John, striding dramatically up and down the bridge had his back to Dave, so missed the gesture, and Dave lowered his hand, realizing the gesture was a little premature, as John carried on, "or, *re*-create, should we say, as far as you know, absolutely *anything*, that he is aware has previously existed.... And *then* you realised that he does not acknowledge his boundaries, and now you think he has ...fallen ...in ...*love*?"

"Erm... Well, I suppose that's a fair summation John, yes. Any…thoughts?" Dave asked a little lamely, but trying hard to sound matter-of-fact, while secretly admiring his colleagues total lack of transmogrifying response.

John was certainly handling his emotions much better these days, thought Dave, as he himself had been desperately fighting the urge to ricochet round the room ever since he had faced up to the need to have this conversation, with his newly calm and understanding colleague.

"Well... it's not good, is it Dave? I mean...Love!" John carried on sagely.

"The most powerful driving force in the universe! And your Heracles now has that driving him, as well!"

"Er, is it...? Has he?" Vastly out of his depth, and for once bowing to the apparent superior experience of his colleague, Dave went for humble and hopeful, "So… any suggestions?"

"Well, obviously, he needs de-materialising, before things go any further," John now tried out the matter-of -fact approach, "and of course, you will have to inform the most Elevated of Elevations, He Who Knows It All what you have done," John charged on quickly before Dave could interject.

"Nothing else for it, I'm afraid! We simply don't have the power to dematerialise the being that he has become, that you have created, by ourselves! And anyway, it's well above our pay-grade!"

Dave practised the recently acquired art of sweating, whilst simultaneously surfing his information logs for 'pay-grade'.

"You do realize he is only He Who Knows It All, if you keep Telling Him It All? Surely there must be other options... you know what it would mean for us?

"For you Dave, not us. For you. This was very definitely an *individual* project! I was running my own experiment!"

"Speaking of which, John, I've just done a little check into that, just watching your back, you know, and *apparently* the Neanderthal lecture *does* actually cover *any* sort of *relations*. You did say you were in a *relationship* didn't you, with your ...*wife*... was it?"

"Oh, erm... frowned upon, is it...?" Starting to practise the said frown.

"Bit more than frowned upon I'm afraid, old chap, in fact I think it would be safe to say, *very much more* than frowned upon! And obviously I'd have to mention it, as it was that whole 'significant other' thing that you mentioned, when you referred to your 'wife', that put me on to what was going on with Heracles."

"I had asked Eric, I mean Heracles, I mean the avatar, what he had meant when he said he felt she was 'significant', he just kept repeating that she was...*significant*! *She* is significant *to him* John! What else could he mean?"

"You don't say?" John said, "Well let me think!" Dave was surprised to see that John seemed to have mastered the sweat facility of his corporeal form with little, or no practise. "There are one or two things we could try, I suppose."

"Such as?" Dave's sweat started to dry up, realizing John seemed to be back on his team.

"Well trying to de-materialise Heracles might be a bit tricky, actually, bit dangerous, if we tried it on our own, and he didn't want to go back to, you know, wherever you pulled him from."

"So?"

"Well...what I was thinking was, well, have you tried explaining the whole problem to the avatar, Heracles, I mean? He does seem quite good at coming up with reasonable and responsible solutions, doesn't he?"

"Well the thing is, I have been trying to get him to come in... for a chat, but he said he was ... busy… so I thought I might pop out to the island."

"Ah, I thought I had heard the thunder! Well, taking the whole Neandertal thing into consideration...

"Popping over to the island would be frowned upon, yes, I know... but..."

"No, Dave, not where I was going. I was going to say...wouldn't hurt."

"Oh! Right, then! I'll get right on that then. When I've just finished my cup of tea…"

Chapter Thirty-Three

Her own common sense told Cece that the rescue party, having set up camp, were obviously going to be there until at least the following day, and so still curled tight against a chill which seemed to be attacking her from outside, and in, Cece eventually allowed her exhaustion to get the better of her, and fell into a deep, unhappy sleep.

Her dreams swam with confusion, realizing that she loved Heracles had brought her only temporary relief from her misery, as his continued absence had allowed her time to reflect, again, on her feelings.

When he had not been there to hear her words, and to at least *accept her* love, even if he did not reciprocate the feeling, the difficulties she had been prepared to overlook, whilst caught up in the moment of her own epiphany, had drifted their way again to the forefront of her mind.

She had fallen asleep certain that she could never be happy again.

But then, even as sleep took hold of her, and despite the storm raging outside her flimsy shack, she became aware again, of light around her; not the false, and intrusive lightning strikes, which had continued to bombard her senses until she had given in to sleep, but a gentle, pulsating, twinkling light.

Still more in the grip of sleep than not, Cece gradually became aware of a visceral warmth, spreading from her core, and permeating into her limbs.

She felt herself floating on the waves of the endorphins which were suddenly coursing through her body, flooding her semi-consciousness with electrifying sensations of bliss and comfort.

The ensuing floods of oxytocin, lapping and washing through her system, meant that despite the terrible storm that continued to rage throughout the night, Cece awoke the next morning not only feeling strangely content, but also, overwhelmed by feelings of love, and being loved, confident that Heracles would be coming back for her.

And as though a weight of uncertainty and indecision had been lifted from her shoulders.

Cece did not really feel that Heracles had been away from her all night, but felt she had been aware of his presence about her.

The doubts that she had had, about what she thought she would be missing if she stayed on the island, seemed to have disintegrated with the tempest of the night before.

Cece felt calm, relaxed, and in love, as she sat with her arms wrapped around her knees, staring out onto the golden sand-filled sea, beautifully painted against the backdrop of the most breathtaking after-storm re-birth of a sunrise, that she had ever seen, as she sat awaiting the return of the being that she knew she loved, and with whom she knew she wanted to spend the rest of her life.

Chapter Thirty-Four

"I thought that was going to get a bit tricky there for a while, didn't you?" Dave swivelled on his swivel chair, cup in hand, flask containing top up at the ready.

"Yes, it could have, couldn't it?" John had just about relaxed into the idea of the second swivel chair, if not the spare flask, in time for them to be wrapping up mission control, to go back to being, well, something other than John and Dave. "I'll miss this old ship," said Dave after a while, fondly stroking the plastic effect console, "and reading the reports, and especially, I think, I'll miss Heracles!"

"Don't be getting sentimental Dave, over what turned out to be just a projections avatar, as we first surmised! Maybe one who, by chance, had a knack for copying or mimicking the right words, and actions, at the right times, to give the impression of, well shall we say, developing a lot more personality than he actually had!"

"Well, I do seem to remember telling you that he did not have an original thought in his head! Certainly no active intelligence going on there!" Dave made the most of looking superior, while he still had a face with which to practice the look.

"Well, certainly no emotional intelligence, anyway!" contributed John, emotional intelligence expert, since his brief marriage and divorce, and having finally got the hang of a sardonically arched eyebrow, he practised the gesture one last time, in Dave's direction, although behind his back.

Not too much of it going on here either, the eyebrow said.

"Damned good researcher though, don't you think?" John said, leaving the expressions of sarcasm to his eyebrows.

"Oh yes, damned good! And brilliant at coming up with solutions too! And such a good sport! I mean he was right, of course, it was the most energy efficient, ecological, and practical solution!"

Dave was feeling quite smug again, about the various protocols he had put into place whilst programming the avatar, now crisis had been averted.

"I thought he might have had a few qualms, you know, about leaving the subject behind, when it came to, but it didn't even seem to be an issue for him, did it?"

"Listen to yourself now John! As *you* have just reminded *me*, he was just an avatar! Qualms indeed!" Dave tutted, and laughed as he sipped the cold tea.

"He did a very thorough assessment of the situation, and quite rightly forecast that the only reasonable solution was for him to provide the subject with a supply of all the bits and bats she might need, for the foreseeable future, and for him to then re-distribute himself, across half the universe, to the various picks and pockets from where I got him!"

"Absolutely! And I thought it was a nice touch too, for him to take with him, anything he'd picked up from his experience on this assignment, moral codes… ethics and ...what-nots...so that he can share his understanding of humanity with any of the species that develop from the bits of the cosmos that he turns back into."

"Well, yes thank-you, I think I *was* having a stroke of genius there, letting him do that, wasn't I? But it did seem like a reasonable request. And what harm could it do? If the test subject was a typical example of the way humanity is progressing, and we have no reason to suspect she wasn't... I mean, look at your good lady ...wife... another sterling example of humanity..."

John nodded along agreeably to the description, savouring the thought of having managed to tuck this small inconsequential indiscretion discretely under his belt, "Quite right, quite so!"

"So, continued Dave, if he does carry the memory of what he learned here, back to the developing civilisations yet to come, it's not really likely to do any harm is it? To the Final Outcome, I mean?

"No, not at all! Well, not on our shift anyway!"

The End

Epilogue

Star-filled, and water made, the shape of a merman, that wasn't a merman, suddenly spun out of the water, executing a dolphinesque pirouette for the entertainment of the laughing figure that was definitely female shaped.

As he dove ever higher, she put down the clam comb with which she had been untangling her beautiful long hair, better to be able to applaud his joyous performance.

She then looked to her companion, on the rock, who, due to resurfaced, and residual feelings of self-confidence, from it knew not where, had decided to throw all unadulterated caution to the winds, and was enjoying, for once, being able to actually catch a break, and an impromptu show, alongside his new found friend.

"What do you think?" Cece asked.

Enthusiastically throwing all eight limbs up in the air simultaneously resulted in an ungainly slither into the brine, which he felt was worth it, in order to get his score counted.

"Yes, I'll give him an eight too! Well done, Eric! Full house of eights! Now stop showing off, and get your tail over here, and brush my hair, please!"

As the shimmering figure settled on the rock behind her, Cece leant into the firm, starry form, and thrilled to his electrifying touch, as the astral hands gently glided through her sea drenched golden tresses.

"You did check that he had actually gone, didn't you?" The none corporeal voice of the entity formerly known as John briefly echoed around the sky.

"Of course I did! Well, actually, I checked that all the stars and various bits of what-knots were back where they should be, and they are. Down to the last cosmic grain. Exactly as was. And without anyone being any the wiser! Why do you ask?" the echo that was once Dave queried.

"No reason, really. It was just that as I was having a quick scan round to make sure we hadn't left anything, I saw the ship that arrived just before your storm, as they were sailing away.

"They were using what I believe is called a telescope, to look back at the island as they were leaving.

"They seemed to have been watching something pretty intently, I thought, so I just thought I'd check," no-longer-really-John's voice explained, starting to take on a faraway quality.

A telescope appeared in the sky, and focussed in on the shore line.

"Ah, I can see what they were observing, it's nothing, it's just an octopus, sitting on a rock, sunning itself… quite unusual behaviour for an octopus, is all."

"Where are you looking?" Was-John's voice was so faint it almost wasn't even there, already on his travels. "...I can't even see anything, anyway...."

"For an almost all-knowing entity, you can be a bit obtuse sometimes, John," used-to-be-Dave, muttered to himself, in the wake of the departed no-longer-John.

"Well, *I* can see it! It's right there! On the large rock… just next to the mermaid…."

The Other End.

A note from the author

Jules would like to thank the reader for taking the time to read this work of pure fiction, and to point out that none of the characters are based on actual people, living or dead, especially Dave, and that any resemblance to actual people, is purely co-incidental.

Jules would also like to take this opportunity to apologise to the reader for any inaccuracies in the narrative, which may have occurred because of her limited knowledge and understanding of astro-physics, physics, archaeology, paleo-anthropology, ancient Greek and Roman mythology, botany and ornithology, natural history, anatomy, biology, geography...

Jules Oliver Wilkinson

Printed in Great Britain
by Amazon

57169822R00159

Deserts

The world's hot deserts

Hot deserts cover about one eighth of the land surface of the world. These deserts are found in areas of the world where there is very little rain, and where the air is hot.

The word *desert* means a place where there is very little life or growth of any kind. But none of the world's hot deserts is completely empty. In most desert areas, a few plants can grow and a few animals can live — even in places where there is hardly any rain at all.

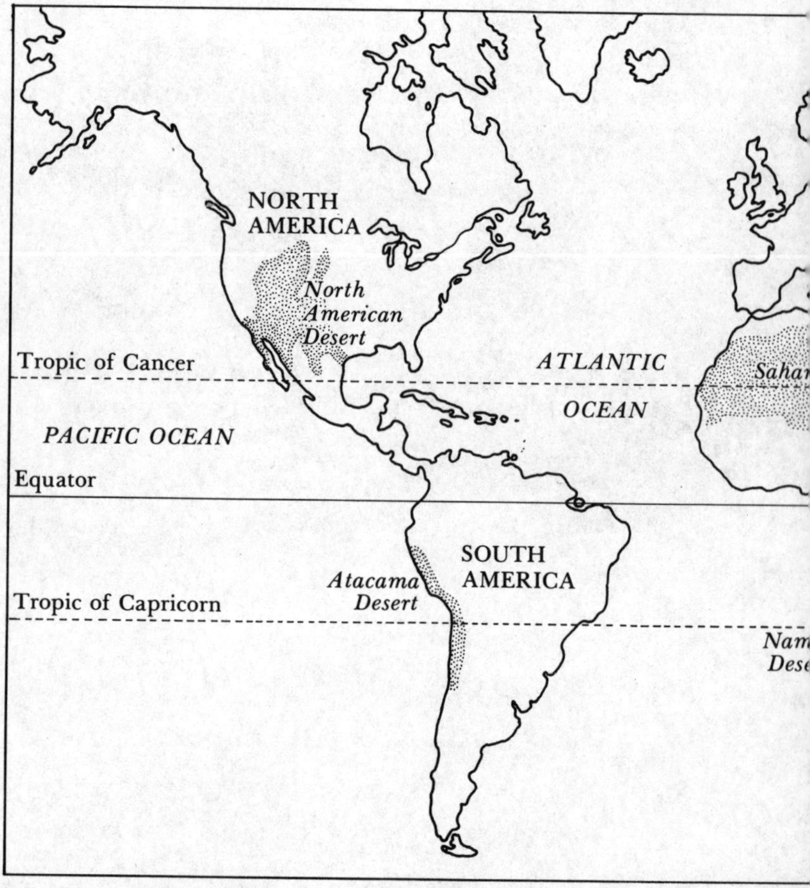

The world's largest desert is in North Africa, and is called the Sahara. The Sahara desert covers more than 8½ million square kilometres of land. It does not rain very much in the Sahara. In some places, it has not rained for at least 11 years!

The map shows the world's main hot deserts. This book explains what hot deserts are like, and tells about the plants, animals and people who live there.

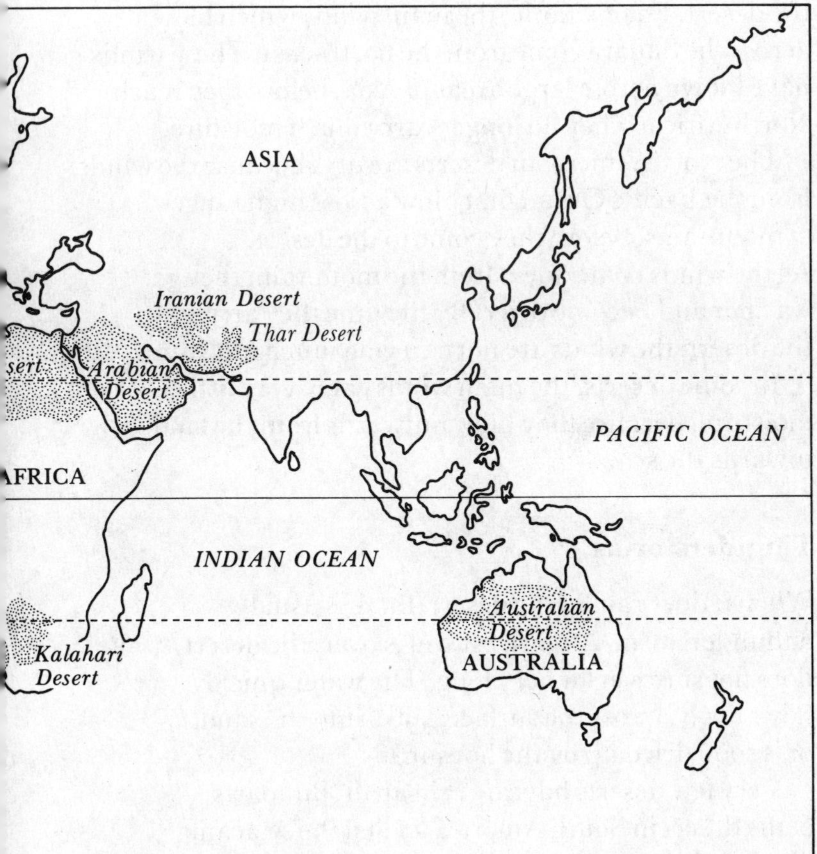

Desert climate

Rain

Deserts are dry, because the air movements in these areas do not often produce the weather conditions that cause rain. In deserts, there is usually less than 25 cms of rain each year.

In many deserts, the winds are dry because they cross thousands of kilometres of land before they arrive at the desert. For example, the main winds which blow across the Sahara come from the north-east. These winds have blown across large areas of Asia, before they reach North Africa. They no longer carry much moisture.

The North American deserts are dry, because the winds from the Pacific Ocean first blow across high ranges of mountains, before they come to the desert. As the winds come down from the mountain, they get warmer and become drier. By the time they arrive at the desert, the winds are not carrying much moisture.

In some deserts, the main winds carry very little moisture, because they blow outwards from the land towards the sea.

Thunderstorms

When it does rain in the desert, there is usually a thunderstorm. After the storm is over, the desert does not stay wet for very long. The water quickly flows away across the surface, sinks into the sand, or is soon dried up by the hot sun.

Very few deserts have no rain at all. But parts of the desert in South America, called the Atacama desert, are said to have had no rain for 400 years!

Desert temperatures

In the hot, dry deserts, the sun blazes down from a clear sky. There are no clouds and not many plants to protect the desert surface from the sun's heat. So, during the day, the ground gets very hot. The temperature of the ground can reach over 75°C. The rocks can get so hot that you could fry an egg on them!

Because the ground gets hot, the air gets hot too. The temperature of the air can reach over 50°C. But at night, the ground and the air lose their heat very quickly. There are not enough trees and plants to trap the heat, and there are no clouds to stop the heat from rising. So the temperature falls rapidly. The temperature of the air can fall from over 50°C to under 20°C. In some hot deserts, at certain times of year, there may even be frost at night!

Mirages

When hot air rises from the desert ground, it can play tricks with the light. Rays of light from the sky are bent by a layer of hot air close to the ground, so that they look as if they are coming from the surface of a pool of water. Desert travellers think that they see water in the distance. But the light is playing a trick on their eyes. They are said to have seen a *mirage*.

Sometimes, a layer of hot air acts like a mirror. It reflects the images of distant objects, such as a group of trees, which normally would be out of sight.

Desert landscapes

There are several different types of desert landscape: rocky deserts, stony deserts and sandy deserts.

The Sahara Desert

The Sahara Desert covers 9 million square kilometres. Much of the Sahara consists of areas of bare rock. There are also large areas of stony desert, where the rocks have been broken into pieces.

In sandy deserts, the landscape consists of mounds or ridges of sand, known as *sand dunes*. The Sahara is famous for its sand dunes, but only about a tenth of the Sahara is covered by sand dunes.

Some desert areas are flat, but many are mountainous. In the Sahara, there are mountains which have snow on them for several months each year. Some of these mountains are over 2400 metres high.

How desert landscapes are formed

Thousands of years ago, many desert areas were not as dry as they are today. The areas were covered with forests, rivers and lakes. When the climate changed, the trees and water disappeared. In deserts, there are often dry river valleys, and large dried-up basins, where there used to be lakes.

Today, when there is a desert thunderstorm, the water pours across the land. There is not enough soil, or plants, to soak up so much water at once. So the water floods across the surface. As it floods, it fills up channels that have been dry for months, and carves out new ones. The water sweeps along everything in its path — stones and boulders, plants and animals. It sometimes carries them several hundred kilometres.

The flood lasts for only a few hours, so it is known as a *flash flood*. But, in those few hours, the desert landscape is shaped by the water.

This dried-up stream bed is known as a *wadi*. Its steep sides offer shelter from the desert winds. But wise travellers do not shelter in a wadi, in case there is a storm!

In sandy deserts, the strong winds blow the sand into dunes. There are two main types of dune.

This dune is shaped like a quarter moon, and is called a *barchan*. It is formed in deserts where winds blow strongly in one direction. Barchans are common in the desert called Turkestan in south-west Russia.

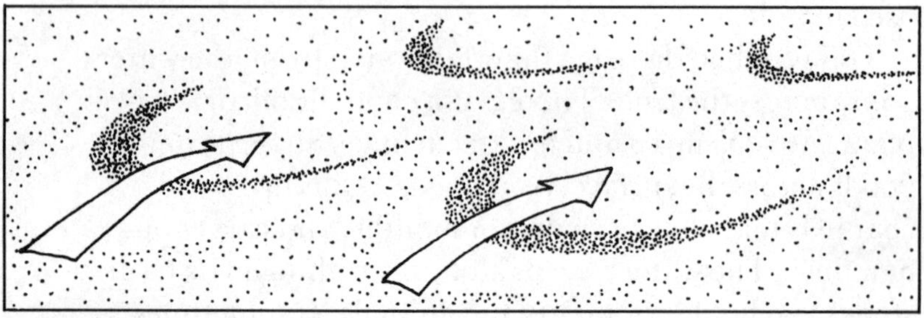

This dune has a long ridge with sloping sides. It is common in the Sahara, and is called a *seif*, because its shape is like a sword blade. The main wind increases the length of the ridge, while winds from the sides build up its height and width.

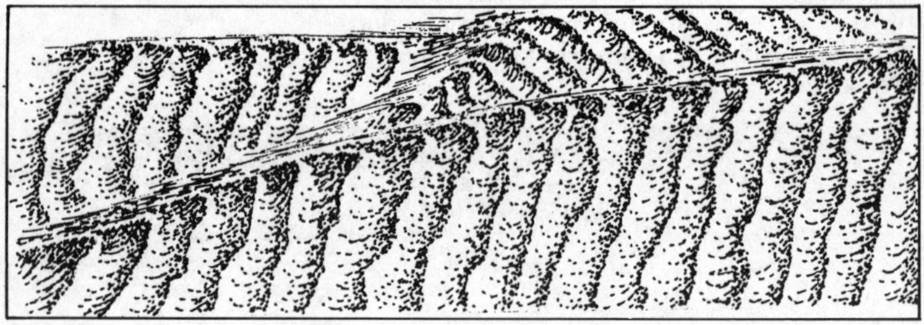

Duststorms and sandstorms

Winds also change the desert landscape by causing duststorms and sandstorms. Dust and sand are blown against the rocks. The dust and sand rub against the surface of the rock, and wear it away. Rock is worn down in this way by the process called *abrasion*.

During a duststorm, particles of dust can be blown hundreds of kilometres across the desert. The clouds of dust can reach up to 3000 metres, and may even blot out the sun.

In a sandstorm, the sand stays close to the ground, and does not travel so far. But sand driven by the wind has tremendous cutting power, and can sometimes cut through stout wooden posts.

Over thousands of years, water and wind have carved out the desert landscape. Because soft layers of rock wear away more quickly than hard layers, rocks are sometimes worn into strange shapes.

Desert plants

Desert plants have to be able to survive for long periods without rain. Many desert plants survive in the form of seeds.

After a heavy rainstorm, the seeds of these plants start to grow. Within only a few weeks, these plants flower, produce more seeds, and die. Some of these seeds are eaten by birds or small animals. But other seeds get blown across the desert, or lie on the surface. These seeds lie there until the next storm makes them start to grow.

Many of these plants have bright flowers. So, after a storm, the desert sparkles with colour for a while.

Desert trees

A long dry period is called a *drought*. Desert trees survive periods of drought by pushing their roots deep into the earth to find water. They are able to collect moisture which other plants cannot reach.

This tree, called the *mesquite*, is common in American deserts. Its roots sometimes go 30 metres deep.

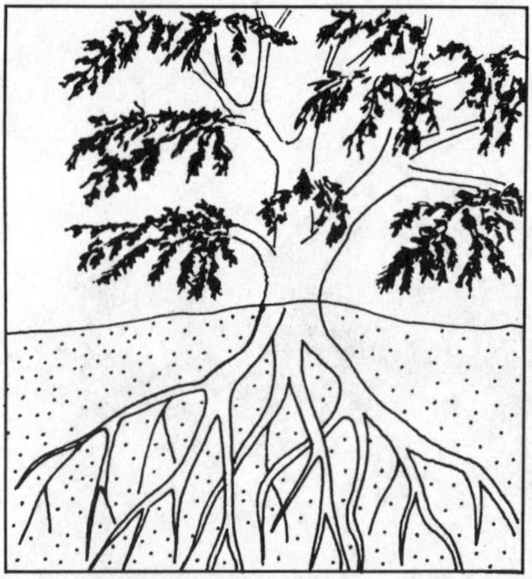

The *date palm* grows to a height of about 10 metres. Its thick bark helps to protect it from the drought.

Some plants survive the drought by storing water underground. These plants use their bulbs as containers. Some of these bulbs can swell to enormous sizes. One kind of plant has a bulb which can weigh 18 kilos when it is full.

Other plants live through the drought by storing up water in their stems and leaves, and by growing very slowly. This group includes those plants known as cactus plants, or *cacti*.

The *barrel cactus* stores water in its stem. As it uses up the water, it shrinks. It has a web of roots close to the surface, ready to use any rain which does fall.

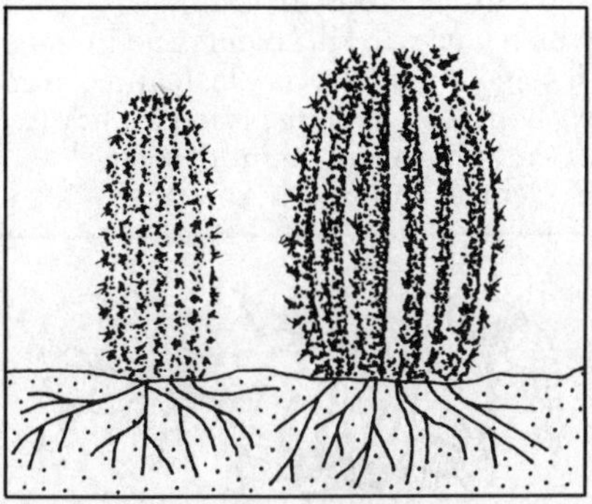

This plant is called the *prickly pear*. Like many cacti, it is covered in sharp thorns. The thorns protect it from being eaten by animals who are in search of water.

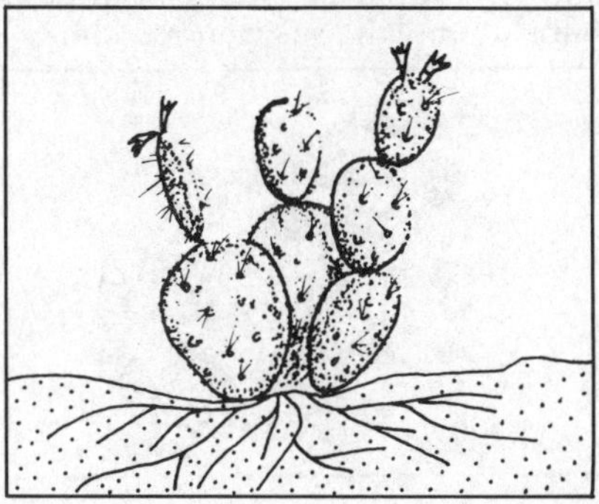

This giant cactus is called a *saguaro*. The saguaro grows so slowly that after 25 years it may be only 60 cms tall. But, eventually, it may grow to 15 metres. Fully-grown saguaros can store hundreds of litres of water. They sometimes live for over 200 years.

Desert wildlife

Hundreds of types of insects live in the desert. They feed on the plants, and carry pollen from flower to flower. The insects provide food for small animals, such as spiders, scorpions, toads and lizards.

Animals living in the desert have to be able to survive the great heat and the shortage of water. About 5000 different types of animal live in the world's deserts. There are more different animals in the North American desert than in any other desert.

This insect is called the *termite*, or white ant. It lives in the Sahara, and eats dried-up plants and dead wood. Termites' nests are full of passages and cells, and can be six metres tall!

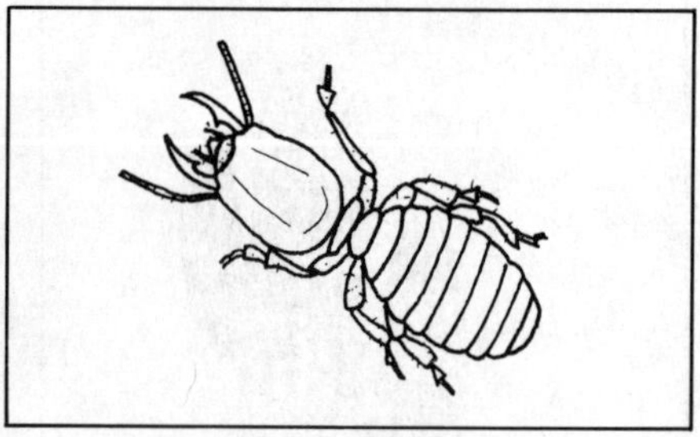

Lizards are common in the desert. This lizard is called a *chuckwalla*, and is very timid. When the chuckwalla is afraid, it wedges itself in the rocks by swallowing air. In this way, it makes itself so fat than no enemy can drag it out.

The *scorpion* has powerful pincers and a deadly sting in its tail, which it uses to kill spiders and insects. Scorpions can run very fast, and can go without food for long periods. They live in the Sahara, and in the deserts of Central and North America.

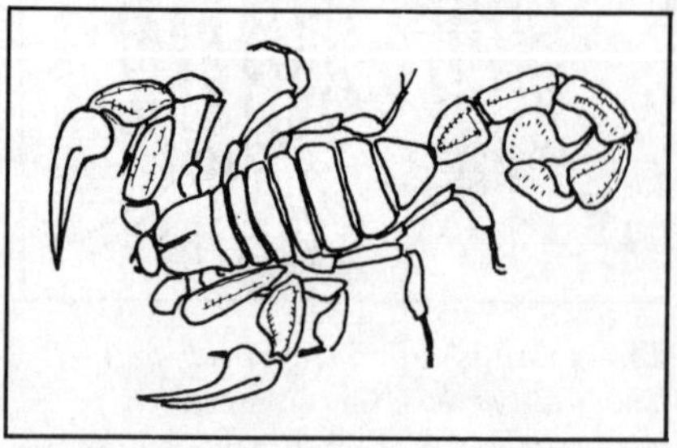

This toad is called the *spadefoot toad*. In a long drought, it digs a hole, and covers itself up. It lives in its damp burrow, until the rain comes again.

Several types of snake live in the desert. This *diamond rattlesnake* can be found in the North American desert. It kills animals for its food, by injecting them with poison from its fangs. When an enemy is near, it rattles the scales at the tip of its tail.

Birds of prey, like this *vulture*, get the moisture they need from the flesh they eat. They keep cool by gliding in the cooler air 900 metres above the ground They have very good eyesight, and can see food many kilometres away.

The *desert tortoise* is one of the few desert animals that moves about during the day. Its thick shell protects it from losing moisture, and from other animals. It never has a drink of water, but gets the moisture it needs from the plants it eats.

Some desert birds save their energy by hardly ever flying. The *road-runner* can race across the desert at 25 kilometres an hour. It uses its long tail to change direction and to brake to a sudden stop. It stabs insects, lizards and snakes with its sharp beak.

Mammals

Animals which have fur and produce milk for their young are known as *mammals*. Several kinds of small mammals live in the North American deserts. They shelter during the day, and hunt for food at night. Animals which rest during the day and come out at night are known as *nocturnal* animals.

Rats escape the heat by spending the day in underground burrows.

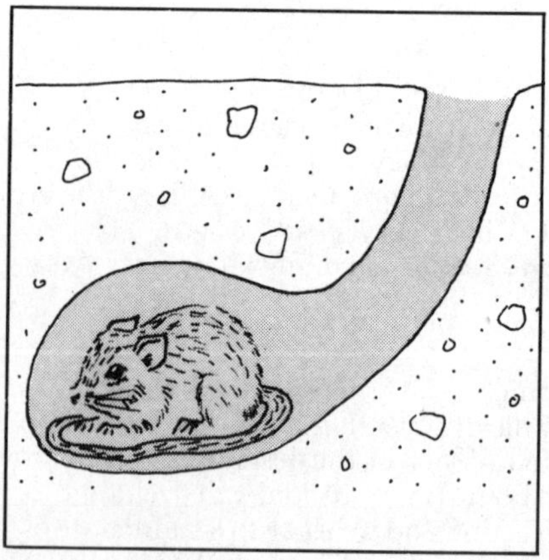

Hares and rabbits shelter from the sun in the shade of plants.

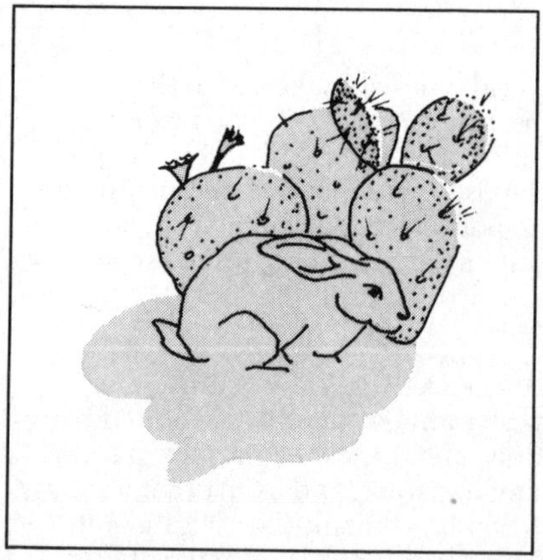

The kit fox has huge ears, so that it can hear the slightest movement of its prey.

The camel

In some deserts, the most well-known animal is the camel. The camel is very strong. For thousands of years, men have used camels to carry them and their belongings across the deserts of North Africa and Asia.

A camel can travel for days without taking a drink. It stores fat in its hump. When it gets no water, it uses the fat to produce the moisture it needs.

The camel has broad padded feet, and so can walk either over soft sand or bare rock. In a sandstorm, it can close its nostrils as well as its eyes; and its hairy coat protects its body from the sand.

This camel has one hump, and is called the Arabian camel, or *dromedary*. The dromedary lives in the hot deserts of North Africa and Arabia.

This camel has two humps, and is called the *Bactrian camel*. It lives in the cooler deserts of central Asia.

Living in the desert

People have lived in desert areas for thousands of years. Some of the world's first cities were built in the desert areas of the Middle East. Today, about 4% of the world's people live in deserts.

Some people who live in the desert have no fixed home. People who move from place to place, and who never have a fixed home, are called *nomads*.

Oases

Desert villages and towns are situated at places where water is found. In such places, there are underground springs and wells. A place where there is enough water for plants to grow is known as an *oasis*. The picture shows one of the oases in the Sahara.

Rivers

Although deserts do not get much rain, they are sometimes crossed by rivers. For example, the river Nile starts in the wet areas of central Africa, then flows across the Sahara before it reaches the sea.

The Bedouin

Groups of people called *Bedouins* have lived in the deserts of North Africa, Arabia and Syria for thousands of years. They used to be nomads, but now many Bedouins live on farms or in towns. A few groups are still nomads. They keep flocks of sheep and herds of goats. They travel between oasis towns and markets, never staying in one place for very long.

They live in simple tents of material made from goat's hair. The material is just stretched over poles, so the tents are easy to put up and to take down. Rugs are spread on the floor to cover the sand.

The Bedouin use camels to carry their tents, and often ride across the desert on horses. Their clothes are made from wool or camel's hair. They often wear a cloak with a hood to protect themselves from the sun, wind and sand. This cloak is called a *burnoose*.

Their main food is a type of stew, made from camel's meat or mutton. They also eat cheese made from goat's milk, and drink very strong coffee.

Aborigines

For thousands of years, the only people who lived in the Great Australian Desert were groups of nomads called *aborigines*. Today, most aborigines live in towns and cities.

In the past, each group of aborigines had its own area. Within this area, the people moved from place to place, taking their few belongings with them.

The aborigines were hunters, and did not keep any animals, except dogs. The men used spears, and special throwing sticks, called *boomerangs*, to kill animals such as kangaroos, snakes, lizards and birds. The women used digging sticks to search for roots, and collected insects, grubs and seeds.

Young aborigines were taught where all the water holes were to be found. They learned how to suck up water from wet sand through a hollow reed. They also learned how to collect water from certain roots and underground plants. In some groups, at a certain age, each boy had to make a journey on his own, to show that he knew how to look after himself in the desert. This journey was known as a *walkabout*.

Developing the desert

Minerals in the desert

In recent years, several desert areas have been developed, because the rocks happen to contain valuable supplies of minerals. For example, there are diamonds in the South African desert, and silver is mined in the Mexican desert. The desert also provides an important part of the world's supply of the mineral called *uranium*, which is used in nuclear power stations. In the South American deserts, there are valuable copper mines.

Oil

Oil is found in some desert areas. Several of the world's chief oil-fields are found in the Arabian and Sahara deserts. Money from the sale of oil has made some countries, such as Saudi Arabia, very rich. Huge modern cities, with new factories, hotels and office blocks, have been built in the desert.

Farming the desert

Large areas of the desert have been turned into farmland, by providing them with water. The process of taking water to a dry area, to make it possible to grow crops, is called *irrigation*.

For thousands of years, people have been taking water from rivers to irrigate the land nearby.
The picture shows men getting water from a river by using a bucket fixed to some poles, called a *picotah*.
The stone fixed to one of the poles acts as a balance.
The men are able to dip the bucket into the water, then raise it again when it is full.

Today, machines are also used to pump water from rivers and wells. The water flows along ditches, or is taken across the desert by pipeline, and sprayed directly onto the crops.

Often, the water for an irrigation scheme is provided by building a dam across a river. In Egypt, a huge dam, called the Aswan High Dam, has been built across the River Nile. The lake formed by the dam has provided the water to turn 1 million hectares of desert into farmland.

Ways have now been found to transport water for long distances across the desert. As a result, more areas can be farmed, and new towns can be built. The picture shows a modern desert town in Libya.

The future of the desert

Modern developments have already brought many changes to the desert. Modern transport makes it possible to travel across the desert more easily by land or by air.

Crossing the desert by land rover

A desert air-strip

But vast areas of the world's deserts are still undeveloped. Until the problem of how to provide enough water is solved, these areas cannot be developed. It is not easy to use sea water, because all the salt has to be removed, before it can be used. One idea is to tow huge icebergs from the Arctic to North Africa. Some of each iceberg would melt on the way. But the icebergs are so vast that each one would still be able to provide the desert with millions of litres of water.

The size of the world's population is increasing. Some areas of the world are overcrowded, and about one person in three in the world does not get enough food. But there are still huge areas of desert where no one lives.

Glossary

abrasion (p.8) the process of rubbing, which causes the surface of something to wear away
cactus (p.11) a type of desert plant with thick stems and leaves, protected by sharp thorns
desert (p.2) a place where few plants grow and few animals live, because there is little or no rain; the deserts described in this book are *hot deserts*, as opposed to the *cold deserts* found in such places as the Arctic and Antarctic
drought (p.10) a long period of dry weather, when there is not enough water for things to grow
dune (p.6) a mound or ridge of sand, piled up by the wind
duststorm (p.8) a violent wind carrying clouds of dust
irrigation (p.20) the process of bringing water to dry land, usually using a system of streams or canals
mirage (p.5) an effect caused by the hot air in deserts, in which the images of distant objects appear
nomad (p.17) a member of a travelling group who do not have a fixed home
oasis (p.16) a place in the desert with enough water for plants to grow
sandstorm (p.8) a violent wind carrying clouds of sand
wadi (p.7) the dried-up bed or valley of a stream in a desert

First published 1983 by
Edward Arnold (Publishers) Ltd
41 Bedford Square
London WC1B 3DQ

British Library Cataloguing in Publication Data

Crystal, David
Deserts.—(Databank)
1. Deserts
I. Title II. Foster, John L. (John Louis)
III. Series
551.4 GB611

ISBN 0-7131-0828-2

Acknowledgements
The Publishers would like to thank the following for their permission to use copyright illustrations:
Barnabys Picture Library: Cover & p. 7;
Popperfoto: p.p. 1, 151 & r & 16;
United Nations: p.p. 6 (Unesco/Dominique Lajoux) 9t & b (Unesco/Dominique Lajoux), 17t (FAO/Vaughan-Whitehead) & 20;
National History Photo Agency: p.p. 13tl & r, br & 14;
The Zoological Society of London: p. 961;
Mepha: 17b (P. Ryan);
Camera Press: p.p. 18 & 221;
B.P. Photographic Library: p. 19;
U.S.T.S.: p. 22r.

Text set in 12/14 Baskerville by D.P. Press, Sevenoaks
Printed by photolithography in Great Britain at The Pitman Press, Bath